MONODROMOS

Marian Engel

Anansi

Published with the assistance of the Canada Council
and the Ontario Arts Council

Design: Walter Dmytrenko
Photo: Graeme Gibson

Typesetting by Foundation Press
Printed in Canada by The Hunter Rose Company

ISBN: 0-88784-427-8
Library of Congress Card Number: 73-85572

House of Anansi
35 Britain Street
Toronto, Canada

1 2 3 4 5 77 76 75 74 73

For Howard and to the memory of Chris Savva

Anything can be killed, except nostalgia for the Kingdom.

—Julio Cortazar

MONODROMOS

I

JANUARY
SUNDAY

The bastions of the city are called D'Avila, Tripoli, Roccas, Mula, Quirini, Barbaro, Loredano, Flatro, Caraffa, Podocataro and Costanza. They are shaped like arrowheads, and they project level with the top of the walls into the broad ditch that was the city moat. The Venetian Savorgnano designed them, and Barbaro engineered them. They were supposed to save the city from the Turks.

I think it was on Barbaro that I saw the cockfight.

The walls of the city were still incomplete when Mustafa Pasha and his men scaled Costanza. In the battle which followed, Roccas, Tripoli, and Podocataro died, leaving only their melodic Venetian names behind them; with them died Nicolo Dandolo, de Nores, who was perhaps the last of the royal Lusignans, da Rimini, and the little Count of Treviso.

Rupert Gunnis, guidebook-maker, likes those now meaningless names, and so do I.

Lafcadio asks me where I am going and I say "out" like a flippant and sulky child, and I do go out, and I stand by the city wall, and I am free.

They've broken the wall here where I am, and over there, and along there, and made big roads and bridges across the moat, and put up modern buildings with neon signs and mosaic fronts. And the palm trees are shaggy, and the eucalyptus trees rattle and peel and I don't much like old women thrusting their wrinkled dugs and empty jaws and old clawed hands at me saying "Baksheesh, baksheesh, lady," and I suppose this modern version of a city others loved before it changed, before "progress" arrived, and odd ideas that the friendly natives might like independence and power and television—I suppose it is, as a lot of people say, an awful place.

I love it.

I came down our street as far as the main street, walking, because it is Sunday and anyway the sidewalk is too narrow, in the middle of the road; and I looked at the old houses whose oriels lean together like mating flowers, and out into the bright vulgarity of this attempt to make an Omonia Square, and I saw the shoe-shine boys and paper-sellers, the taxi drivers and the serious old man who takes photographs with a pin-hole camera down in the moat, and a cloud pulled away from the sun, and I was suddenly warm and happy, and I said, "My place."

By now, I have had the official tour of the island: the slippered visit to the mosque-cathedral, the insipid curry lunch at the deserted English Club. The quick run to the west to see the deserted winter beaches—a flash of blue, a hint of treasure, a scent of orange blossoms, and a view of a forest of iron windmills bearing the faded word TORONTO on their tinker-toy sails—these are all the experiences I have been allowed. We went over the northern mountains to Florinda's at night in the dark, and I could feel the peaks closing around us and sense them as they leaned away at the top of the pass, but they were impossible to see. I might have been in Aden or Gib or Hong Kong.

But now I am here, alone, in the brightness of day. I am going to circumnavigate the walls. Though it is hard to begin.

I stand braced against the wall. Here where it breasts the

boulevard it is almost up to my waist. Down in the moat, where once a great river was re-routed to encircle the city, there are tables, chairs, public lavatories, lawns that have never seen that river flow, and, its pathetic punning legend askew, a tin shack of a restaurant with a deck and a wooden smokestack, the ''Ship-Kebab''. At night the city air is fragrant with bay leaf and the grilling flesh of the Mediterranean fat-tailed sheep.

The moat cuts the old inner city away from its suburbs, and gives the houses along the wall a spurious angular dignity, as if they leaned against some northern canal.

It is winter, and colder than I had hoped it would be. The cold, stone Mediterranean chill. There was ice in the puddles of the courtyard this morning and frozen grit in the corners of my eyes. Even at noon, when a cloud passes across the sun, it is footstamping weather.

But it is good to be out in the open air. I had forgotten what it was like to be day in, day out with him, under his unforgiving eyes. I can't assume any dignity with him. We knew each other when we were children.

Old, old warped stone. The walls were never much use, it's a wonder they've kept them. They're good, though, they make a strong image for the place, tie it together. To walk beside them is to forgive all emperors a little.

The island has passed from hand to hand with history. Only Napoleon and Kubla Khan seem to have neglected it. It has been an adjunct of every other empire; it's out of its British phase now, waiting for history to clear and clot again, to see what it will become. It has a wan look in the winter sun: this desirable property to let. I hope the islanders are shrewd about the rent.

The stone is yellow as butter. Inside the cincture of the walls, the word ''bastion'' flaunts itself against reality like a banner, and on the arrow-headed height that is Quirini I see a woman hanging her washing out between two eucalyptus trees.

MONODROMOS

Down in the moat, you feel as if you are in the bottom of a well. Two rakes, a hoe, a forgotten cap lean against the wall. Mustard spills out, and moss, from between the stones. *There is sweet music here that softer fall / Than petals from blown roses on the grass . . .* My mother taught us Tennyson while we were doing dishes.

Choose your mythology: Pygmalion, Aphrodite, Cleopatra, Ptolemy and Arsinoe, St Paul and Barnabas, Harun al Rashid, St Helena, Richard and Berengaria, Othello, Rimbaud, Kitchener, Lawrence Durrell: all of them have been here. The population is considered by sophisticated travellers to be squalid in comparison with its history.

I read too much. Already antiquarians are taking away my eyes. Gunnis hates the varnish in Greek Orthodox churches, Gordon-Home inveighs against non-Etonian Greek, Strabo found the citizens lazy and lascivious. Florinda says they are too idle to whitewash their horrible old yellow stone like decent Greeks. I haven't met any of them yet.

My bump of direction is good but it was formed in a grid. I can't make out round towns. Now I have been somehow shunted away from the walls, walking by dull and curtained commercial buildings, shops advertising bicycles, cameras, ladies' ready-to-wear, dusty luggage. And across the road there is some kind of yellow official building, the same stone as the walls, but sharply cut, and it doesn't look right put together with white English mortar. I can tell from the map in the guide book that somewhere in here the Greek quarter ends and the Turkish quarter begins—this is one of the islands the Turks conquered and never left, so they live restlessly side by side with the Armenians between them, and fight a lot. The British left them with a strange constitution giving the Turkish minority a veto. The first thing you learn about this place is that no one is satisfied, they feel bereft of their chance to fight it out, they're aching for some kind of revolution. It's one of those regions prey to passionate dissatisfaction, like Ireland.

Strange Sunday morning emptiness: closed shutters, fastened gratings, a great wide dusty street without traffic flowing around the traffic island. I'm sure I've seen it crowded before with buses and motorbikes and donkeys. It might lead up to the cathedral. It might not. It is empty and shut and full of possibility.

I stand on the corner looking up and down. I am an ordinary human being standing on a corner, and the corner is deserted and vibrating with life for me. To my left there is some kind of official building, to my right a closed cafe with a curved front window. Across the road, a modern Italianate church. In front of it, two women in flowered hats shaking hands with a Franciscan. To the left of the church, a cafe with a painted airplane on it and an easy-looking Greek name: Sigma, Pi, I, T, Phi, it's like deciphering fraternities, I, Rho, Epsilon—Spitfipe?—Spitfire? In the left-hand window a row of old men sit smoking hubble-bubbles. Their eyelids are heavy. They watch me blandly as I cross the road. There are pool-tables and a Coke machine inside. A place to shout outside for your husband. I wonder if they put pot in the water-pipes.

And when I am half way across the road I look down it, and it disappears through a great thick gate in the walls, and I know that the Spitfire Cafe sits where the royal palace once stood, where the king kept hawks and leopards and extravagant court.

The road that goes uphill beside it leads to a denser, older quarter. The streets are named for Victoria, St Francis, Our Lady of Tyre and Catherine Cornaro, the duped Venetian queen. The buildings are old and unenlightened by plate glass. They are heavy with age, their single front doors have become double gates. Their windows are cross-barred in thick soft-looking iron, as if the smith who made them had pressed each juncture with his giant thumbs. Old palms project above the courtyards, plumes in their hats. This is some upland heartland, here where Venice and Araby and William Shakespeare meet: Illyria, lady. Or what Max meant when he said, "You have received an invitation to Byzantium."

High walls on either side of me. I venture between them with high hopes, a high heart.

The houses are not old, nor, though they look it, French. Dates in their fanlights made of bent wrought iron or punctured tin are 1891 and 2 and 1885. The French haven't been here since the 14th century.

Big brass hands on the doors. A feeling that the streets are closing in behind me. Through open doors, small glimpses of flowering courtyards, grand staircases and great tiled halls. Niches for statues. At the corner of the street, a small domed Turkish tomb prinked out with pieces of mediaeval Christian tombstones, which I think at first is a fountain.

Shaved-headed kids clustered around a bicycle look up at me and stare. In the moat, an unmistakable edifice of higher education flies a star-and-crescent flag. So this is Turkey-town.

Two old men with rags around their heads: curtsies to the memory of fez and tarboosh. The children have such large eyes.

In mediaeval times the city, Gunnis says, had a mixed population of Franks, Venetians, Greeks, Maronites, Armenians, Copts, Nestorians, Jacobites, Abyssinians and assorted monophysites. The Jews had been wiped out by then, the Phoenicians had disappeared on their own, and the Doukhobors had not yet arrived to complain about the climate and move on to Canada.

Max said, "Find out if there are any Nestorians left— " he makes a hobby of heresies—"and look for the ikon of the dog-headed saint." So I said to Laddie it was a wonderful place, there were survivals of heresies and animal-Gods, there must be folkways that have died everywhere else, the island was somehow culturally stranded, like Australia with all its strange animals, and Laddie said, "Shut up if you're going to talk like a tourist or a child." I love Laddie, he's good-natured and kind.

MONODROMOS

I am in an open space, back near the walls again, though they barely rise above-ground; in four hundred years the city has silted up to them. The narrow northern gate stands isolated like a once-triumphal arch between the roads that have been cut through the walls on either side of it. This is a huge open square, crowded with sweet-sellers with coloured glassed carts like popcorn wagons, all kinds of vendors and hawkers and strolling men. Beyond them is a kind of park set on a bastion.

There, within a perimeter of rattling gum trees, a circle of people, forty, fifty, a hundred of them, in clustered groups. Men. I move to see what they are watching: a cockfight.

They have intense, wood-carved faces. Wood-coloured as well, sallow under winter-faded tans. Sunday: serge suits. Again, the oldest ones have rags around their heads. The young, in open-collared shirts, have long necks and vulnerable collar bones, Greco-Semitic beauty. Long, hard, white teeth, perfect noses; long, sharply delineated upper lips. Some have round Praxitelean eyes, some are green as fish. There are good weathered country faces, city lounge-lizards, muscle boys and rumpled businessmen.

Where there is speech, it is a collective rumble. Individual words come up in Greek, though this is plainly still a Turkish sector. The only Turkish words I know are *yok*, which means no, and I learned it from a detective novel, and *tek yol*, the phrase on our street sign: TEK YOL / MONODROMOS / ONE WAY STREET, it reads.

There are also two chickens.

Fowl, then, if not chickens, but not the fighting cocks of paintings on black velour. They are as lowslung and broody as barred rocks in a barnyard, they are reddish in colour, but not majestic, not glossy in the feather. They have big, bald, pendulous rumps and collapsed combs. Everything about them is couchant rather than rampant. Their eyes are drunken, glazed. Their fighting-spurs make them clumsy on their feet. They must have begun their battle hours ago. One is badly gashed on the breast and indifferent to everything but death.

They move languidly, as if they are on slow-motion film. Their managers crouch by them, making clicking noises with tongue and teeth, forcing them towards each other. They shy away, are forced together again and peck at each other wearily. The men take their underbodies in cupped hands and speak soothingly to them, place them face to face. Nothing happens. They avert their eyes from each other. They are half dead.

Suddenly, one finds a lost well of aggression in himself. He preens and gashes at the other with his sharpened beak, and moves away. The other settles despondently in the dust and then at a push from his manager moves in to peck pettishly at his opponent.

At every move they settle lower on their legs. Their underparts swing swollen after them. They are scrawny, the iridescence of their feathers is an old memory. They have not chosen to be martial. They are chickens.

I do not see the end. It might go on for hours, this feeble contest of the not-quite-dead, but I heard a whisper in Greek, again collective, and it is a word I know, for I came to the island armed by Max with the works of Mr I. Kikkotis, grammarian: "a woman". A woman is here. I look around. There is no other woman. The interior lens closes. I move off.

I choose my street badly, and fail to finish the circumnavigation of the walls. I drift self-consciously southwards instead of to the east. Beside the shrine of the Whirling Dervishes, where dervishes are said no longer to turn or dance or whirl, there is a kebab-vendor with two sick-looking sheep tethered to his folding charcoal stove. He cooks three sticks of meat for me, and slits elegantly the bladder-bread called *pita* that they eat. I look in through the arches at the beehive tombs of Turkish heroes. They are raised like flatbed English tombs, but at the head of each is a round cement post wound with a turban of green cloth. The kebab-vendor shakes his head when I gesture that I want to go in. He whips my meat off the skewers by grasping them through the envelope of bread, slit-slot cuts celery, parsley, onion and tomatoes; sections a lemon. I pay him and go with my portable sandwich and the sick sheep call after me.

There is no one in this street to stare. It is as silent as if the building were up to their necks in snow. I come to another square, in the middle of which stands a conquistadorial marble pillar. The lion of St Mark once stood upon it, Rupert Gunnis says. Venetian imperialists are comfortably likeable and dead. When will we begin to invest the English with such sentiment? I pass an English pillarbox now painted independent yellow, and under the new paint trace with my finger the letters GRV, the English coat of arms. Might as well be SPQR.

Where to turn now? Don't choose, go: everywhere is promise. Here a small cruciform church, looking as ancient and comforting and small as the Mausoleum of Galla Placidia, is sunk six feet below the level of the street. There are steps down to the front door, and over that door an arc of mediaeval carving, bands of flowers and geometric forms, supported by Corinthian capitals. Over it is a sign saying "Hamam—Turkish Baths". I wonder if I would dare.

Across from the church an old woman sits in the street, facing her doorway, knitting, on a straight wooden chair. The door is half ajar. I can see arches, tiles, a courtyard and a lemon tree. Beside her on the ground a nondescript bird sits silent in an unpainted wooden cage.

Why hasn't he let me out to explore before? Where I go, he goes, rushing me past the outposts of Elysium into tea-shops. Tomorrow I must have an explanation from him. It isn't good to walk only on a Sunday when the stores are shuttered and unrecognisable, this is the Middle East, you need the excitement of its commerce to have any sense of place. Everything is different today. If I knew enough about shutters and doors, I could make a sociological study of shutters and doors, a compendium of the history of galvanised iron, sheet aluminum, and patched and weathered wood. But I want to linger in open doorways and watch the coppersmiths, whose street is called Hephaestos after the smith-god, and hold my nose at the tanneries and find out how they make halvah. I am six years old again and curious, curious; I love being alive and having a pair of eyes; my favourite subject in high school was geography. I have to cut loose from Laddie, I don't want to know this place through him and Rupert Gunnis and I. Kykkotis and Kevork K. Keshishian and Robin Parker, I want to see it myself, without benefit of guidebook, grammarian or jailer.

&

Hell, I know where I am now. It's my own street. I've gone a half-circle, not a whole. There's the sign, MONODROMOS half-wiped out with red paint, Tek Yol partly erased with blue, and One Way Street so faint it's lost the battle of the paintbrushes. (They love each other here, they play a haunting game of French and English, Jew and Arab, Catholic and Protestant, Prisoner's Base.) The real name of the street is endecasyllabic, and I will never master it. I realise now that I must have come down Arafat Pasha and turned into St Skolastikos without even knowing it and thus arrived back home again. It isn't even two o'clock and I said I'd be out all day. If he thinks I'll get lost and never return, he hasn't a hope, not in a round town.

The street is awash with Saturday's rubbish—flying papers, filthy deposits of old tires and boots and boxes and cabbage leaves. The garbage men are on strike. From this corner, I can see the cloth-merchant's, the wool shop, the perfumier, the cadaiffi maker's, the jeweller's and the barber's shop. Then a gap for an unlabelled side street, and our building. An ordinary-looking commercial block with a wine shop, a tailor's shop, two empty boarded-up archways, and an insalubrious grocery shop called Phaedra's; but if you raise your eyes you'll see where the plaster has peeled off over half-timbering.

And the last archway goes through to the courtyard behind that shop. It isn't sensational to look at, just one of those squat Gothic-looking arches you see here, that give a touch of Jerusalem to everything. There's an ordinary-looking brass plaque fit to break his mother's heart screwed into the stone: L.G. Moore, A.R.C.T., A.C.T.M., Piano Lessons, Mathmata Piano. And then, as you glance through, a hectic vision of piled wheelbarrows, ladders, old chicken coops and a riot of geraniums among crazy ruined arches. It's like nothing a well-groomed person from the new continent has ever seen. People just come and leave things in the courtyard, tin barrels and old tin signs, and once last week a man arrived with four old telephone poles and threw them on the pile. A curious white dust accumulates on the garbage and in a week the poles will look as dignified and abandoned as the pyramids.

We live over the row of shops, but our lives face inwards, over the courtyard, for the building is an abandoned caravanserai.

"Good Audrey," Max said, "good Audrey, think of the sun." A mere ten days ago.

Bitter English weather. We'd both been ill. I took to walking home from Pye's on Goodge Street because it warmed me up: the length of Regent's Park, wishing we were still meeting after work at The George, except that it would have killed him. That night arriving with chattering teeth, and Max showing me a coal-fire and a cable: LADDIE DIRE DISTRESS COME SOONEST FLORINDA POWER.

Max is long in the leg and short in the body, he dangles from himself like a kind of marionette. He got up and shuffled and huffed in a kind of excited dance and sat down again. He fed me hot claret cup, which he cooked in his silver wine bucket with a poker. "An invitation to Byzantium."

It was out of the question to go. Dire distress is never health; it's always love or money. I didn't owe Laddie love or money.

Max huddled under his grand Adam ceiling. "You're a fool if you don't go."

The misery of the cold and London running out of gas, coal, electricity, pink paraffin. The misery of thinking again of Laddie. "I'm not responsible for him. I'd rather stay with you."

"Elizabeth's invited me to Scotland."

"The Argentina List's come in. I can't leave Pye with that in his lap."

"You protest too much: think, think of the sun. I'll fix your Mister Pye."

For all that he is half Irish and half Jew, Max has a high-bridged Highland nose. He began to bray through it: Byzantium and Alexandria, the Templars, ancient Greece. "Think of living," he said, "under the pontifical thumb of an autocephalous ethnarch."

He stood up and shivered. I knew from his face that he was going to have to admit something. That he had been ill, that he had been frightened (Christmas was crisis, this time, and it was very close), that he was fifty, that he was frightened enough to think of changing the way he lived. "Elizabeth," he said, "has heat. I shall never be well this winter without heat. I must go to Elizabeth in Scotland. I should be much happier if you went south to Laddie."

"It's ridiculous to go back to people—me to him, I mean."

"You can settle his hash in a week, I should think. Then stay on for the sun, Audrey, stay for the sun. You don't know that part of the world, do you? You've only had that package trip to Mykonos. He's bound to have some kind of digs to put you up in if he's been there that long. There'll be sun and wine and the olives crushed with coriander you get in Great Tichfield Street . . . '' He began to stride in the room and swing his long arms; then he marched over to the phonograph and put Laddie's one record on. He swung the jacket from his fingertips, leant his head to the music, twitched his ears, looked at the photograph. ''Not bad, not bad. You're hard on him. He lacks nuance, but how old was he then, twenty-two, twenty-three? They're wrong when they say Chopin is a young man's composer. It's a pity you don't know any Greek—I suppose we could start you on some—ah—put your coat on.''

He swept me out, and in spite of the dying coal fire it was warmer outside than in. His long legs scissored Regent's Park and I trotted behind him. He talked and he talked. ''Henshaw's the man for us, Henshaw's the man.''

And Henshaw was, of course, in The George. ''Henshaw. Maurice. There you are!'' They had been at school together. Henshaw is a journalist, a bibliophile. When he heard that Max was packing me off to the island, he rushed us down Great Portland Street to his flat. Just the thing, just the . . .

''I knew you knew Sir Harry,'' said Max happily, fingering Sir Harry's book. ''Is it a first? Was there a second?''

Henshaw broached a bottle of dark brown brandy that tasted like Christmas cake and varnish. Max gangled and scuffled among Henshaw's stacks of books and hummocks of pamphlets, exclaiming over an Imperial treatise on locust control. Henshaw winced. He is a passionate collector; the uncracked spines of his books are the unscarred faces of his children. He grumbled, ''Seven at a blow,'' as Max knocked pillars of first editions over. ''Don't bash the corners, Max, there's a good fellow. You don't need to take that home, you can get it tomorrow at Bumpus's. I did my military service there, you know. It's one of the grotty islands, some say, but it looked jolly good to me after North Africa and there are some bloody good ruins to boot.''

"She's off tomorrow, Henshaw, tomorrow. The need is urgent."

"Not tomorrow, Max. I have to give notice at work."

"Nonsense. 'Mergency. Fix Pye myself."

Useless to argue with him.

"Here, you'll need this." The first sight of Gunnis's insular encyclopaedia, for every village a separate listing, the work of a lifetime. The possibility of thoroughness in small compass his challenge: he accepted it, became a classic. No building was too small to have an opinion of, and this at a time when the islanders were too busy surviving to be interested in their architectural inheritance. Who else but these odd Englishmen, ink to the elbows, would take it up?

Henshaw's bookcases were full long ago, his books have silted up the corners of the flat, the cupboards, all the floorspace. He wrestles a tattered Baedeker out of Max's hands: "Too rare, that." He does not like to part with books even to his oldest friend. And Max is in a delicate condition, he has drunk enough to be rambunctious and in his loose-limbed way he is dancing the stacks down around him. "Now Max," says Henshaw.

"You're an old woman, Henshaw."

It is after midnight. The brandy has driven away some of the cold but when it wears off I shall be miserable. Max is white and ill. We get him, drunk and bookladen, into a taxi finally. It is he who should go to an island and the sun.

&

In the morning I find him naked to the waist when I wake up, sitting shivering in the armchair reading a Latin history of the island, under the eiderdown, poking with one hand at the extinct fire. "You must go," he croaks at me. "You must, must go."

"I can't leave you here to die of pneumonia."

"I'm going to Elizabeth."

"I wish you'd come with me."

"Ah, you are going, then."

"If I can fix it with Pye."

"Leave Pye to me."

Damn these men, damn even Max. "It's my job. I'll fix it with Pye." So I did.

&

I had worked with Pye for four years and it was the best job I ever had in London: Pye Information Ltd. Good wages and a decent electric fire so the typists' hands wouldn't seize up, and a boss with a sense of humour. I went to it from teaching little British blighters their own language for the London County Council. They threw their boots at me.

Pye Information is a credit business. Max didn't like the sound of it when I took the job, and I was shy of its lofty financial pretensions. Henshaw, too, thought it indecent of me to have to do with snooping and debt-collecting, but we all found out that the business was innocent on the whole—X is not going to send bicycles to Y in the Upper Volta unless Pye tells him Y can pay for them—and the stories the files engendered were lovely. There are hundreds of firms like it, and some are fairly shady, but Pye's was practically By Appointment to Her Majesty.

I expected to spend an enjoyable day sending out to Pye's foreign agents the names of firms that the government of Argentina wanted information on, and when I got tired of that, dabbling in the Old Perennial, the Extraordinarily Smelly Leather Case, a file that had been started long before my day. A tanner in Lincolnshire was bound and determined to be paid for his leather by a cobbler in Germany and had been working to this end for many years. His every approach to the cobbler through Pye's went to Pye's people in Berlin, who wrote to the cobbler, who replied in Old Low German (handwritten), and the letter was forwarded to me to translate. I liked to work at it neatly and slowly. By now the tanner had spent five hundred pounds to fail to collect fifty. I was fond of the cobbler and his excuses, the main one being that the leather was extraordinarily smelly, and aware that the action was paying for the office tea.

But instead I was closeted with Pye himself. Max had telephoned as soon as I left the flat. "So," he said, "you are having an emergency. What's it about?"

I showed him the telegram.

"Money," he said, "come a cropper with money, I should think."

"Me too."

"Have we anything on him in the files?"

"No."

"Have you finished with that business of the Scientologist's yacht?"

"Can't get a thing on him in Europe. I'll have to write to his credit bureau in California."

"They'll send us a form full of typos and charge us five pounds for it. Can't do a thing with bloody Americans. Drop it. When are you off?"

"I'll send out the Argentina List."

"How many are there? Four, five thousand? No, tell you what. Our Marlene's had her baby and she's weary of home life already, these modern girls. She says her mum can look after the baby. These girls will go off, then want back. A woman's privilege, eh? I should think our Mr Speridakis could use you on the island. What he sends us looks as if he has five incompetent Levantines typing with their toes. Here's a shilling, you can buy him some new carbon paper. Interesting chap, Speridakis. Not sure of his politics, but from a business point of view he's straight. Need to support yourself, there."

"I'd only stay a couple of weeks, Mr Pye."

Pye twirled his ex-officer's moustache and looked over his National Health glasses. Great goof, the look said. "Eight years," he said, "is about as long as you can be expected to tolerate an island. You're inclined to be impatient, I'd give you six. After all, it won't cost you anything to move in and live with the bugger, will it? Give all his creditors a pound on tick, and live happily ever after. Get Max down there to visit you. Ought to do something about that chap, else he'll never get out another book. He should get some sun, he's had pneumonia twice already this winter."

"He's going to Edinburgh; his wife has heat. But he wants to join me on the island in the spring, if I stay."

"Good for him."

"I don't really want to leave."

"Don't get stuck, stale. Giving your life to Pye I. isn't going to do you much good, is it? Come half the way round the world to be an office slavey? Get on with you. Pick up your cards at tea-time."

I spent the day on the files referring to the island, going over Speridakis' faint carbons. There were hundreds of small-traders, the place lived on export-import, bearing out Pye's view of the ant-like business instinct of the Wog. Most of the big firms were Greek, though there were a few Turks in textiles and ordering equipment for big estates. The main banks were those staples of the East, National & Grindlay's, the Ottoman, and Barclay's District, Colonial and Overseas. The money seemed to be in cars, in oil refineries, in machinery agencies. There weren't many bad records. The islanders seemed on the whole to be honest, or as Pye would have put it, clever.

The office did a whip-round and gave me a book-token as a farewell present. I went to Foyle's and got my own copy of Gunnis's guide. Pye's eyes were dry.

Passport, money, letter of recommendation to Speridakis, self-written, signed by Henry Pye. "In the end," he said, "we'll see you back. Islands pall. Get some sun, girl."

In December, thirty babies died of hypothermia in Brighton and the Home Counties. Their mums put them out in their prams as usual, not knowing what below-zero was.

Henshaw and Max bought more island brandy to see me off with. I was nervous at the airport and fought down the thought that I had invested ten years in England, and England and I were glad to see the back of each other.

Laddie said, "So you got that telegram and you let two men pack you off. You were always weak, weren't you?"

&

On the stone balcony of the extraordinary building we inhabit, Laddie has set out a table for tea. Later, he will have to move it into the music room, because it is too cold to sit outside: God forfend his visiting ladies catch a winter chill. It is enough imposition for them to have to avert their eyes from the heathen garbage of the yard.

Structurally, our caravanserai is a hollow square, a once-arcaded assemblage of the sort you find under different names from China to Peru. It is the form of the Alhambra or a palace in India, a crusader town in Aquitaine, a monastery cloister: two storeys of shallow Gothic archways face the courtyard, in the centre of which a knobbled tree and the ruins of a Moslem well can just be seen under the rubbish. It was built, I have been told, as an inn for itinerant cloth-makers from Turkey, but it is in much worse condition than the Inn of the Travelling Musicians down the street or the Khan of the Gamblers. Two sides, in fact, have almost fallen down and the third is dangerous. Only the row of rooms that fronts along Monodromos is usable.

You glance through the archway at it, and it is just a beautiful jumble of old stone, lath, and fiercely red climbing geraniums. You glance again, and it's a ruin of the nastiest—dampest—kind.

But somehow, Laddie has made one side of it civilised. I like him for that.

It is nearly time for his ladies to come to tea. On his mother's petit-point tablecloth sit my mother's cups and saucers (because I took nothing when I left him, not even my own mother's sacrifices to my attempted domesticity), and the translucent tea-plates with turquoise painted doves Uncle Will gave her for a wedding present in 1932. The black cup has a green and orange bird of paradise in its bowl. It is shallow, and Mother always kept it for people who did not take milk in their tea. The pink one is a dusky rose colour you don't see any more except on Australians who knit their own pullovers. She always liked it, because it was a bridge prize from Mrs Devitt, who died when she was only forty-three. The fine flowered one, old enough to be without a maker's mark, and from her mother, was patterned with a sepia transfer which seems to have slipped. The petals of the flowers are coloured with transparent inks. The fourth cup is fat with roses and gilt. It is too vulgar to have been my mother's; he must have bought it himself, or got it from his own mother.

He has also put out my mother's souvenir spoons, and my aunt Lynn's silver cream-and-sugar she sent us for a wedding present. The silver teapot is his. Maybe he got it from his rich friends in France. I saw him this morning folding the purple and blue flannels the silver lives in. Then he picked up the silver spoon from Sacramento, the one with the poppy on it, and asked me the story of it again. I pretended I couldn't remember it.

He is expecting ladies to tea. He wants to explain to them the curious North American custom of collecting souvenir spoons. I have promised not to come, because I do not like tea, or ladies, or, really, souvenir spoons. I only like this island I cannot get him interested in.

The courtyard is oddly silent. This morning before I went for my walk, with much noise and shouting Mrs Phaedra and her husband departed in a hired car, she fat in a clean wrapper and giving orders, he frightened and fussed, a respectable foot behind his Mrs Moneybags. The part of the neighbourhood that was awake gave them a noisy farewell and went back to bed. Laddie and the Phaedras are the only people who live in this enormous columbarium, though a mountebank named Flores is said sometimes to ascend a hidden staircase from a boarded-up store on the side that has almost, but not quite, fallen down, and crouch in the filth of one of the upper rooms.

I have just time to dash into the bathroom and then to my room to get a warmer coat, and down the stairs again before they come, but I am a little too late. To avoid an embarrassing encounter with Laddie's ladies, I retreat to the centre of the courtyard and crouch down where, beside a kind of summerhouse that was once the fountain (the Turks use criss-crossed lath as though they were underlining Canadian verandahs), there are piled as well as wheelbarrows and ladders six enormous clay jars, each of a size to accommodate forty thieves. From behind them I can watch him receive his guests.

You have to admit he has taste, Laddie. I couldn't have turned ten cells of what the funny tailor downstairs calls an old Turkish monastiraki into a civilised apartment. His mother, Rosa Trethewey Moore, daughter of the finest Cornish counter-tenor in New York, called him Lafcadio as if that one touch of romanticism would get her out of a bad marriage and a meagre farmhouse. To survive public school he had to re-christen himself Laddie, the dog in the Grade One reader, and I saw him polishing his silver and cutting dandelions out of the cracks in the worn stone steps (though he couldn't reach the rooftiles to tear off the mad carpeting of mustard that sprouts there, thank goodness), and trimming his geraniums, and I thought, how right, how good, here's where he belongs.

He and his great friend Edward paid a thousand pounds for a fifty-year lease on the place four years ago. They sank the rest of their money into plumbing and electricity, they scraped rotten plaster off the stones, they scrubbed the balcony white, they put in a hot-water heater and had new shutters made for the windows. The ten rooms were just stone cells. They made one into a kitchen, made a bathroom in another, installed in the third Laddie's elderly Pleyel. A fourth became Edward's bedroom and if they had had enough money they'd have fixed up the other rooms to let. The walls are a foot and a half thick and made of that stone I love, soft, pocked and yellow. The roof extends over the balcony and is held up by pillars with capitals that are shaped like a dim memory of the Ionic order. I have to congratulate Laddie.

The courtyard is not paved: there are hollows of sticky clay that collect the winter rain and freeze in the night. I muddy my shoes in them squatting to watch over the bellied amphorae the arrival of Laddie's ladies: two stout women in good knitted suits, upholstered, in good grey calf leather shoes, heavy. Of the kind who gave me the recipes at the dinner party he played at: take twelve eggs, three pounds of hazel nuts, three pounds of honey.

The introductions resound in the jar below the balcony. Mrs Haji-Blank, whose family has made a pilgrimage to the river Jordan; Mrs Andreas-who-is-related-to-a-priest, and, smaller, catching up with them, Mrs Who-comes-from-Mitsero. She is younger than the others and more sophisticated, she looks as if she reads *Elle* rather than the perennial *Romantzo*. All of them will have children of pianoable age.

I used to look at Rosa Trethewey Moore and think her the very embodiment of the bourgeoisie. I know better now, for it is taking tea on the balcony.

He is speaking to them in a special language that I too shall instinctively learn, English for Foreigners, the language of *For Whom the Bell Tolls*, with much emphasis on the use of the past-perfect tense. "My mother also has very much liked green tea," he says.

MONODROMOS

From here he still looks very beautiful. The hair, though there is less of it, is golden and well cut. The physical consolidation that took place in his twenties has replaced his wasp-willow look. He looks stronger, now, and oddly sexy. His suit is immaculate. He had the ironing board out this morning, flashing me ironic looks referring to the one year of our marriage, when I scorched his dress shirts. I don't like the way he flashes his bum like a child coquette when he walks, but that's a kind of race prejudice in me, I ought to be above feeling like that. His nervous arrogance has given way to an adult authority and he is good now, in the way he deals with these women, exchanging courtesies and the smallest possible jokes. Now he is carrying the tea table to the music room, letting them flutter and help with the cups and saucers. I wonder what he will play for them?

It must please the women to be chauffeured from their dodecasyllabic suburbs in big grey cars to visit him, take tea with a genuine gentleman musician in a former caravanserai. Now that the English lord is gone, he has his sister living with him. It would be more romantic if she were blind like the sister in Lawrence Durrell, and instead of hiding, stayed to listen admiringly to him playing Chopin after tea. The notes have an extra poignancy as they fall disorderly from the sticking piano keys.

Florinda met me at the airport, a fat-fleshed mother-figure, now the proprietor of a teashop, once a dancer. An anagram of Heidi, who met me when he wired me to come to Frankfurt. I ignored his telegrams from Ajaccio and Uppsala.

At the airport, I was disoriented. It was dark, and I was in a new country and I could not see it. I had not had time to think, I had left Max, left Pye, left England, left even Maurice Henshaw, come to the unknown suddenly, fallen into the arms of a large active person who packed me into her little car and took me to him immediately. We looked at each other and nodded formally. It gave us both the miseries to see each other again, but she was so pleased with her efficiency we didn't let it show.

Out again, into the cold streets and alleys. The thought of hot tea and music makes me feel exiled. I wish I could curl up on Edward's bed and read, but the ladies would think it rude and queer.

&

Last week, on Friday, I went to look up Mr Speridakis. The girl in the outer office is a moustached Alexandrian of seventeen called Bibi. She said, "Oh, are you the lady from Pye Information? Do you like it here? I do not. I am from Alexandria. It is a much better place. It is very old-fashioned here, my uncle will not let me go out to the cinema at night even with my brother. Mr Loizos has not yet returned from Addis Ababa. Do you wish to talk with Mrs Barnes?"

Since under the initials HP / AM and LS / DB Mrs Barnes and I had corresponded for some years, I said I wished to meet her. Bibi ushered me into a large office that had once been the drawingroom of the house the office is in, which is dominated by a huge equestrian portrait of some Greek king. Bending over an enormous desk spread with the raw material of the Argentina List, a blonde with enviable legs was checking names from a sheet of paper. She looked up: pretty, and somewhat predatory about the mouth. "Oh," she said, "you must come to lunch. Monday. We're on ex-Gladstone Street near the Russian Embassy. Number thirty-two. About one. I don't expect Mr Speridakis will be back for an age."

Laddie waited for me across the street in a coffee shop. We had coffee together when I came back, and sat drinking the sweet stuff to the lees, staring at the low roof-line and curved verandah of Speridakis' umber-washed Colonial house. "It needs gingerbread, it's carpenter-Gothic," I said. "It used to be the

British Council,'' Laddie said. ''Your Mr Speridakis has come up in the world.''

Sunday afternoon: I could be drinking tea with those women, I didn't want to. The sun's going down already; even with a duffle coat on, I'm shivering. I have lost all my enthusiasm for continuing the trip around the walls. Splendour could not absorb me now. I want my comforts. I come into the main street, and join a queue at the English bookstore, where Sunday Timeses and Pictorials, Observers and Expresses are selling as fast as tickets to the Irish Sweeps. An Englishman mumbles that the plane was late this morning. The man who is selling the papers from the doorway has a kind of standard storekeepers' face: Mussolini-shaped and sloe-eyed and unsmiling. His customers are out of Grahame Greene, there's even a little Englishman in a kilt who looks as if he would know Laddie, and a fat woman on a bicycle who says ''Ta-ta'' for the Sunday Telegraph.

The teashop next to the paper shop is necessarily pricey, and there is a choice of Earl Grey and Typhoo. There doesn't seem to be an open bar around, the British have left their mark. There are many varieties of gargantuan sticky cakes. I hide behind my paper, looking through it to see if Max has written a review, listening to the English making a kind of shorthand conversational hum. Nobody says anything interesting. Better to watch the sweetshop man set out trays of Turkish delight with sugar-lust in his eyes.

&

For supper he makes the same kind of shepherd's pie his mother made, onions and meat hashed with leftover gravy, good creamy mashed potatoes on top. The meat he uses is a kind of Danish Spam called Hamlet, ounce per ounce the cheapest meat on the island. There are good-looking butcher shops in the main street run by great hammy men who lounge between hanging carcasses, but he marches me past them into a little store that is no more than a covered doorway to buy this Hamlet, ignoring hams that are black with sumach and coriander, and strings of spicy sausages, and big pungent tins of anchovies. He says I don't know how to live off the land yet, and when I say he certainly cooks with a lot of onions, he says, "All foreigners eat onions."

The kitchen is neutral territory and we are relatively harmonious in it. We were, after all, brought up in kitchens. He cooks meticulously, though rather unimaginatively considering all the gourmandistic paradises he has lived in, ignoring the treasures of the Indies to reproduce his mother's food. I wash the teacups and stack them to drain on the wooden counter. I say I wish there was more storage space. He says "You can't teach an old khan new tricks," and that is the one and only laugh of the day. He lays the table the way his mother did, with the spoons across the top of the plates. He dishes out the food.

We sit erect in our chairs like good children, our knees together prudently. We miss our napkin rings and are ashamed of not saying grace. I look at him. He is forty.

Close up, you can see that he is going bald untidily; there are wisps of hair isolated on his cranium. That must pain him; he was always neat. Women lose their figures, men their hair. He isn't now the youngster chided by the music critic of the Guardian for condescending to his audience at Wigmore Hall. His fingers are all gnarled with rheumatism. You can't heat a place like this in winter.

We have heavy lemon pudding for dessert, made with thick malty island bread. There's a French bakery in Grammos Street which makes croissants and white bread, but Laddie says it's too expensive, and anyway the other day when I sneaked in on the sly, the woman behind the corner said she wouldn't sell me anything because I was wearing jeans.

I clear the table. He fills the kettle from the tap because

the water can be used when it is boiled. For cold drinking water we use a terra-cotta jug of ancient design: where neck and body meet there are vestigial pottery breasts. It keeps the water cool and sweet. We buy it from a water-carrier who comes down the street with a tank on a cart pulled by a small black mule he calls Lumumba.

When I am sitting here with him like this I feel my own invasion, I know Florinda's wire was a mistake, I am not needed, there is no dire distress. He is poor, certainly, and lonely, but no poorer and no lonelier than I was sometimes in London. I feel a big blank between us and the disgraceful knowledge that he has amputated his social life because I am here. My instinct was right, I should not have come. I'm still fond of him, but not in a good way, there's a malicious edge to everything I think about him because it was so stupid of me to marry him and I've never got over the humiliation. I wish I could afford to get a room somewhere else—because as Pye said it's foolish to come for just a week—but I'll have to wait until I find out if I have that job with Speridakis, keeping company with misery.

Tonight he has to talk, he has to tell me what he wants of me, on what terms we can continue together until I am financially independent. I'll get him going. "How was your tea party?"

"Weren't you there?"

"No, I told you I was going out and I went, except for coming back to the loo."

"And hid behind the wine-jars."

"They're marvellous aren't they? Could you see me? I'm sorry. If I had gone straight out I'd have run into them."

"Well why not? Why couldn't you've just walked by them and nodded politely like a real person? Why do you have to be such a slob?"

So we are at it again. He turns away to make the tea. I begin to rise in response, because I am angry with myself for still wanting to please him, and then I use my head. "You couldn't see me without leaning over. You did lean over to fold the tablecloth. They didn't lean over, ergo, they didn't see me."

"Oh yes, they saw you. They were too polite to mention it, but I could tell from their faces."

"How?"

"They wrinkled their noses."

"Maybe the place smelled of onions. It generally does."

"It does not."

"It does."

"I was most careful to air it. Probably you sitting all that time in the bog."

"I'll make the tea if that's the way you're feeling." He is waving the kettle dangerously at me. I take it from him and find that it is off the boil. I go to put it on the gas. "Anyway, you can't see the side where the jars are from here, I know it. You're lying to put me in the wrong. You always do."

He is about to reply when I try to light the gas and there is a juvenile pop, an expiring hiss: the butane cylinder is empty.

"Thirty shillings," he shouts. "Thirty goddam shillings. Seven and a half fucking piano lessons." He puts his head on the table on his arms. His back hair is still soft and fine and golden, like a child's. His shoulders shake.

There is water hot enough in the boiler to make instant coffee, but is it safe to drink? He never drinks instant coffee. I begin to wash the dishes. I don't want to look at him. The rain that has fallen in that life is chosen rain, and I don't want to think about being broke and exiled, it's a place I've been too.

When I've washed and dried the dishes and he has seen this, he goes out to the toilet. He returns with a clear face and sits down at the table, working his hands together. I leave and go to Edward's room and come back with pencils, paper, and a bottle of island brandy, for which I am acquiring a taste. "Shall we talk?''

Old attitudes hanging around us like shrouds on a clothes-line: and then he talks.

&

Edward is nondescript, he says, although, as the Germans would put it, highly well-born. Edward is youngish, quite young.

Is Edward not Hatch, the music critic, with whom he lived so . . . ?

No, no, Hatch was years ago. No, Edward is, or Edward was . . . look, Edward is gone.

Gone where?

Ah, there's the secret, the mystery, it's rather beautiful, but . . .

But what? Get on with it, Laddie.

The day he brought the Turk I was in misery. He had been gone three days. Things were going badly for us. Edward's guardian had cut off his allowance, and the last of my royalties had come months ago. My agent—if he had found me a circuit how could I repair my clothes and buy my ticket? No, we were both of us washed up, beached. Then Edward . . .

Edward who has accoutred his room with the heaviest treasures of the Biedermeierzeit, whose few books are ancient leather-bound treatises on the Papacy bought for their spines, on whose crested linen I . . .

Then Edward having walked out to buy oh, lunch, cigarettes, drink, something, and been gone three days—in the summer the weather is unbreathable in daytime, one lives at night—and the heat here . . . I had moved my mattress to the verandah, (a mistake, it is cooler inside, the walls are so thick . . .) and I didn't hear them. They were beside me, suddenly, Edward looking—he is not as young, now, of course, but he still has his hectic schoolboy rosiness—Edward looking excited and the man with him, a big slow, ring-fingered Turk, full of exquisite compliments, heavy-eyed, a type who is classic but still: courteous. Oughtn't to have trusted . . . but all of a piece, you understand, consistent with himself. In the night you cannot say eunuch, pimp, court procurer.

We sat where we are now, between the stove and the doorway, cramped, domestic. I made their kind of coffee. I make it as well as the cafes, you have to take their mysticism seriously and let it come to a foaming boil three times. Then you pour it ever so carefully a little into the bottom of each cup, then around again, so the dregs are fairly distributed. Beautiful coffee very sweet. There was music, I remember; not the three old fellows downstairs—though I do like Aristides' flute, don't you?—not that nasal yelling the other two do, but from far off, from one of the clubs, probably the place along the way, the House of a Thousand Bottles, and every one of them empty, as Teddy used to say. Bouzouki, from far off: it was very dark and magic. I don't mind Greek music in the heat. In the winter it . . . never mind.

It's something in the beat, the way they yowl with it. Good enough stuff as folk music goes, but . . .

I made them coffee. Edward got out the brandy as usual; he'd been drinking rather too much all summer, but of course, the heat . . .

The Turkish gentleman: look, you mustn't take me for an utter fool; it's not that I'm inclined to trust fat Levantines who turn up with Edward when he's drunk and been away three days and in the middle of the night. But to give him credit, he seemed no more inscrutable than anyone else here. We're not popular, our sort, you know: might as well be in England sixty years ago. Everything is officially organised along quite other lines: dowries, prostitutes, the male-oriented bit, *our* kind of Hellenism doesn't go down at all well with the church. Oh, there are places, resources, but nothing Arabian Nights, as I do admit

I had hoped once. The whole society's very bourgeois. I saw you glaring at my tea-party and I thought my God, I've come full circle and I'm the image of my own cousin Permilla, genteel, and the finger crooked and the sharp nose peering at the rosebuds in the bottom of the teacup, dear—but really, in Rome, the Romans, it's all quite, quite necessary. What else to do? Stuck here, beached. Six years, now, and we *made* this place, it was an absolute dump when we took it and put everything we had in it. And then something legal happened to Eddie's entail. We thought we were going to be in heaven. Lonnie Fogart, the architect who used to live in the Armenian quarter, drew us up the plans, and I suppose I've rather let it go, but a year ago this place was paradise, paradise, and we were going to keep on with it. I mean, the least one can do is keep on, make the best of it, isn't it? So that one invites the dear ladies to tea to discuss their infants' progress, and attempts to trust oily gentlemen in the night.

Teddy had been drinking, but he didn't look scruffy. He was as sweet and clean as a Sunday School boy. Perhaps they had stopped in at the hammam. His eyes were shining. I don't know when I've seen him so happy. They told me about the proposition.

I ought to have known. It was so—so Kiplingesque, so Empire-ridden, just the right mixture of adventure and anthropology, and out of the way—and I thought, the women will appeal to him—Teddy's bi, though he didn't get much of a chance here, the way they lock up their daughters.

I met him at Aix, the year I played at the Festival, and got the awful, really shocking, I hope you didn't read them, they would have made you even more bloody-minded, notices. A little apple-cheeked Eton boy, failed his A levels, staying with an old woman in the Quartier Mazarin who was a friend of Jean-Philippe's. It was a low point for me, I had left Hatch. You can't live with critics, they turn into dreadful nags. I was cruising a little and I was just on the point of taking up with a rather dreadful Algerian when I met Teddy.

Terribly young, I know; but it was his initiative. I've never known anyone so thoroughly *schooled*. Trade secrets you'd consider unsavoury, I'll change the subject. We went to Corsica with Jean-Philippe, then I left to do a dreary tour in the North of England. Edward did me the compliment of meeting me in Leeds. He said he was miserable without me. So until he came of age we had to come somewhere, his father didn't seem to mind where as long as it was good and far away and he pretended he was doing something. We thought of the Greek islands but they said there wouldn't be anybody for me to teach, and this place looked so wonderful on the map, and Eddie thought with his title and all he might get something . . .

It was hot, that night, hot, and not a dry heat. This island sits in the middle of a sea of warm soup. It was August, and there was music from far away. I wouldn't have believed them if they'd told me about it in the daytime.

He was to go to an island off the coast of Turkey and become a factor in snails. It has to be hot, with music from very far, if you want to believe that. Of course it is true that the best French snails you get in tins are imported from Turkey. And you can see why he was excited. The Turk was a big, slow fat man, he called one my dear and made very slow gestures with his hands that had big rings on them. And he told us about the island and we sat like the two young boys on the dock in that picture about Sir Walter Raleigh that was in the history book at school, drinking it all in. It was a very special island, inhabited by a race of troglodyte gypsies. He had photographs of marvellous conical hills with doors and windows in them, naturally weathered dry mountains, well, tiny little ones, more hills or hummocks, and the gypsies had hollowed out little caves. And the gypsies were snail-gatherers.

It does sound odd, doesn't it? I mean, the point of gypsies

is that they don't live in houses. I remember your father teasing your mother because her maiden name was Lee, saying she was a gypsy, if she didn't like the house she should go and sleep out on the beach. But the night was magic and he had a map. He pointed to a quay and said, "You, my dear, will live here." And then he explained that that island, like this one, was bisected by a low but precipitous range of mountains, and that at certain times of the year Edward would be in charge of accompanying a group of natives, Turks, over the range with a caravan of donkeys, to buy the harvested snail crop from the gypsies. This was necessary because there were tribal wars between the gypsies, who lived on the non-agricultural side of the island and the Turkish villagers who made periodic raids on the snail-bearing lands, hoping to cultivate the slopes where the wild thyme grew.

He was fascinating. He had words from old-fashioned geography books and much persuasiveness. And Edward was to be a factor for him, to live in isolation with a selected library, of course, and carry out his duties like a true English sahib. How could he resist?

He went to his room and came back with a rucksack stuffed with pyjamas and underwear, and his favourite books and the picture of his mother. They left, then. Just like that. Edward smiling as I'd never seen him smile before, the seraphic bitch. And it was weeks before I realised that I didn't know the island's name. If it was on the map I hadn't noticed it. The Turk said his name was Ismet Bey. There's a needle in a haystack.

Not a word from him in over six months. And now it transpires he never paid any of the bills. I didn't expect much, but when he had money I thought he could put some on the grocery account. I started the lessons again after he left. When he was here I was a bit capricious about them, because he hated the noise when he had a hangover, and they were certainly capricious about coming. Florinda found me at Christmas, sick and starving on the floor. She's been a boon, Florinda; they're the only ones who care, you know, the old hags with no hope but mothering left to them. I don't know why she wired you. Perhaps I was weak, and told her to. But you're no good to me if you've spent all your money on your ticket, are you?

There's nothing even remotely like it on the marine charts. I heard last week he'd been seen in the Northern Range. There are a million villages there, needles in haystacks again. If he'd wanted to go he could have just gone, I wouldn't hold it against him. He wasn't faithful, he'd disappeared for days before, and there are certain ships that come in, I've had my pecadillos. But my God, he isn't here now, is he?

Below us, in the courtyard, Aristides is playing. By day he goes out in his wheelchair to sell lottery tickets and reed shepherd's flutes in the street. At night he comes to drink with his friend the tailor downstairs, and Mr Flores, and they play and sing together. The notes of his flute are eery. They make you think that only a poor man can make such sweet sounds with that crude instrument. They are like cool water.

II

JANUARY
MONDAY

There are no lessons before school today. Laddie snores in bed, exhausted by confession. Early, I go down to Phaedra to enquire about getting a new cylinder of gas. She in her shapeless dirty housedress jerks her shoulder at her husband, who propels his little graceless body quickly away. She claps for coffee. How do I want it? Sweet? Medium? Very Sweet? Moderately sweet? Naked? Medium. *Metrio*. She is pleased I know the word.

She smiles. While we wait, I purchase cigarettes from her, English ones made under licence here and sold in maddening packages of fourteen. If I liked black tobacco I would buy Papastratos, which come in exquisite little boxes containing maps of the world. A boy appears with a bicycle, holding a round tray suspended from three wires: my coffee.

I am given a chair, I sit to drink my coffee as she carries on a loud conversation with someone in the back of the store. Then she pats me on the shoulder, smiling, friendly as can be, and hands me a small black notebook. On the first page I can decipher the word "Ladi", and numbers in Greek and English and in all salient principles the same.

There are many pages and few of them are marked to indicate that the account has ever been paid. Impossible to decipher most of the words. She translates for me (they all, inside the walls, have acquired a little English in order to survive commercially), "Tomatoes. Cigarettes. Oil. Brandy. Nescafe. Cucumber. Hamlet. Rice." Mostly, cigarettes and brandy. "Mr Edward?" I ask. Yes, she says hopefully, and flips to the back of the book, where the sum has been totalled and is enormous.

I have travelled hopefully and arrived with a thud. I love this place, the people all look wonderful, except one. She stands in front of me smiling the vestige of a schoolgirl's propitiatory smile, among her dusty sausages and filthy candles, old bread, decaying produce. I have already noticed that she sells more dearly than her neighbours. In addition, she is indubitably dirty. For almost two weeks, I have heard her hectoring her husband. In any language, those personalities are the same. An overwhelming smell of anchovies and perspiration envelops me. How could anyone owe this woman four hundred pounds, half a year's wages at Pye's? An awful snobbishness engorges me, I could play the conquering English lady, I don't want to pay her, I'll eel out of it.

Her husband returns, shuffling. Behind him, a young lad trundles a tank of Butagaz on a trolley. "Thirty-five shillings," says Mr Phaedra.

"With the old tank, thirty shillings," I reply, proud of my business acuity.

"Old tank is seven shillings, sixpence," the delivery boy says. "Pay me, missus."

The Phaedras glare at him and me. I go around through the archway and through the courtyard and up the stairs to the kitchen with the boy, pay him his thirty shillings, receive seven and a half for the empty tank, and am refused when I offer a tip. "They are bad people," he says, jerking his thumb downstairs.

The street is seething when I go out again, with bicycles, mules, trucks, mini-station wagons. I push my way down the street to go to lunch with Dympna Barnes, walking circumspectly, for the clang of bicycle bells is frightening and piles of china, enamelware, hardware and drygoods are thrust unevenly into the street. I am still seething at the encounter with Mrs Phaedra, and, afraid of my balance in anger, I walk gingerly. Suddenly I hear running feet behind me. It is a woman who runs a little knitting shop and sells safety pins and zippers, a woman with a crimped ex-blonde permanent and a knitted frown. "Mrs Laddie," she calls, "Mrs Laddie. One pound, please, one pound."

I slink into a stall to get away from her and find myself between stacks of red hospital blankets. A beaming clerk with a Clark Gable moustache approaches. "How much?" I ask. "Ten shillings per lib," he says; "very good blankets, best English quality, let me show you." He spreads his treasure out, caressing the indifferent wool, extolling the evenness of the commonplace weave, extending the label to show the Britishness of the product. I ask, "What is a lib?" He shows me the label: "Pure wool, 4 lbs." I thank him, resist a vagrant female impulse to embrace him, leave wondering if I would have found Phaedra's mistake in English as adorable.

I am late when finally I dawdle to the ex-Gladstone Street side of the moat. Hurrying past a walled English cemetery, I rush by big Embassy houses to a little villa with a neat sign on the door, "Terribly sorry, have had to go away, DB." Phooey. The museum is closed on Mondays, though it is not far away. The section of the city is arrantly, heavily commercial. If I go home, "The Happy Farmer" will be rocking the courtyard during noon hour piano lessons. There is absolutely nothing for me to do. I must find friends.

&

Dear Max, dear splendid Max, Max capital, Max Esquire, Max: Lemons, fat-rinded oranges, bay on the branch (Daphnis), tomato paste on paper squares, Jerusalem artichokes, purple French artichokes, onions, potatoes, carrots, tin toys, frozen octopus from Greece, dead hanging sheep on hooks, rice puddings, Indian custard like rosewater junket, Armenian pancakes spread with meat and sumach—like the socca we had in the bar in Nice, behind the lawcourts, with wine mixed with lemonade—cheese pies, pumpkin pies, and curled sheets of dried apricot paste that look like sheets of fly poison put out in summer in a pie plate; water jars with vestigial penises and breasts; pinheaded penny banks like the Venus of Willendorf with the slot in the wrong place, Lapithos jugs with splashed copper in the glaze, bowls, plates, casseroles, yoghourt pots, all undecorated, spindles, hand-made whiskbrooms, whorled. Poets don't know the domesticity of Byzantium, they're all too busy looking for mosaics, gyres and mechanical birds.

The bazaar, once the souk: the lid has been taken off, it's now an ordinary quadrille of streets; but there are silver and goldsmiths, coppersmiths of huge dimension, rug-vendors, hardware stores and haberdasheries, candle, ex-voto and string-makers all combined, halvah-moulders, bootmakers, perfumiers, busmakers: all still to be explored.

And the countryside contains the whole of history and I haven't been there yet.

And you sent books from Edinburgh. I'd be afraid to go to Edinburgh, it's the iron in the blood of Canada, and the snow in the veins, they'd kill me dead, they'd look and say "That one's unworthy," and send me to the gallows before you could say . . . what? "She's worth sending books to." Thank you. The funny man in the kilt who came last night to see the Lad said the old guidebook that mentioned dragomen and native porters was immensely valuable. I shall treasure the book on flora. And I am halfway happily through the Iris Murdoch.

The kilted man who came to see the Lad brought cats with huge Egyptian ears. Not Siamese, mind you, but not English either. Egyptian in the department of the ear and intelligent-looking, though not necessarily intelligent, knowing cats. "If you don't take them I've got to do away with them," he said pathetically. "In the end, they run your life." I was much tempted but there were nine of them, and Laddie, whose problem is not really love but money, resisted. "Take them to the vet, Percy." Off the kilt flirted. In an hour he returned exhausted and tearstained and drank a great deal of brandy. "It always happens," he said. "You take them in and they eat you out of house and home." He looked profoundly sad, but somehow not penitent. As a conversationalist he was otherwise uninteresting.

I notice that when you take this place apart with words it ceases to exist. You'll have to come. The cost of living is as high as that taxi-driver said; as high as London. It's not, either, all of a piece, eye-wise, like Mykonos. I don't know where the charm quite lies, but I bathe in it. It simply floods in like the light. I think it belongs to the conjunction of images; it distills itself as you stand on the street corner thinking of all the poetry that ever tried to exist.

I've been so bad about writing, saving my impressions up, and now I feel too paralysed by the richness to put them down. It's simply and utterly beautiful. It has a sordid edge as well—you think of Durrell's Alexandria but of course it's on a different scale. All the *English* travel books prepare you for a disappointment, they expect you to be some kind of purist for whom everything must be the Taj Mahal—phooey on them. This is much, much better, not a monument but a whole place with its evolution showing. And since it's not on a grand scale it is possible to dream of exploring it. I won't be satisfied until I know both the city and the island like an encyclopaedia.

But I haven't met many people yet. Speridakis is still away and his secretary Mrs Barnes is one of those blonde evasive superior English girls who don't give anything away or turn up to lunch. The most vivid person in Our Khan (I shall fix up one of the empty rooms for you, tent it in stripes and carpet it with orange sateen mattresses they make beside the cotton gin in Baffo Street, for when you come) is Laddie's absent Edward, a real English milord, if you please. I'm the daughter of the Earl of Oak Acres, myself. I bet Elizabeth has a Debrett's and you can look him up to see if he is lying. I know I'm not, but he may have reason to, considering the structure of debt he has erected all about us.

Laddie was not pleased to see me. I was wrong to come, I suppose, from the point of view of psychological game-playing. The only justification is my selfish enjoyment of this place.

The sun is getting stronger every day. Tomorrow I plan to rent a bicycle and ride into the country. Laddie says the shepherds will goose me. I suppose shepherds do goose people, it's quite in the fabric of the pastoral mode.

Laddie's protectiveness is like my mother's, I think. She had me wear running shoes whenever I went out alone at night, which kept me pure and saved her worry. For a while, I thought Laddie was hiding something, he seemed so furtive about what my relationship with this world was to be, but now I think he had nothing up his sleeve but his own comfort. If he discourages me from doing everything, he doesn't have to worry about whether I do the wrong thing. I don't know, though: how can you tell what the reticent are thinking? I don't really believe that still waters run deep.

Yes, I am happy here, though I miss you a great deal. I would like to see the island from your eyes, which have seen so much else besides. So I am glad to have the head start on you and will poke and pry against your visit in order to dig out treasures of imagery and design. If you promise to come very soon I shall send you a beautiful cat's pelt from the Pharmakia as a chest-protector against your voyage. If you tarry, I shall run away with a shepherd.

MONODROMOS

With all love, heightened emotion, and beaten gilded birds, your A.

III

FEBRUARY

They knew how to build once. Think of a city block as a thick-sided lidless shoebox, the kind you divide up inside to make a peep show. Put doors, weathered deep into the grain and latched by breastplate fastenings with frayed edges and twisted hanging rings, and wide shallow archways at intervals in the outer walls (chipped stucco, ashlar corners, mud-brick and rubble-fill, thick, cool). Looking down from your Olympian position, divide your shoe-box into compartments large and small. Roof over as much of each compartment as you think your family will need; make three rooms here and five there, with a hutch for a kitchen. Partition the back half of the main room of the oldest dwelling horizontally also, to form not a sleeping platform but a classic grain-store. Where the roof does not cover the entire enclosure make a courtyard garden, setting out wild cyclamen in old Spry cans, wiring a chicken run, training a vine or a fig tree, making sure to plant a lemon tree. And where the beam ends of the roof have decayed in the stone and adobe wall, lodge tumbling doves.

When your daughter marries, roof over another section of the courtyard for her dower house.

Aphroulla's outer gate is an old plank door flush with the street. The house is at the back of the courtyard and consists of two rooms, hers and her son's. It is simply roofed with beams and tiles and rushes. A shed alongside houses a kitchen which has running water and a shower stall, and a toilet you flush with a pail of water.

"I've never thought of housing as interior geography before," I say to Laddie.

"What do you mean?" Looking up from an old green Penguin book, annoyed.

"When we made villages out of blocks when we were kids we started with solid forms. Here you'd have to think differently. Exterior and interior meet. The garden walls are also housing walls. Each city block is also a house in itself "

"You have travelled in the realms of gold, haven't you?"

A dried vine hangs limply over the arbour beside Aphroulla's lemon tree. A dead-looking arthritic fig tree presides inside the gate. White doves round as puffballs hide under the edges of her faded rooftiles. In the courtyard there are benches and plaques and modernistic plaster statues and a sundial made from a Byzantine capital capped with a bronze slab that she cast herself. The inscription is in an ancient language and obscene.

I found her by a kind of psychic coincidence and I hope she will be my friend.

After the first fortnight here I thought a hundred times of going away; but there seemed no point in leaving the island unexplored and returning to an England empty of Max, heat, work, fantasy. Laddie and I paced the stone galleries of the khan like a pair of leopards. Outside, the town was beginning to develop itself for me as a compound of undigestible images, fragments of eye-shapes, cornices, siren-songs. I began to want badly to know it, and in that intimate way which consumes time, perhaps lifetime.

On the balcony of the caravanserai, the once-oriole turned crow thought differently. "Where are you going?"

"Out."

"You can't go out alone at night."

"Just to a movie."

"They'll rape you and cut you up in little pieces."

"For godsake Laddie, I'll wear my running shoes and take my bow and arrow."

"It isn't done, you know."

"Nobody anywhere really gives a shit what other people do. You just think so."

"They watch everything you do here."

"You're paranoid."

"When in Rome . . .I thought you were the experienced traveller."

"Come with me, then."

"How can you waste your time and money at the movies?"

"How can you sit and moulder here every night waiting for Mr Halley's Comet himself?"

"Anyway, you can't go out."

The year we split up—I found him in a poor position with John Snow Lowden in the loo—I was sick with agonies of humiliation. I was wrong. "Do you have any friends we could drop in on? I'm stir-crazy."

"No."

"Let's go for a walk."

"I'm too tired."

Mr Speridakis has not yet returned from Addis Ababa. I feel now that he will never return from Addis Ababa. I decide to use my time to venture forth, explore the island. It is small enough, it seems, to be explorable.

In reality, I find that it is immense, that car-hire is beyond my pocket, that bus schedules are impenetrable and geared to getting the workers to this city at 6 a.m. There are virtually no hotels in the delicious-looking villages you can get to on the workmen's buses. Communal taxis, are, however, available to the other cities. I travel south to Scala, an ancient seaport, on an idle day, and spend it walking on the seedy promenade. Perhaps in summer it is a pleasant place, but now it looks like a bewildered imitation of Nice. Most of the old town was knocked over by an earthquake, and the rich archaeological diggings are locked behind Frost fence. Gunnis tells me it was founded by Chittim, son of Noah. A bust on a plinth proclaims that here Zeno was born. It was a great port during the Crusades and during the Turkish occupation that filled the period from the reign of Elizabeth to that of Victoria, it housed those foreign consuls who negotiated safe-conducts between travellers and the Porte. The beach is stony, the principal treasure of the town now seems to be an American convent that grooms students for the American University in Beirut. *My name is Ozymandias, king of kings . . .*

&

We pass and re-pass each other on the gallery, and sit brooding in our arched doorways, staring vacantly at beams and columns and plaited rushes above us. The roof leaks. Laddie has been told he ought to have spread lumps of clay upon it in the fall, to melt in the winter rains and seal it. He doesn't like heights. He spends his evenings staring at the wall as if it were a television set. I loathe his idleness, it is seeping into me. "Let's go to the movie-house around the corner."

"Why?"

"We can't just sit around and do nothing all the time."

"When in Rome . . . "

"Are they all sitting staring at their walls? I don't believe it. They're always busy. Why don't you play?"

"My hands are stiff."

"Well, let's go out and peek in windows."

"They go to bed at nine in the winter."

"I can't stand this, Laddie, I'm going out, the Devil finds

work . . . ''

''Well, go then. If some wily Pathan carves you up, I'm not responsible.''

''I should think not.''

Out. At last. It is black, but surprisingly fine. Not a soul in the streets, busy buildings resting. No sound, even from behind the doors of the taverna. Maybe he's right, they've gone to bed. There is light, though, faint, coming through broken hinges and half-plugged holes.

I am still unused to the city in the dark. I fumble left, right, left again, and almost trip over the manager of the cinema I am looking for. He stands ingratiatingly under his tin marquee, grinning hopefully in a waiter's cummerbund and dress suit, ready to sprint into the cashier's box. There is no competition for tickets. Yesterday's bill, *O Tpitos Anøpoπos*, with Opson Ovels and Tzozeø Koton, and *Sian,* with AAan Aantt, has disappeared in favour of an Indian double bill with Greek and Chinese subtitles.

I head wilfully into the unknown, hoping to find again that sector of the city where a streak of Arab fatalism has preserved the older buildings. The mere arrival of February has softened the weather. Walking alone at night, warm and mysteriously comfortable, one can possess this world.

Damp winter sacredness of wood and clay and somewhere a great grille-screened house of mediaeval proportions once seen from a side street, empty and possible, for whom? for what? Somewhere, too, a pair of high wooden towers like grain elevators, and a church with a sunken courtyard, a vine-covered mosque.

My footsteps echo. If they have electric light in this quarter they are saving it. The streets are canyons. Old oriels loom, their wooden corbels creek. Behind the buttresses of the old Bedestan beside the cathedral, there is a house with a round mediaeval window, can I find it?

MONODROMOS

The alleys smell of pee. Above me shuttered balconies meet and close off the roof of the street, blotting out the quarter of a gibbous moon through cross-lathed screens. In a doorway, I hear low voices. I pass foundations sunk beneath the level of the street, look up at huts on roofs, spy out small slatternly houses crammed between great decaying mansions. Who lives in them, squatters or disgraced daughters? The widow of Mr Rochester?

Curtains are pulled as my shoes resound in the street, but I see no faces. Once I turn my ankle in a puddle and swear: a light goes on behind a shutter. There is music, but from very far away. Nearby, there is the clacking swish of falling palm and eucalyptus leaves.

London is never dark at night. From the Heath at one in the morning you see the city outlined in a hellish glow. Streets here are dark as lentil soup. Women do not go out alone at night. Here be purse-snatchers, as in Arva Township.

Noise behind. Light. Oh God, let it be a corsair or a eunuch servant, at least a Bishop's nephew pimping for his lord: make it something southern and corrupt and not banal.

Earth. Wood. Iron. Beside a minaret (the circle of the loud-speaker outlined in the moonlight), a Gothic doorway. Behind it, a cemetery containing turbaned styles and cypresses. Walled. Gated. Padlocked. Climb.

Car lights, car lights stopping. "Lady?"

The vehicle is a jeep. The lights are blinding. I take my foolish feet off the fence. "Lady, we are tourist police, are you losted?"

"Just out for a walk, thank you." Severely: the voice of Lady Hester Stanhope looking for the loo. On her way to tame a sheik.

"You must not walk out in the night by yourself, Lady."

Lights dazzle, then I see the outlines of their caps, the shiny reflections on their obviously genuine badges. "I'm quite competent, thank you.''

''What are you seeking, Lady?''

For no reason at all: ''I'm looking for the house of the lady who is a painter.''

What I love about Max is the head on his shoulders, his refusal to have to do with waffle, tripe and spooks in a world that is larded with them. So I know that what I said then came from a faint memory of an article in a colour supplement, that it did not rise from the collective unconscious or the influence of anybody's private holy well. His is a view that limits the circumference of eternity and comforts me.

Because they hand me into the jeep, the junior officer tumbling clumsily into the back, the driver carefully assisting me to arrange my skirt, and changing gears with his knuckles in my thigh, repeating his lecture against nocturnal peregrination. ''The Turks is a very violent people, they rubs their bodies with blood from the bladders of a pig before they goes to war, they loves women too much.'' Banging into gear again, and, in a swirl of headlights over arches, oriels, flying buttresses and minarets, setting out for the house of the lady who is a . . .

''Mrs Aphroulla, Mrs Aphroulla, the sister of Mr Ladi is coming to visit you.''

''Oh . . . '' They have invaded her courtyard with me, stuffing me gently enough, but stuffing me, through her wooden door. ''Oh, Costas, Eleftherios, thank you, thank you.'' The voice is deep and disembodied and crisp. ''Good. Welcome, welcome. Did you get lost, trying to find me? It is not very far, but the streets are crooked. It is worse than the Left Bank of Paris, do you not find? Good night, Costas, good night, Eleftherios. Yes, you can go now, she is safe with me. I hoped that your brother would bring you to me last week, but he has not done so. But it is perfect that you have come tonight, for we are having a small party and you will make some friends.''

After the chill of isolation there is the warm air of human

breath. I sense the trees in the courtyard, I smell black village wine. "Come into the studio," she says, "and join our circle. It is not yet warm enough to be outside. They say in the travel pamphlets that we have 340 days of sunshine per year: they do not mention the cold nights of January and February, when the villagers suffer because they have no European winter coats. It is only a small party. What is your name?"

Her studio is a little house in itself. *Monospitos*, one-house, is the word for it in Greek architecture. The form is simple and age-old: a roof, four walls, a door, beside the door, a hearth, into which is now fixed a green porcelain French stove. An oblong ten feet, perhaps, by twenty, and very high, containing the necessities. There is a scent of firewood, there are sheep and goatskins on the floor. When she closes the door the smell of wine and fire and warm bodies is very strong and good.

A circle of faces: you say you go for the weather or to see the landscape but without people you do not survive. A circle of faces backlit from small lamps made of water jars with raffia shades, faces with dark eyes outlined as in mosaics or figures on Coptic altar cloths. Megas, she introduces them, Megas, her cousin, Maro, his girl, Michaelis (separating the syllables), Ahmed, with a breath of a C before the H. An English girl, Petronella, what all English girls should be to girls who grew up on boarding-school books: body and bones, blue-white skin, yellow hair, protruding teeth and joints. Lurking, someone called William, William Pender (and she always uses both names when she speaks to him as if there had been another William once): English, languid, in a dark suit stained white along one edge from leaning against the wall.

A door opens, and a boy in a dark pullover and the Minerva badge of the Greek Gymnasium comes in. An extraordinarily beautiful face, adolescent and beardless. "I came to say good evening, Mama."

"Ah, *mon dodo*, Alexi-*mou*: my son Alexis. Will you stay

with us? This is Mr Ladi's sister come from England. The others you know."

He holds me out a grave neat hand and lowers his lashes. He looks to me as if in about six month he will explode in pimples and whiskers and big coarse bones, but now he is perfect. "I have lessons to do, Mama."

"Do them, then. But it is cold. Mind you keep up your fire."

"We have no more paraffin, Mama."

The face is grave and full-lipped. It has the perfect nose and sensual mouth of Apollo Belvedere but not yet the heavy musculature and chin.

"Then I shall soon bring you some hot milk. Off you go then, and goodnight."

"Goodnight, Mama." Shyly waving at the rest of us, turning gracefully—though there is nothing unduly feminine about him—and one of those slots of understanding opens up in me and what I have read and heard falls through it, and I understand at last the attraction for women of a certain age of such young boys and wish I had a son. Or a lover.

Aphroulla settles on a bench, pours wine into a pottery glass ("Iannakis made them, you will meet him, he does good things"), and explains her friends. Petronella teaches at the British school; Michaelis is not from here but from Athens and works for the United Nations measuring water; Megas operates an actors' group from a post in the Post Office; Maro is his fiancée but their fathers cannot agree on a marriage contract; she should not be out at night with him, but Aphroulla has made it all right with her father, because a Minister of the Government should understand that his daughter must be allowed to move into the modern world. William is William, and at the moment he is pretending to be a newspaper reporter. Ahmed is not a Turk, he is an architect from Libya, he is quite all right.

She is fond, motherly, possessing these people as she encloses words about them with her hands. But she herself is not quite explicable: tall, hieratic, stylised, a woman in a film or on a deck of Tarot cards. She wears a long dress in rich colours, her hair is in big loops over her ears, and black as pitch. Long, thick, stained fingers; big rings in scale with the Elizabethan houses of another quarter. Was she born with this dignity or did she make it for herself?

"He has kept you to himself, your brother. I am angry with him. Very frequently I invite him but he does not come."

The walls of the room as plastered with pictures, hangings, small Persian carpets, shelves that hold pots and pieces of clay figures. What furniture there is is low and I think home-made, benches covered with blue and ochre and striped local cloth, little stools like dock-cribs, some kind of pithy sticks tied together, little ricketty tables of the same stuff. "Have you been introduced to anyone?"

"I have met Mrs Power, and the mothers of some of his pupils."

"The nouveau riche and Mrs Power. Mon dieu, you would not have to leave England to do that. Mrs Florinda, she is not bad. She is somewhat too eager, but she has a good heart and she works very, very hard. Petronella, when she was young, my mother says she was like you. Do not fall in love with a penniless shipping agent with four daughters, or you will spend your life making English teas to pay for those daughters' dower houses." She speaks English correctly and emphatically. I imagine that she speaks five more languages with the same agility.

One has here, too, the sense of being in heartland: these are the high plateaux of the Peruvian Andes, the uplands of the Himalayas, places of exploration and pilgrimage, where the seeds came from. Merely because it is dark night. It is an old house and a simple one. The floors are beaten earth beneath the goatskins. The ceiling is the same uncovered beam-and-matting that we have. It looks better when it is not lowering over Edward's Wagnerian mahoghany bedroom suite.

In the dimness I begin to be able to pick out one hanging object from another. If she has made all the things in this room she has worked like a slave. Very high there are large dim oil-paintings, egg-shaped tunnels and green vortices, young and self-admiring but tense with subdued vitality. There are also pierced hand-thrown hanging pots with strange greenery hanging out of them, and pieces of embroidered gypsy-like costumes (Oh, in the old days, she says, on a feast-day, the men of the villages . . .), vests hung expecting arms and flapping embroidered collarless shirts, as if the hired man's body had withered away inside them. Banners in rows or flat: faint forms, ancient and hieratic. A scarlet lion has the nostril of a bull.

It is always easier to start with objects than with people. "Did you make the hangings?"

"Oh yes, they pass the time, they sell." She points to a cloth collage: a fat tourist on a woolly beach beside a Coca Cola beauty in the arms of a black serge priest. "The tarts and the tailors in the quarter, they save me their trimmings. I am not richer than they are, so we share."

Megas and Maro, sitting side by side, are dark squat twins. Ahmed has, beside the memory of Alexis, an elderly beauty: a neat skeleton and thick, fringed Coptic eyes. Michaelis has a cockade of hair and iron-rimmed French glasses. He plays with Petronella's hem and makes her squirm. He says, "So you are the sister of Mr Lafcadio who is to go to work in the office of Mr Loizos Speridakis?"

"What a lot you know."

"There has been much speculation about you. It was Mrs Florinda who decided to telegraph to you. It was from me and from Aphroulla that she asked if she should do this. We decided that it was good, there are never enough persons to talk to on this island."

"How did you know I'd be talkable-to?"

He shrugs. "One could be wrong, of course. But he assured us that you were younger than he, and not too fat."

"Your brother was much upset by the departure of Edward."

Michaelis makes horns with his forefingers, rolls his eyes. "Cocu, cocu."

"Michaelis is very clever and very bad," Aphroulla says. "He has studied irrigation and women in France. He believes that he is a great lover and a great engineer. In fact, one day he will be the government inspector of houses of ill fame."

A voice from far away in the background, drawling, with one of those English accents so smoothed-over as to be almost indecipherable, says, "Has there been any word from our dear Eddie, then?"

"No, nothing."

"Poor Laddie has made himself ill with worries," says Aphroulla. Michaelis giggles. "Do not," Aproulla says to him, "amuse yourself with the perversions of other people. You would take a goat if you could get one."

"A moufflon, perhaps," says Michaelis, "but not a common goat."

Maro and Megas begin to talk in Greek to each other. Petronella says, after all, Edward was unfailingly polite. A presence, supine and sepulchral, makes itself obvious on the floor by the wall across from us by rolling out from under a bench. "Fine chap. Old Etonian. Should have gone on to Cambridge. Couldn't do French. Stepmother was French. Wicked woman. Mental block. Come into a bloody great castle one day, if he's still alive. Lucky bastard." The form rolls and collapses into the shadows once again.

Aphroulla switches to a softer tongue and speaks with Ahmed again, then says to me. "Don't bother about Roger. My half-brother, Loizos Speridakis, returns tomorrow from Addis Ababa."

A grey-white arm rolls forward, holding an empty tumbler

as if it were Excalibur and he in a pond. Aphroulla shakes her head. The bag of laundry—no, one of those stuffed hanging forms footballers practise tackles at—rights itself gradually and says, "You'll find that this is a better bloody climate than England, and the wine is cheap. You aren't a sociologist? Good. Last wandering American gel we had asked the High Commissioner if the natives were cunt-fuckers or bum-fuckers and it took him a week to get over it. Salmon, Roger. How do you do?" He fills his glass himself. He looks like Max, a little. Same liquid weathering.

"*Exodus* is coming to the Grammatika Kine," William Pender says. "Do you think they'll blow it up again?"

"I can't see why they did it last time," Petronella booms.

"I have a rule against talking politics," Aphroulla says. I take more wine and inhale the smoke, the minute silence. My head is swimming a little, I haven't been warm and wine-filled for a very long time. They all look as if they are going to say something significant, but they don't. Aphroulla looks at her watch, "Megas, it is almost eleven. You must take your Cinderella home." Maro has the grace to giggle.

They get up and put their coats on. "I promised your father," Aphroulla says. "Go straight home. I cannot afford not to keep my promises."

William Pender follows them aimlessly, the whitewash mark down his suit seeming to weave after him like a neon sign. I have a feeling he is practising to be Roger Salmon. Petronella refuses a lift to Michaelis, and offers one to Ahmed, who says he has an engagement. Roger Salmon snores. Aphroulla goes and pokes him. "Wait," she says to me, "and I will show you the short way to your home. So you do not lose yourself again. So you can come back to me. She pokes Roger again. "Roger, you cannot stay here."

He pretends not to be awake, curls foetally against a bench. "Roger, wake up."

''What? Who?''

''Opa. Allez-oop. Up with you, Roger.''

''Ho? Fuzz? What?''

''Roger, go home.''

''I haven't got a home.'' Somehow, it does not sound pathetic.

''Roger, I am warming Alexis' milk and I am taking this lady to her house and you will go home. I will not have scandale. You know my mother watches me.''

I sit by the stove while she warms her Alexi's milk, staring at her ranked objects, wondering what was going on between the people, wondering if because I came the electricity was blocked. Feeling good because it felt like being back among musicians drinking austerity Espresso and feeling important because I was with them and they said one day they would make Mahler the most important musician London had ever heard. I look benignly at Roger, he winks, and gets up to go. ''Good night,'' he says, and shambles out. His walk is drunk and springy at the same time, quite an accomplishment.

Aphroulla comes in stifling a yawn. ''We get up early here. I will show you where you live. One would need to be Asmodeus, to take the roofs off the houses as one flies over them, to find one's way down these complicated alleys. They are all old camel-paths. And between such walls there are no perspectives.''

She walks me down a street, an alley, through a passage. I hear the tailor's music. His doors are closed, but his music seeps through zig-zag patches, through vestiges of indigo in the grain of the wood. He is singing to Aristides' flute and the carpenter's nameless instrument. ''I like that,'' I tell Aphroulla.

She frowns. ''They are peasants. They drink raw spirit, and it makes them sing. Wine would improve their voices. I will leave you here. I must help my son with his Ancient Greek. He finds it very difficult. Give my regards to your brother, please, and come to my house whenever you wish.''

''Perhaps I will go to see your brother tomorrow.''

''Mr Loizos is my half-brother. He is not very nice but I believe he is somewhat honest. It is better to wait until he has been returned a day or two. On this island, we interpret every situation by saying slowly, slowly. Impatience makes life difficult. Good night, new friend.''

&

In one of Max's poems, notes fall from a pianist's fingers like fish-scales. In the courtyard, Chopin is dropping thin plates of gold into the night.

Laddie plays better now. Although it has been pointed out to me on many occasions that I am not musical, that I can tell neither the keys nor the études one from the other, he plays better now. In spite of the stiffness of his hands. He has grown up, traded drama and arrogance for maturity. The notes he lets fall are precious things now.

Outside, downstairs, the shepherd's flute makes coarser counterpoint. The tailor's nasal bagpiping accompanies it. Their cadence is archaic as the khan. The keys of Laddie's pianola are pressed to the service of a different history.

I can hear them both from the archway where Aphroulla has left me. Laddie playing softly to himself, his shutters closed to drown the native musicians out. His music is for night and silence and sensitivity. Theirs shrieks booze and belly and dry roots. A phrase of his floats ballerinas through my head, the miracle of first theatre, curtain rising, grace going on. But their music has not forgotten the thump on a hollow stage of human feet. ''Ay-ay-ay-ay, Mar-I-na Mas,'' they shout, pulling their wattles. The sharp sound pierces his room and he stops playing.

MONODROMOS

Yesterday as I was passing his one-room shop, Pambos assaulted me with the sacred word "Kopiaste"—sit down and share. He put forward a chair for me, clapped his hands, ordered Coca-Cola from the street-boy, motioned me to sit; drew a smile on my face with a finger, and, grinning behind his sewing machine and scorched crumbling ironing form, tapped away at a piece of shoulder pad with the point of an iron plugged in to the ceiling light-socket. He began to sing. "Music," he said. "Music. Good. You like?"

"Yes, very much."

"I like, you like, we like, she like. Music is good. Po-po-po-po, Mar-I-na Mas!" Which is the theme song of the island radio station.

The shop is a filled-in archway and he is framed by a Gothic point. Behind him, curling on a wall once painted umber, ochre, indigo, and white, and now a flaked rainbow, hang brown-paper patterns labelled and numbered indecipherably. The floor is littered with scraps of men's suiting, a bolt of yellowing striped sateen lining slants from a broken shelf like a half-drawn curtain. Hanging from nails are half-finished jackets and trousers and vests heavy with whitewash and dust. Pambos is perhaps fifty. He says he has five sons and two daughters.

The Coca-Cola comes, and with it a bald parrot of a man wearing lederhosen who introduces himself. "I am Costas Costakis, Polyglot. I speak many languages, English, French, Greek, Russian, Persian, Hebrew and some Swahili. I have been in many places. How do you do?" He is bland and condescending. He settles on Pambos' other chair, crosses his bleached winter knees and commands a coffee for himself. "I hope you like our island. Is it not fine? I speak many languages. I have studied much. I have travelled far. I have come to be your interpreter. What was it you were wanting to say to my disgusting friend?"

"I like Mr Pambos very much. I also like his shop."

Costas Costakis repeats this to Pambos, who grins wider and

throws his shoulders back like a delighted ten-year old. "I call him my disgusting friend," says Costas Costakis, "because he disgusts too much—degusto, degustare, to disgust. Is greedy man, Mr Pambos. But with good heart."

"Yes, indeed."

Pambos, who has missed the irony of the conversation, is peeling a cucumber with his pocket knife. As his knife moves, he slides his tongue carefully along his lips. He holds us out a piece of cucumber each and says he wants to sing. "What would you have my disgusting friend sing?" Mr Costas asks.

"What does Mr Pambos wish to sing?"

Mumbling and shrugging ensue. Then Mr Costas says "He says he will make you a *chatista*, a song of his village. Is very interesting, *chatista*. Is made of what he who is singing is thinking."

"I would like that."

Costas Costakis, secure in his superior position, looks at me as if I am mad. "He could also," he says, "sing to you, My Bonnie Lies Over the Ocean. Is much better song."

"I would rather hear his *chatista*."

Pambos begins slowly, humming to himself as if to start the engine of his thoughts. He unplugs his iron, waxes the end of his sewing-thread, threads his needle. Costas crosses his bald knees again and twiddles his thumbs, lowers his lashless eyes. Then the words begin, in a deep and affectionate bearish hum. "The sister of Mr Ladi is come from over the sea..." with a pause for Mr Costas to translate.

"... The sister of Mr Ladi is wearing a blue dress and has dark hair. She is not young and she is not old..." picking up volume in the chest... "The sister of Mr Ladi lives in the old Turkish monastery over my shop. At night she will come and my friends will make music for her."

"We will sing because the almond trees are soon to come in bloom and in the fields there will be poppies and asphodel.

It is time for the orange harvest and the goats are glad that the barley heads soon will be full.

With intensity: ''The spring is come and the sister of Mr Ladi is come and she will take care of him, and she is in my shop drinking . . . .'' (flourish, crescendo,) ''Coca-Cola.''

Costas Costakis springs to his feet. ''That is all, I am busy man. I shall hope to meet Mrs Ladi again, good-bye.'' Machine-gun Greek to Pambos and a whish of disappearing bottom.

Pambos asks with a wide, shy grin, ''You like?''

''Pretty, Pambos. Very pretty.''

That is how they made the Odyssey.

While the *chatista* has been going on, the fourth runner-up in the International Chopin contest of fifteen years ago, sans tail-coat, has been pulling a pretty child called Efy through the usual melodic knot-holes. When he emerges perspiring he delivers his minion to a proper gentleman in a bowler hat who is filing his nails on the verandah. He growls at me, ''Late again, and where's my dinner?''

&

Now he plays a broken piano with stiff hands and to no audience. And I come in from Aphroulla's and put the kettle on. ''What movie did you see?'' he asks.

''Didn't.''

''Where did you go?''

''Ran into somebody called Aphroulla something. She knows you.''

''Oh God, you would, wouldn't you?''

''I liked her.''

''You would. Who was there? What did she say about me?''

''Oh, some English people, mostly drunk, and a couple called Megas and Maro. Megas is a nice name, isn't it? I figured it out, it has overtones of nutmeg and big.''

"Big ass, that's what it means. He's all right, Megas. Bit of an enthusiast, but really . . . . Was Ahmed there? Did he say anything about me?"

"He didn't say a word. They talked about Edward. She said she'd asked you to bring me round."

"If you really want to spend your life with a lot of art-tarts."

"They're not art-tarts, they *do* things, most of them. She's quite good, I think."

"Turns her hand to anything to make a buck."

"Like you. They asked if you were better, I said yes."

"You'd have to, wouldn't you?"

"Milk or lemon tonight?"

"Anything's better than that goddam sweetened condensed milk. What are you paying for lemons?"

"Three for half a shilling. Cheap."

"Grab some off Aphroulla's tree when you go next time. What's she working on now?"

"Weaving."

"She would be."

"I heard you playing when I came in. You sounded good."

"You have no ear, and no fundamental feeling for music. You don't know what it's about. Repeat that three times a day and you'll be a better woman."

"Thanks, sourballs. I was listening to Pambos and his gang, too. What's the other instrument?"

"*Laouthi*, lute. Blondin passed through, remember? Actually, it's a completely eastern instrument that the English wove into their history to justify the takeover of the island. Who was playing it?"

"I didn't look in to see."

"Puts me off, their rattle. Nothing but noise, except for the flute. In daytime it's their blasted trucks and motorscooters, at night if you're not yammering at me, they're singing."

"I liked Aphroulla's studio."

"Nice, isn't it? Did you see her son?"

"Alexis. He's beautiful."

"He'll be in his puberty rites now, being taken around to elderly tarts for his lessons. Maybe he'll be brought to you."

"Or to you? Do they still do that sort of thing anywhere in the world?"

"Sure. Everywhere."

"I don't believe it."

"I suppose you don't. Anyway, your friend Max might object."

"Have you been reading my letters?"

"Only the ones you leave lying on the kitchen table. Why don't you want Alexis? He'd be a dream."

"Honestly, Laddie, you are the limit!"

"Or you could have Aphroulla. Man, woman or goat, it's all the same to her."

He sees my eyes flash and moves away from me. "Oh, she's all right," he says, "If you like that sort of thing, but watch her, or she'll get under your middle-class pretensions."

There's nothing you can do with a man like that except sit with your face buried in your tea and hope you don't kill him. I have been trying since I first came not to use my advantages, play on his weaknesses. Coming here was doing that, I have to hold off saying what I think. But he has no decency.

"What happened to Meadows?" he asks.

"I decided not to tie him down."

"As soon tie down a whale, I'd think." He curls his hands on the kitchen table and beats its formica lightly with his fists. I wish it was a wooden table. "Old times," he says. "Old, lovely times. I must remember to thank Florinda for sending you. Tell me what really happened to Meadows?"

"Got a job in the Philadelphia Orchestra."

"Went off without you."

"No, I went with him for a while. It didn't work."

He wants to hear about Charlie Meadows, I don't want to give over that private winter's tale to him. Aphroulla's village wine has stimulated a jumble of unpleasantnesses, if I open up to him I will spill out two decades of bad blood which is, or was until I came here, in the process of drying up. One was foolish, once, one has felt victimised ever since. One ought to be able to pass by on the other side of the balcony, one's piss-pot held genteely high. "Lets's not talk any more. We ought to have better things to regret."

"And yet," he says with his old twisted smile. "You'll find that you and I have better things to regret than any of the people you met tonight. Islands are funny places, sister-*mou*, first you love them, then you hate them. They were pleased to meet you at Aphroulla's weren't they? It made you feel good. You came in lit up like a seven-branched candlestick. They'd be pleased to meet a one-fingered badminton player with athlete's foot. God, even I was pleased to see you when you came. For a full five seconds I was raving with joy. Anything, for another human face, a story you haven't heard a million times before. But it never lasts, it never lasts. Islands are too small. Goodnight, love."

Why did he mention Meadows? I haven't thrown Edward in his face—much. Downstairs the songs are still going on, jagged and rambling, their softer edges gone. It's cold. In bed I lie shaking and uncomforted, alone. Still, I could be wearing Phaedra's housewrap, shaking my mop out of my mother's second storey window with my hair in rubber rollers. Here, my dreams are hieratic (but what are Phaedra's? cross-dog dreams interspersed with signs and astrological portents?) and explicit in their sexuality, but costumed in the heraldry of landscape: great gulches red as Petra turn into dream-Japan (whereas in France one's dreams are stately and palatial and in England gorsey and familiar); where I am is not banal to me.

But there are no dreams. My body has not forgotten Charlie Meadows, flautist, boxer, light on his balls. What about Aphroulla? Could one, if one . . . no, one needs a genuine inclination. Meadows, now, the thought: he did it as if it were the most natural thing in the world, it wasn't work to him, it was swimming, and you swam with him, down . . . if you could catch him between the gym and the concert hall and the other women and find something to do while you were waiting for him to come home. You couldn't resent the way he spread his talent around, he was . . . Charlie Meadows.

They don't have sewers here. Piss in the dark and send it down to the foundations of the city, which sits on a cesspool.

Music's gone. Still a noise. Almost dawn, too. Where? What? Laddie. Jerking off. No. He still bangs his head against the wall in his sleep, and these are stone, poor bugger.

&

Mr Loizos Speridakis is as broad as his desk and very short, and much younger than I had thought. Heavy-lidded, clever eyes, a frizzy tonsure. Sucks Peppermints, calls everyone "My dear". An undertaker's manner, but there is rigidity under it. Unhealthy. Pouchy, puffy, yellow. Frightened, almost. When he is not powerful. Only about the eyes like his half-sister.

Four pounds a week for five half-days, not enough to live on, but not bad. Working on the Argentina list from another angle, just helping Dympna pull old reports from the files and update and retype them.

He does the Middle East. His people in Lebanon are not the same as Pye's, though they use the same typewriters: old Underwoods that skip. Maybe the same outfit using two different styles. There's something endearingly hamfisted about the thin paper and the worn carbon paper, the way they go on typing Al Bader and El Bader and El Badar and Bader Trader for the same company regardless of the screams of the British Board of Trade which wants everything spelled correctly and consistently. Unable to keep in its head the fact that the Eastern Wog cares not a fig for vowels.

England isn't the only nation of shopkeepers. The island runs over with commission agents and indenting agents—importers who don't need much in the way of capital—little fellows struggling valiantly along, like the Armenian Pambos gets his suiting from. They couldn't live if their wives didn't come provided with houses.

The interesting thing is that they have cousins all over Africa and South America. The British Empire is over, but the Greek commercial empire is a significant underground. Speridakis and the Israelis can get information from the strangest quarters, they can tell you which Ibo won't turn up at the warehouse to claim his shipment of bicycles, but will rather wait until they're sold as unclaimed goods and be the only one to turn up at the auction; and which Jewish South Africans are selling out to risk small-trading in Israel, and who pays his bills in Australia. All over the world, "Subject has no known capital; office premises consist of a rented room and typewriter; no assets; do not recommend dealings."

Speridakis sits scowling under King Constantine II. Scribbling on slips of paper and talking very fast in Greek, English, Turkish and Hebrew on the telephone. He has assets. When he is listening, he stares at Dympna Barnes. Her hair hangs over her face and she chews it when she is typing very fast. "Yes, Mr Loizos, no Mr Loizos," she says, like an automaton.

I came to meet him, he showed me the desk and typewriter he had got in for me. On the fourth afternoon he rose portentously from his desk and said, "And now if you have a moment, Mrs Moore, we will look into the business of your brother." He snapped his fingers, and Dympna Barnes, expressionless, produced a file and left the room.

"Did you know this Mr Millington-Sandys, Edward?"

"No, Mr Speridakis."

"Good. He is not a nice character. Very British, very charming, very upper-class, in fact, actually a viscount. But not a good man. Not good for your brother."

"So I gather, Mr Speridakis."

"He has gone, and your brother owes much money."

Yes, Mr Speridakis."

"Call me Loizos, it is better. Or Lewis, if you would like to. I have, here, a partial list of his creditors. You would not recognise the names, not knowing the orthography. I presume you have become aware of those in your neighbourhood to whom moneys are owing? Good. You wish to help your brother?"

"To a degree."

"So do I, to a degree. I do not approve entirely of your brother's perversion, but there are those who believe he is an asset to our culture. One thing is obvious, he knows no arithmetic. Has he any income?"

"Only from piano lessons. I have a little money."

"Would you advance him some?"

"I have agreed to assist him in return for my accommodation."

"The people to whom moneys are owed are simple people, small grocers, wine-merchants, barbers, jewellers. The government will not expel him, even if he does not pay. We are very tolerant here, and the people of the quarter are fond of him, he is very picturesque to them, they do not wish to harm him. But they are poor people, and they must pay for their children to go to school. There is no future for a poor boy who has not gone to school. The priests are hard on them. One week behind in the fees, and pop, the child is out. There is no credit. Come, we will settle with them."

The first discovery is that Phaedra had been overcharging them by half a shilling for cigarettes and two shillings for a full bottle of brandy, padding even the price of lemons. Her account is reduced from astronomy to twenty pounds in cash. I leave with spittle on my shoe.

The caverns of the quarter: old wine shops dug into primeval clay; tarred barrels marked XXX and XX and X. (X is for Moslems who drink no wine, but slip watered brandy through the Koran rules.) Small disproportioned tables tippy on earth floors. Speridakis bargains, spitting out words. Account books are produced from behind plastic signs that say NO CREDIT in three languages. Speridakis drinks coffee or sweet pop and goes over the shiny accountbooks, licking his pencil-stub. He crosses out a dozen semi-legible M . . . Sandys, makes separate columns of figures, and hands out huge elaborate notes from an outsize billfold. "Ten pounds. Five pounds. Will that do? I know you, Leondias, you put water in sealed government-inspected wine. Your ouzo is no good and you trade under the counter in raw spirit. How can I trust this book? Get me some wine—the best —from your brother Gerasimos' highest field before Easter and I will pay you cash if you let me taste each bottle. Make sure the corks are good. Get long corks. Here, I will give you five shillings towards the corks, I know you have many obligations. Tell Gerasimos brandy must be made at the co-operative. If you see Mr Millington-Sandys, tell me. You may consider Mr Laddie paid in full."

"For the account of Mr Laddie, Canadian, two pounds, Mrs Marianna? All clear? Good, now?" A handful of dried peas or passatempo as he passes the barrelsful. Beeswax kidneys amongst the twine. New amphorae and old cheap Japanese dishes with a transparent glaze.

It would be possible to adore this man with a dog-like devotion. He strides the quarter, passing out authority.

We return to the khan at seven. He pokes his head between the aggressive beads of Mrs Phaedra's curtain, rattles them, calls out to her. "Three coffees, medium, Johnny Walker, ice, upstairs, get on your feet, old woman.'' Puffs up our stairs, goggles, chuckles. ''Crazy foreigners and their old buildings. One day I will live in a building that is truly modern, with a toilet for every room and electric heat and the wiring inside the walls.'' Laddie brings glasses to the music room.

Loizos toddles along the balcony inspecting us, stooping through the low stone doorways. ''Ah, you have bought the furniture of Lady Tressington, when she died.''

''Some of it,'' says Lad between his teeth.

''What did you pay? Too much. You have always paid too much. You knew everyone was cheating you? If you play grand English and pay always full-price, cash, that is a gentleman's game, but it is not the way of this country. It is forbidden to bargain in the marketplace by the British law, but the British have gone now. You should have tried to bargain just a little.''

''When you have no cash, you pay too much.''

''You are clear, now, for a while. If Mr Millington-Sandys returns, that is another story. You owe your sister one hundred and eighty-four pounds, approximately one year's savings. I have paid the merchants. She will give me a cheque. You will have to keep her here a very long time. How much is that in music lessons?''

''A lifetime.''

''I will get you more pupils. Now that she is living here, you are respectable. The quarter is vile, but you are now respectable. Every child who aspires to be middle class shall now learn the pianoforte in an old Turkish inn.''

''I have a sub-lease from a Mr Ioannides who is not a Turk.''

''Ah, you have been here long enough to know the importance of that? Good. You have learned something. Ioannides is very rich, he is all right. I will employ your sister while there is work for her. After that, you will take care of her. Foreign women are in much demand. Our own are not evolved yet, and the men find prostitutes tiresome. Always the same girls and such big legs. Put a latch on her door and advise her about her friends. My half-sister is not respectable.''

I begin to protest. He says, ''My dear . . .'' and lays a fat hand on mine. I look at him hard and realise again that he is quite young and tender. ''I'll look after myself,'' I say. He winks at Laddie, stands, bows, and sweeps away before I can thank him.

''Where does he get his authority?''

''He takes it,'' says Laddie with a smile. ''Women can't, of course.''

''You'll see.''

&

Aphroulla's friends have lunch in a bar called The Brigadier which was founded by a retired British corporal in order to sit in it and drink himself to death. The current owner has green lubricious eyes, and does not allow women to pay for their own drinks. His name is Fivos, a corruption of Phoebus.

The regulars are William and Petronella and Michaelis, Megas, when he is feeling international, a bunch of journalists and a skeletal couple of old men called Peter and Perry, the White Russian Twins, who have bad teeth and speak atrocious English. When Fivos feels benign, he lets Roger Salmon in as well. There, I meet a Greek poet who also has green lubricious eyes and a virile moustache. The same night he walks into Edward's room and tries to get into bed with me. I push him out, hard, and he leaves swearing. As I lie in the dark shaking, I hear Laddie's door creak. It gives me a dreadful impulse to look through the keyhole. I hate myself in the morning.

(Picture postcard: Gothic window, crenellated walls, mountains,

exaggerated sea, lemons hovering in the blue:)
IT DOES LOOK LIKE THIS. COME AND SEE. YOU CAN DO IT ON THE CHEAP FROM MARSEILLES. SPERIDAKIS IS OK AND HAS BETTER PEOPLE THAN US IN AFRICA. CAN YOU GET DOWN TO BOOSEY HAWKES AT LUNCH HOUR BUY MODERN PIANO LESSONS I & II THREE COPIES EACH SEND POB 2978? WILL REMUNERATE SOONEST. PYE CAN SEE THIS. L. IS OK BUT AS WE THOUGHT DEEP IN DEBT. REGARDS TO PYE. LOVE A.

Dearest Max: Laddie has at last revealed that one picks up one's mail at the post office by the moat. He didn't feel like bothering to go last week. I went today and got your letters. Therefore you are no longer lying dead beside the Flying Scotsman, ravens and corbies croaking your demise, but alive and well and still in the imaginable vicinity of Edinburgh. I'm much relieved.

I like your description of Elizabeth's elaborate domesticity. I like elegance too, but as you know I can't for the life of me make it. I used to think housekeeping was something one just did, one did it better if one had money and good furniture etc., but I have lately come to the conclusion that like everything else it needs talent if it is to be done well. All the goodwill in the world would not make me good at running a castle. Laddie, on the other hand, has really managed the khan very well. Since what he and Elizabeth seem to have in common is a vile temper, however, perhaps you and I should just lie contentedly in our sweet, good-natured mess.

About myself: I'm working, I'm beginning to make friends. But everything that is happening is happening very slowly. You can't whiz in and out of a place and expect to know it. I get, periodically, little intimations of the immortality of certain customs—a lewd irrigation engineer the other day, for instance, told me that since a pilgrim to the Jordan or Mecca is entitled to put "Haji" in front of his name, to get one's Haji means to have been cuckolded, for what it's worth—I drink sweet coffee and am learning to accept forms of courtesy I used to resist—doors opened for me, chairs offered in shops, shopkeepers clapping for coffee. I am learning, too, to reconcile the endless bustle of this quarter with the islanders' reputation for lascivious laziness. Everyone who aspires to middle-class western prosperity has at least three jobs; others, like my tailor friend downstairs, adhere to a fine old tradition of doing things "slowly slowly". Fuss replaces lost ceremony. Hospitality is an old touchstone. It is unthinkable to have someone in your premises without offering a sweet or a drink or a sweet drink. It's very nice, it makes one long for ownership of the Coca-Cola franchise, but what would happen to such a system if they brought in American cost-accounting?

And wouldn't it be nice if some day someone discovered American cost-accounting was totally wrong?

I try to live here without counting the cost, though the cash-register numbers sometimes flash in my eyes when I see Laddie in the morning: money is power, isn't it? I suppose about five months' accommodation should settle my account with him. I wish I liked his cooking better. Eddie must have liked English grub better than I do. He knocks himself out to get sausages and mashed while downstairs the street people are cooking the most delicious and deliciously cheap little native sausages—rough, hot things flavoured with quantities of coriander—over a saucer of village booze, which is also used as an antiseptic for burns and to wash the sausages down. Two of those with a cucumber, there's eating, now.

No, I haven't winkled out your dog-headed saint. I have a feeling that all the people I've met so far would be insulted to hear of the dog-headed saint. They want to belong to the *modern* world. The number of cars per capita is what is important to them. They haven't got any workable definition of modernism yet, unfortunately, and my obscene irrigation engineer despairs of them. It seems that since the Phoenicians logged off the central plain for timber for (A) copper-smelting and (B) ship-building, the water table has sunk lower and lower. The situation was not helped by the importation at the turn of the century of Canadian tin windmills, which were so efficient they sucked the water up sloosh sloosh sloosh and the sea ran in and created salt pans where there had been orange groves; and is not helped today by quarrels between Greek and Turk over water-rights in an incredibly complicated land-tenure system. The worst thing, says Michaelis, is the waste: they quarrel over who gets what water and meanwhile don't mend their irrigation tiles, so what little there is is wasted. They are all too stubborn to do what they ought, which is to exchange land parcels so that each man's fields are all together: he says there will be a war over this one day, it's the only way. Meanwhile, that picturesque central desert—now in places hectic green with what I am assured is wild barley—is the playground of herds of roving, spirited red goats, each marshalled by a shepherd with a crook. The land has simply never been enclosed. Which means reforestation is impossible. Again, a choice between prosperity and beauty is indicated: why can't we ever have it both ways?

No, I haven't yet met anyone called Sophonisba. There is a Bouboulina Street, though, named after the Piratess of Byron's war. Someone says he has a good comparative Demotic & Ancient Greek vocabulary in the appendix to Don Juan. Do you know it? It's the English who have funny names here, not the Greeks. They're all after saints, except a lady I met called Galatea, pronounced GalAtea, like a stack of falling pails.

As Mr Laddie and his sister we went last week to a very grand dinner party in a modern apartment in the suburbs. Rich, hearty-looking middle-aged people, fifteen-roomed apartment upholstered with overt wealth, heavy, heavy: damask walls, silk carpets, chandeliers. A woman asked me how much I'd pay for a really good mink coat in Canada: I choked on my beautiful dinner. There was a huge buffet set out with rich heavy food, nothing effete and French but home-made sausages and macaroni casseroles, big salads and stuffed vegetables and vine leaves, everything three bob a spoonful, and for dessert those nut and honey cakes they make. Local wine, but better than I'd had before, which proves that money talks.

Afterwards, Laddie played. It was a little Liberace. Candlesticks on the baby grand, best profile on display, money changing hands as we stood at the door. Men drowsed and women sat enchanted. He will be as much in demand as a eunuch in a harem, but I don't think I did as well.

I like this place, though. I don't want to come to the bottom of it too quickly. I want to know not the bourgeoisie, the well-heeled and well-upholstered who are the equivalent of the people I'd live among at home if I'd made the normal marriage, but the ordinary people. As usual, I'm making more progress among the artists. Aphroulla Xenakis is really very good to me. Her studio is simply open, except when she is tutoring Alexis. Odds and sods of people come into it: strays from other countries, islanders who want to come to terms with l;ife the way she has: non-conformists. It's very hard for them, and, I suspect, hard for her. She makes almost no money. And all her ambitions for her son are bourgeois, therefore expensive. I wonder if her husband gives her anything?

Ah well, there are complications, but the wine is good, the sun is coming on stronger, we've started grubbing around the worst of the garbage in the couryard to get it looking better, and Laddie says it's fine if I start working on one of those empty rooms for you. It will be a labour of love because there are terrifying mini-tarantulas in that picturesque straw matting between the beams, and cockroaches the size of clockwork mice: big enough to pot at with a '22.

If the British Council doesn't come through, do you think

Elizabeth . . . ? not bloody likely. But I long for you to come, I am saving sights for you, we can rent a car and scud around Aphrodite-land. In the mountains to the south they have cherry blossom festivals. The wasted winter beaches are beginning to bloom again. April is not a cruel month. I miss you. A.

&

There was a pious girl at university who wrote, and declaimed after she had written it, this surprising poem:

Love is a red-hot rivet and I got burnt.
Laugh, you damn bastards, that goddam
Rivet is on its waaaaaaay.

It was the only time she was ever known to swear.

&

I find him in the kitchen washing his hair. There is a medicinal smell. I sniff. Herbs on the gas element? A very clean smell. I sniff again. "You don't need to be aggressive about it," he says.

Peroxide.

The vanity of it all sets my teeth on edge. Ladies don't, that's what I was taught at home. I've brought Max's letters in to re-read them over my coffee. The smell distracts me. "It'll turn orange if you do it yourself."

"You bloody puritan, mind your own business. I can see you through my back, twitching your tiny nose."

"Sorry. I suppose it's a professional necessity."

"You're thinking vanity, vanity, all is vanity, if only poor Laddie didn't waggle his bum. Why the hell don't you do something about yourself?"

"Don't need to. Get along quite well as I am."

"Flat as a board in front. Most feminine thing about you is me. You turn your best chances away."

"When I don't want admirers, I send them along to you."

"I'm *faithful* to Edward."

"I'm sure you are, it shows in your temper."

"You look like an old rag doll in a charity barrel."

"You've never seen a charity barrel. And I wish you'd stop telling stories out of Lucy Maude Montgomery when we go out. You've fictionalised our families both out of recognition, which is not very nice to them, and anyway, some day I'm going to forget the fiction and goof. Our glorious brother-and-sister childhood."

"If you drank less, you'd get the story straight and keep it there."

"I love the way, even with the charity barrel behind them, they keep going up the social scale. You haven't mentioned our mutual poverty for weeks."

"I've never heard you talk about your father's store." He moves into the sunshine to dry his hair. "You look twice the age of Florinda," he says. "You should do something about your skin. And buy some decent shoes." And then he turns and smiles. "Remember the summer you hardened your feet up so you could walk on the beach barefoot at noon without wincing, like an Indian?"

"They've never softened."

"They used to scratch my shins in bed."

"At least I never did anything more intimate to you."

He stops and I wonder what tack he will take now. "I wish," he says coolly, "that you would clean out that goddam nest of Sunday papers from under Edward's bed. If you don't have the decency to share them you could have the consideration to fold them and stack them in the kitchen where they are needed. And under the bed there are nests—clots—of slut's wool. What do you think it's like for me living dependent on a woman who looks like a board gone soft in the middle and never cleans under her bed?''

''Lay off, Laddie.''

''And bleeds on Eddie's mattress.''

''Bugger you, Laddie.''

''Don't use foul words to me, Lady Jane.''

''Handsome is as handsome does.''

Soon, Aristides, Flores and Pambos and Costas Costakis Polyglot and Costas the Carpenter and Phaedra and Mr Phaedra are in the courtyard listening. The foreigners are screaming at each other. Costas waves encouragement, Pambos looks gravely concerned. Laddie is laying about me with the broom. It brings out the evil gypsy in me, I dance about rubbing crossed fore-fingers at him and screaming, ''A mother was chasing her boy with the broom, she was chasing her boy with the broom . . .'' and run into a pillar. Laddie runs up against me, panting. I think, for a second, before my head starts to hurt, it is the closest I have been to him for years. I wait. Then he screams, ''Get out, get fucking well out.'' I look up and realise that my nose is bleeding, and hope that in another incarnation I shall have blue eyes to blaze as well as his. He hands me his wet peroxide-smelling towel to wipe my face.

I have learned a thing or two on this island. I say to him, ''Never mind, Laddie. Tomorrow I will go. Or the day after tomorrow. When it suits me. But not today.''

&

There is something stately and dignified about the figure of a woman over a loom. After the emotional chaos of the courtyard I settle happily into Aphroulla's calm. ''You know,'' she says, ''I was always going to be a painter. There were no painters here then—oh, perhaps the old man who is so famous now, and a few amateurs, a few foreigners—but it was not considered something that one could be. Especially a woman. In order to become a painter I had to marry that madman, Alexi's father. who was so weak and so much in love with me that he took me to study in Paris.

"I don't know where I got the idea to be a painter. Perhaps from going once, when I was a schoolchild, to the National Gallery in England, I don't know. But I decided this very young, and as it would have been unthinkable for my parents to send me to art school, I got my husband to do so. I studied, I had Alexis, I put him out to nurse, I painted. I wasn't very good, but I wasn't, either, extremely bad. I did those green things on the wall in the studio there. I thought that if I worked very hard I would become a great French painter.

"Then my husband's business failed. He was no businessman, believe me, only a poor old commercial agent who wanted a new young wife. We had to come back here. I thought I would die of it. Women are not allowed to express themselves here, and merely to pick up a paint brush is a form of cultural rebellion.

"Then a friend of mine from Paris came to visit. He said he had never seen such a beautiful place. He said, 'Never mind about what people say. Remember Cezanne, Matisse, Van Gogh, they painted southern places in southern colours. You are still painting as if you were in Paris, with dark northern colours. In the north, the natural colours you find here are considered vulgar. Don't mind that: you will paint well, if you look around you. You will not be able to avoid it.'

"I was much heartened by what he said. I looked around at my own place, I thought, there is colour here, there is all the material of the painter: terebenth from our mountain trees, terra umbra and ochre from the copper mines, oil of the flax seed: all the earth is painters' earth and before they were Greek nationalists and began to use whitewash and indigo, they stained their houses pink and golden and green. If you want to make tempera, there are chickens, there are eggs. I can show you shops in the old town near here where there is indigo in quantity and very cheap, the same they smear their carts with; and on the south coast, where the salt lakes are, where the shrine of the Prophet's aunt is (it is very Chinese, by the way,) there are still shallow ponds like very small rice paddies where half a century ago they cultivated madder. When we were children, Baba Joannou, my grandfather, used to tell us how when he was a boy he would go to the madder-fields to supervise his father's peasants in the picking and drying of the roots and make sure they dug in the wet sand carefully so as not to open the roots and make them bleed, and that they laid them carefully as babies in straight rows in the drying-sheds. He went, but what he really wanted to do instead of supervise the madder-harvest was to take sticky-sticks and go with the other boys to catch figpeckers in the trees. Very beautiful, very Shakespearean, is it not? There are foreigners who come and find us cute.

''Of course there is no madder market any more. The chemical dyes have taken care of that.

''So, I decided I would continue to attempt to be a painter. For years I worked, accomplishing nothing, damaging other people—the old man my husband is mad, you know; I take responsibility for that though it is a fact his mother and his grandfather were mad before him—and Alexis and I are forced to live like poor people, which he does not like. To live, I had to make the kind of things one sells to tourists, small banners, pots, carpets, tapestries, even little postcards. The things of these I have kept, I did for myself. I watched Alexis grow and did a little of this, a little of that, sold things for less than they were worth, begged from my mother, exhibited at my own expense, and received only scorn.

''I could say this happened because I am a woman, because the climate is unfavourable to my art. But I did not feel certain.

Then one day the American Ambassador came to visit. His wife was looking for some paintings. The Minister of Culture had shown him the usual people. He liked some of it, but he insisted that there must be other artists. The Minister of Culture then showed him an old Turk who peed on forged antiquities to season them, and a hunchbacked woman who makes picture postcards with her feet. It was his wife who brought him here, through Laddie. He looked at what I was doing and said, "But this is wonderful!

"After that, his wife came and talked many times to me. She brought me magazines from New York, she said I must know what was going on there, New York, not Paris, was now the centre. She gave me great piles of magazines, and it took me a long time to go through them. I was very unsympathetic to many things they were doing, but one day I opened an article about a woman who was weaving—my God she was doing beautiful things, God's eye and Aphrodite—and something opened for me. I thought, but my people have never been painters, they have always been potters and weavers. I fell on my knees.

"Now I have changed everything in my life. I have said to my Auntie Thekla in her village, 'You are too busy lending your dowry money at 22½ per cent to weave, old woman; give me my grandmother's loom, and not the narrow one, the old wide one she used before your memory begins.' I have gone to the cloth shops I see you lingering hungrily beside, to find in which village women spin their goats' hair fine, who still makes linen, who still unravels silk worms. Unfortunately, I have found out that there was a reason for the death of the old dyes: they do not withstand the sun. I have found out a multitude of things. I am a weaver now. If no one buys, I do not care."

It is noon. Almost time to go to work. We share a glass of wine. "You have been quarrelling with your brother?"

"Does it show?"

"The woman who brings eggs to me told me. She thought it was very funny, the two foreigners fighting."

"He's a bastard, Laddie, He's trying to drive me out."

"Will you go?"

"Not yet. I have a job, I like it here, some friends are coming from England to visit me."

"Since you came, he has ceased the whole of his social life. Perhaps you should move further away from him. Do you have a lover?"

"I'm fixed up in England, thank you."

"Do you find the men attractive here, or too little?"

"Attractive, certainly. They all look like movie stars. They have good teeth."

"They are very proud of themselves, and rather good lovers, but puritanical at heart. This society is not so free as perhaps it looks to you. When you choose, choose well. If necessary, ask me. I am said to be a crimson woman so I have received visits from them all."

"I think I'll be all right."

"You can have a good time, but you must be careful."

"I have to go to work now. Thanks."

I leave her in a mass of brown and scarlet wool.

IV

March: Bloc-Notes

The guardian of the big mosque, which was once a cathedral and quite a good 14th century one, assures me that the muezzim is very modern and does indeed call through a microphone. In fact, when he can afford it, he is going to buy a tape-recorder. It will assist him to give a more even performance. The sound of the Call to Prayer balloons out of the minaret five times a day like an auditory magic carpet. Greeks find it a constant annoyance, but it's very pretty.

&

The Ethnarch leads parliament five days a week, signs letters on the sixth and is said to preach religious war on the seventh at village church services. Whenever he appears, he is impressive, all robes, ceremony and blessing even when he is plainly dressed.

&

The imagery of penetration and discovery has been made as ludicrous as Little Nell by psychology. In this society I am handicapped by my femininity, I can't take on any male enterprise at all; but I am fairly contented to be surrounded by walls. Perhaps my imagination is so rotted by romanticism that I would rather add camels to the mental map of the town than go out into it and not find them. But no, I think it's rather that if I can't have water to stare across—I was spoiled in that respect as a child—walls are a comforting form of psychic limit. I feel less exposed than I would in an unwalled town on the plain.

&

It is hard not to make other people's religious customs sound cute. Here, times, seasons, birth, puberty, marriage, diet and death are taken care of by religion: it is the culture. Therefore it is also the politics. There are many interesting customs, but no way of marrying transculturally. Civil ceremonies are available for foreigners—for Israelis to marry Gentiles, for instance.

&

At English Easter, the beaches were slathered with white flabby English bodies. At Passover, the stores were full of Israelis who did not look at all like Canadian Jews, if they have a look: dark tanned people who spoke fast and loud and used their hands a lot, like Arabs or Armenians. They wanted electrical appliances and instant coffee.

&

There is a family of black Turks in Magosa rumoured to be descended from Othello. Otherwise there are no Negroes and they are spoken of with contempt. I am reminded of Grandpa Stringer telling us to turn off that heathen jazz. Blacks are heathen, primitive. Africa is too close for liberalism to obtain.

MONODROMOS

&

Seen at the corner of Baffo and Bulgar-Slayer: a sheik in one of those head dresses with cords around them, wearing a heavy dark robe. The selvedges of the material met on his chest and ran down to his feet reading "100% British Woollen, 100% British Woollen . . ."

&

The land looks good. In fact, at this season it looks like heaven itself. The fields a hectic Shelleyan green and screaming yellow wild daisies everywhere. Big wild fennel spraying golden umbels in the air. The central plain is by *Arizona Highways* out of Victorian stage backcloths. Purple mesas, orange hills, oases of eucalyptus trees.

&

Cash crops: lemons, artichokes, oranges, potatoes, carrots, cos lettuce, wheat, barley, carob beans. The latter are like catalpa beans and used for fodder and photographic coatings. The book says.

&

Charm is an old chipped word. The khan is an old chipped place, smelly and tumbledown, sullied and sordid. But it has charm. Any self-respecting Greek who believes in progress would tear it down and erect a Bauhaus skyscraper in its stead. The Turks tend to leave things lay where Jesus, or the Prophet, flang 'em.

MONODROMOS

I love what remains of the old city because I grew up with nothing old except rain and poison ivy.

&

Florinda comes and has long gossips with Laddie in the kitchen. She does not feel I have been a success.

&

Phaedra has a new wrapper made of Hudson's Bay trade goods. When she smiles, the effect is lurid. The dried face cracks around the broken teeth. She's the best spitter I've ever known.

&

Driving in the country: at the edge of a deep red valley, where the wild barley and sprouting trees and daisies made a shocking clatter of impressions, kids at the roadside thrust bunches of wild tulips out towards the car: glaucous maroon flowers with long thin pointed petals—tulips from Persian carpets. In the woods I tried to pull up a mandrake. It's like snake rhubarb, the leaves come away in your hand. The tap root is too long and strong to come shrieking out. The hairy blue flower has nothing to say.

&

Mrs Loizos Speridakis is small, neat, and bouffant in the hair. Very modern. At birth, she says over tea, Loizos weighed one oke (2 4/5 pounds, the local measure). He spent his childhood wrapped in cotton wool, and is still delicate in the chest. Those business trips are a terrible strain. Mrs Speridakis Senior, large and fierce and hollow-eyed with unspent passion, dropped by as well. Aphroulla seems more capable than Loizos of equalling her.

&

Costas Costakis, Polyglot, has a new business card which reads, Costas Costakis, Polyglot, Conductor of Conducted Tours.

&

We were married fourteen years ago today in Hampstead Register Office, herself in a suit from D'Allairds in Hamilton that cost sixty dollars and was a size too large in case she grew, her mother having done the choosing. Witnesses were Rosa Trethewey Moore, daughter of the finest Cornish counter-tenor there ever was, and Henry Newman. After the wedding, which was dignified, if brief (one didn't have to lie about obedience), the boys had a rehearsal and herself and Rosa went to Selfridges to shop for curtain material.

&

The fashionable English who used the island as a jumping-off place for solitary expeditions to the highlands of Turkey and Arabia Deserta have sold their villas. It's not cheap enough to attract itinerant writers and adventurers now. It's easier to visit one's publisher from the South of France, and Mykonos is more picturesque. So that most of the English here are the bath-chair set, whom one never sees, or forces or diplomatic personnel. And, of course, a few castaways.

MONODROMOS

Street cries: *Phos, Phos, echo to Phos* . . . light, light, I have light: not Goethe, but a blind newspaper seller.

"The oranges are one shilling; the bananas are one shilling." Up and down the scale, through the nose, all day, up and down the street. They say the woman is an epileptic who will fall down in a fit if she stops singing. The word she uses for oranges is not *portokalia*, the Greek, but *naranjes,* the Spanish word. Or is it Turkish or Moorish? The tedious song goes up and down the streets like a rusty saw.

&

Q: What do you give to a beggar whom you know socially?
A: What do you usually give to a beggar?
Q: One piastre, if I feel like it.
A: To a beggar whom you know socially you give two piastres.

&

Castles and abbeys, mountain tops, Greek and Roman theatres, ruined hilltop cities, gnarled olive trees and lopping figs, mudbrick farms melting into the landscape of the plain, lost columns, statues of lions: they work on the emotions, particularly those seated between the legs.

&

I have been seen in the Turkish market buying black figs. It is very bad of me to go there, Pambos says.

&

Orthodox Easter is a wonderful event. One day Pambos asks Laddie and me to his village for a day. A rented car arrives early in the morning containing Mr and Mrs Pambos, two daughters and four of five sons. We squeeze in in two layers and drive through the rapturous countryside singing. A record-player under the dash jiggles out bouzouki music. It is a feast day in the village of St Xaralambos, and also Pambos' name-day, there are queues of buses behind us, he was a famous saint. The boys yell "Yasu, Baba" out the window at every shepherd we pass, and there are a lot of them.

The car turns up the mountain. When the road is no more than a goat track the youngest children get out. They shout at the almond trees that have come into bloom.

The village is triumphal, milling with people. The little kids disappear, though the oldest sons, movie-star handsome and very tall, stay with their mother, who is also handsome and tall. On the way to the square we pass a tumble-down house. In one room, exposed to the wind, is a black iron bed. "My bed, where I was born," Pambos says proudly. His wife thinks that is very funny indeed.

The church is quite new and raw, spacious and varnishy and dull. Inside, two priests in stove-pipe hats are holding out an ikon, and the villagers are marching under it in a kind of Virginia Reel. We are pushed into line and assured that for the coming years our ears, eyes, noses and throats will be well looked after.

Women pat my belly. "No baby? No husband?" I sit with them for hours it seems on a verandah drinking orange pop. Inside the cafe, Laddie and Pambos and the men are singing. Then we have a glorious picnic by a sheepfold. Mrs Pambos is built like my country aunts, wide and strong. She points out the names of the mountain peaks and beats her children in a footrace. The girls are very shy, and at the giggly stage, and not good-looking.

&

MONODROMOS

William Pender in the Brigadier: "Snorklest thou?"

"Sure."

Over the mountains in his Morris: from the top of the pass the white peaks of Anatolia are showing clear. "Light up your liver and lights, wot?" We drive down among the lemon trees. "Look," he says, "I'll drop you off at a place I know, come back to you. Something in my secret life I have to attend to."

His place is a monastery beside the sea, empty, perhaps abandoned. A gallery of rooms, like one side of our khan, beside a church whose plaster walls are prinked out with pieces of ancient capitals and mouldings. He unlocks a cell containing a bed and a table and a row of hooks. "Change here," he says, "but don't swim without me." The room looks over the sea, which has settled from a rough winter blue to something more placid and green.

At the end of the balcony there is a washing-trough made of a Roman sarcophagus. To the east of the whole building, a little hill on which sits a small cruciform Byzantine church, no bigger than an outhouse, hunched in its arched shoulders. Very old, and locked.

The ground is dry already and rough; it cuts sandalled toes. Beyond the hillock with the church on it is a flat stretch of ground beside the sea: not a beach, but a series of rough stone terraces. Nearby, as if deposited by a celestial crane, is a large rough red rock. Not at all the same rock as the rest of the landscape, adventitious. The sort of rock desert fathers retired to with scorpions and holy books.

It's hollowed out, too. I hoist myself inside and find broken bottles, rubbish, goatshit, and a quite new knapsack. It is not a pleasant-smelling place. I decide to sit on the flat rocks by the sea.

It's hot, though the wind is cool. I am tempted to swim alone. I put a foot in the water. The stone is rough as coral. A better place to sunbathe would be that boulder out there. Water can't be more than a foot deep around it. But what's on it? A corpse? An anchorite? "Oh, do excuse me. I was washing my smalls."

Roger Salmon's greenish skin turns pink, for more than his smalls needed washing. I gallantly wade away and in a moment he is dressed and clambering along the rocks with me. A rumpled gent shivering in damp underwear. "How very nice to see you here. Did you come with William Pender? Has he left you here, by any chance, while he went to see his Gran? Lucky you—he comes back with marvellous champagne."

"He's been gone rather a long time."

"It's a long way over the mountains." He waves at the grey ridge behind us, the low range of mountains that endearingly never looms and threatens. "Did he leave you here without even a guidebook?"

"Yes."

"William has charm and limitations."

"What's the name of this place?"

"Unpronounceable, my dear, quite unpronounceable. It means, brought over to the plain from the mountains across the sea by the Virgin with her very own hands. One of the many handkerchiefs of the asthmatic Veronica was found here."

"I wish I could get into the little church. What was brought over the sea, the church, the monastery, or the big red rock?"

"The church, I think, the little one. Pity you can't go inside, but the Archbishop has the key. The monastery's quite a posh outfit: the Governor used to have rooms in summer here. Now the Bishop of Tylliria uses them, and William's Gran, who makes good champagne and thus has influence among holy men."

"I didn't know he had family here."

"He keeps quiet about her. Lives in terror someone will ask to meet her. If she disapproves of his friends, she'll cut off his allowance. The *Domaine* is just over the other side of the mountain and a better vineyard you won't find on the island.

These are the fishponds of a city that is said to pre-date Aphrodite. Fancy that. You can pick up bits of mosaic if you poke about. The red rock is—God knows. Straight out of Eliot and Frazer, I'd say, the protective-threatening-sheltering pistil. Could be more comfortable."

"So you're the one living there?"

"Camping out for a spell. For my health."

"Where do you live ordinarily? I've never known."

"I'm furtive by nature. Comes of having once been a small boy. Here's William now. Oh, you are in luck, look at the size of the hamper."

The sea is salty and cool. I slide in off Roger's washing rock with crossed fingers, blessing the first immersion with superstition. William dives for amphorae and brings handles and necks up, lamenting their newness. The picnic, after swimming, is Lucullan. William's Gran, it turns out, is French. Her husband brought their vines from Champagne a long, long time ago. You can't buy her wine, *Domaine d'Agridaki*, in the shops, only in the best restaurants. "You're really well connected," I say to William.

He grins and shyly shrugs. "She's an old curmudgeon, but the wine is good, isn't it? Finer than the stuff the co-operatives make. She'd have been nationalised years ago if the bishops weren't so fond of her stuff."

We leave Roger behind with a heel of a bottle of champagne. William says he is camping out to avoid his creditors.

&

To:

One orange sateen mattress:	30 shillings
One *ditto* comforter:	*ditto*
One Van Gogh chair:	25 shillings
Costas, for labour:	2 pounds.

MONODROMOS

I am independent. I have cleaned out the room furthest from Laddie's along the balcony. We see much less of each other and are better friends. Aphroulla has lent me a tapestry, and William got faded curtains for me from his Gran. I am undecided about whether to put a lock on the door. I am advised to do so, but I wonder whom it would keep out. The wrong one, probably. What do I hope for? Nothing I would accept.

V

GOD'S PLACE

Today I am lunching with Efy's father at God's Place. Brains and sweetbreads are on the menu, and zucchini flowers stuffed with meat, lamb braised with artichokes, kid skewered with bay leaves and grilled over charcoal; cucumbers in yoghourt, grilled mullet, stuffed eggplants masquerading as "little shoes", the first new carrots, and heaped plates of stuffed vine leaves. The wine is served in gourds that have been dried, scraped clean by shaking broken glass inside them, decorated with a hot skewer, and kept stone cold full of white wine in Theo's cavernous refrigerator, which he is said to have purchased from a bankrupt undertaker. The sun is beginning to be very hot at noon.

Anyone will point out to you the name of God's Place on a tin archway near the post office: look, there's the name—O Theos: God. He tries to live up to it.

I am hunched behind the menu, trying to pretend I do not know anyone here, but that is useless. Theo has already shown with a broad grin that he knows me. Efy's father, X (that is of course not his name but it does begin with X and I think from the position of his left knee that we'll soon have a relationship that admits of pseudonyms), owns a bank. A very small one, but good for open credits of 200,000 pounds a year. I've never known a banker very well. I've met men here who are perhaps more interesting, younger, more attractive, but it is nearly May, the season is working on me. The handsome lounge-lizards glued to the walls outside the taverns and barbershops and pool halls of Monodromos are beginning to have an effect on me. Their teeth are very white, their skins are brown, going down the street to work is like passing through a lifeguards' convention. I didn't feel this way in England about men at all. On corners I am pinched and pummeled like a fresh tomato. I have begun to enjoy it. It is time to choose before one is chosen. X has long graceful hands, fish-shaped intelligent eyes, a shock of prematurely white hair.

We are in the best weather now, they tell me, and the populace responds. The restaurant is crowded, though mostly with foreigners: in one corner the gang from the French cultural centre are eating quickly and seriously, and by the gate, where she can see Alexis if he passes by on his way from the Gymnasium, Aphroulla is sitting with Maro, who is twisting her napkin. Waiting for Megas? Dympna is lunching with her beef-faced husband, Major Peter Barnes. She smokes, while he eats and talks at the same time. People who live with the silent are desperate conversationalists.

Who else? A tall fellow X knows and bows to, local, with a beard, unusual in one not a priest. Two Greek journalists. A Turkish civil servant. Roger Salmon in dirty whites drinking with the White Russian Twins. Payday at their embassies, perhaps? The last day of the month, anyway. At home, the daffodils will be coming out.

Laddie and Efy are to join us when the lesson is over.

X recommends the fish and claps his hands for Theo, pours out more wine. Our paths first crossed in the wintertime, when he came early to pick up his daughter. He was wearing a proper English suit and a bowler hat. I offered him a drink to ease the agonies of "The Happy Farmer". He said it was called "The Merry Peasant" when he took piano lessons from two fierce Greek ladies who lived in a house with a tower. It was unusual for women to work then, but they were from a very good family and taught piano and violin. All the children were very frightened of them.

Speridakis caught me looking into X's file. "He's very nice," he said, "but not quite typical. A little too English." Speridakis is not fond of the English. He claims they did undignified things to him during the war of independence, things one would not recount to one's mother. He knows how to handle them, however: he gives them things and does not allow them to pay him back, which humiliates them.

Easy to see what he meant by English: the careful accent, the tailoring. But the knee is not English. I have a letter in my purse from Max beginning, "I am glad you have found what appears to be an eating society but do not, I pray, forget The Dogheaded Saint. He is vital to my life, my heart, my prosody. I will not be able to reach you for some time." I order sweetbreads.

X passes the order on unsmiling and sticks to his fish. He looks at Aphroulla. "That is the sister of Mr Speridakis who employs you."

"Yes. Do you know her?"

"Oh, she is very well-known, everyone knows her. We have not so many painters who are women that we can ignore her."

"She has a marvellous studio—just about the nicest place on the island: doves, hanging baskets of flowers, sculptures . . . "

"But then, you are something of a Bohemian."

"I guess so. Do you know her brother?"

"This is a small island: if you went to school, you went to school together. But later Loizos and I diverged: he studied in Athens and I in England."

I have heard him before on the subject of going to the University at Durham. The attempt to place his long hands and limpid eyes in the vast stumped-legged cathedral and the midget northern tomb of Bede confounds me. "Have you seen Aphroulla's work?"

"Yes, she is very well-known. My wife at one time wanted to buy one of her paintings. But it was at the time she left her husband, who was an old friend of ours."

"Isn't he dead?"

"No, but he is a very ruined man now, a mendicant at her door. Perhaps you have seen him. She was very cruel to him, and now he goes about in rags. He has a long white beard like a priest. It was a very sordid, rather Middle-Eastern marriage."

"Arranged?"

"There are some quite intelligent arrangements, but this was not. She would marry no one, she wanted to study in Paris. He was a fool, he offered to take her there, so she accepted. She used him badly."

"Among artists it's always *sauve qui peut*."

"One does not forgive people for driving one's friends mad."

"Wasn't he old and senile anyhow?"

"He is one year older than I am. His name is Mammas. He calls himself Ayios Mammas, Saint Mammas. You must have seen him. He wheels a little cat around in a broken perambulator and pretends that it is the lion who helped St Mammas escape from the tax collector."

"But that is a very old man."

"I am forty-five years old; Aphroulla is forty-two, Loizos two years younger. Adversity can do many things."

"She said there was insanity in his family."

"Oh, that is true. One of his aunts was quite a famous madlady. A hereditary disposition was there, perhaps. When you see Ayios Mammas you must remember to throw a piaster in the perambulator in memory . . ." He fumbles with his cutlery.

". . . in memory?"

"Of a poor choice."

We both stare over at Aphroulla. In this light she is handsome, but not very good looking. Her features are so strong as to be almost cruel, like her mother's. "I saw that old man outside her doorway one night."

"If you see him again, tell him to go away. He has been a very great nuisance in the neighbourhood."

"Where does he live?"

"Oh, who knows? The back part of the town is a rabbit-warren. One lodges anywhere."

"Someone has tethered a sheep in our place. It bothers me, it looks so dirty and sick."

"You are very English."

"I'm as English as you are."

"There is none of that blood in my veins, and only eighty years of the government. And I abhor animals. When we want to get rid of kittens here, we leave them in front of a cinema that is playing a British film. It is bad luck to drown them, and someone always takes them home."

"The cats are beautiful, very Egyptian."

"Efy will bring you a kitten if you wish. Are you comfortably arranged in the new room? Did Costas do the work as I told him to?"

"Yes, thanks, you're a marvellous interpreter. I hate the look of his wiring but everyone assures me it's safe. You were right about the lock, by the way: there were squatters along the west gallery last night. We've no right to put up a barricade."

"Oh yes, it's a very well known place to go if you've nowhere to go. Do you feel better now that you're further away from your . . . brother?"

"Yes, and so does he. One had not quite enough privacy. And the room with the enormous furniture gave me claustrophobia. I hate that big Victorian stuff. All marble and hanging knobs." He is human. Furniture bores him. He looks at his watch.

"Ah, here they are," he says.

Laddie mincing, Efy skipping. A picture of innocence together. X rises and embraces his daughter, shakes Laddie's hand delicately, turns to me. "I am very sorry that I must excuse myself, but I have an early appointment. You must tell your friend Aphroulla to go to my Uncle Achilles' shop. He has some old yarns that will interest her which he cannot sell: I will have him give them to her. Weaving is better for a woman than sculpture in cement." To Theo: "You will serve a dinner to Mr Laddie and put it on my account. Come now, Efy, it is time we kept our appointments. Mrs Laddie, at seven I go to a meeting that will interest you. I will pick you up."

Exit. Very quickly and efficiently, a female child skipping behind him. Laddie whistles. "A hit, a palpable hit."

"You're looking chirpy."

"He paid me, my dear, he paid me. And she'll have lessons twice a week. I've no doubt you'll wind up singing for my supper—but better for pounds than for pence, eh?"

"I like him, actually. I wish he wasn't married, but they all are at his age. He asked me what it was like to grow up without the sea and the olive trees and Bouboulina and Barbarossa the pirate."

"What did you say?"

"I can tell you what I didn't say. I told him about the lake and the apple trees—they're crazy about anything to do with fresh water, aren't they? They all want to hear about Niagara Falls—but I didn't have the heart to tell him about Laura Secord. Your Mum was the only legendary person I was brought up on."

"She was something, wasn't she? Look, Aphroulla's waving. Do you mind if we . . . ?"

So we join Aphroulla and Maro and Megas, who has come at last and squashed his post office cap in his back pocket. Peter

Barnes hunches their table next to ours, and William Pender and Petronella come in off the street. Everyone is suddenly jolly and laughing. So jolly that for a moment I wonder if I have committed some hilarious public gaffe. Then I realise that is is I who am happy, and I am giving them my glow.

Because he also said to me, "Do you find us more like *South Wind*, *The Rock Pool*, or *The Alexandria Quartet*?" And, "In novels, and in poems, everything is always rich and strange, but not quite as rich and strange as it is if you really know it," and, "I come from a city once sacred to Aphrodite. More recently my family were foreign consuls in the town of Scala. We have had many names in our family, and no doubt many religions. We have managed to survive without ever being quite reduced to the peasantry for at least six hundred years. But you must not think of us as either aristocratic or rich. There is no aristocracy here, no regime has lasted long enough for that. And our money does a merry dance from hand to hand: we have more than the peasants, not as much as the big bourgeois. I think we are rather like Americans, we mercantile Greeks. Our forms are always being created new, we flee from island to island with commerce as they flee from state to state. When times are bad here, we go to other islands, we send our boys to trade in Africa, in Lebanon. Nationalists like Loizos Speridakis will not admit it, but we are a mixed race, partly by rapine, partly by the desire to survive. I have a young cousin who resembles astonishingly a Syrian tomb-figure, and an aunt called Loulou who writes romantic novels claiming that we all of us descend from the aristocracy of Troy. She is wrong, but she has energy. He is not your brother, is he?"

"Why do you say that?"

"You do not at all resemble our long-resident Mr Lafcadio. In physique or in character."

"Brothers and sisters can be very dissimilar."

"He is not your brother."

"He feels exceedingly like my brother. He has told the government labour office that he is my brother."

"He is your brother, then. But you and I know better."

"They call me Mrs Ladi on the street."

"You have not remarried. Why?"

"I don't know. The time. The place. I don't know. All the good men are taken, now. I was married, but I didn't like it. When we were fifteen, we were all sorted out in couples in school. I had enough of it then."

"They were not successful in teaching you to be dependent?"

"It never lasted for me. Anyway, I was taught to pay my own fare on the bus. It's better . . . when you can."

"Why did you come here?"

"It says in the brochures you have 340 days of sunshine a year."

&

Laddie is in great high spirits. Maybe he sees me taken care of now. Money always does him good. I feel taken care of, and it's good, for the nonce. I don't know what I'll think of it when Max comes, but Max is dawdling, if I don't do something about taking care of myself now I'll do something foolish later. And why rationalise on a happy day? Laddie is telling them gorgeously about Miss Errol, the piano teacher on the Indian Road, and I can hear her fingernails clicking on the keys, and her gum popping, and feel the fat pads of her fingers as she crosses my hands on the piano for some idiotic exercise. I can smell her hair, as he talks, the purple rinse she used. He is telling her story well, the White Russian Twins are popping up and down and spitting out German shrieks of joy, and everyone is laughing. Then Peter Barnes is funny on the subject of being moved up to the part of Cassius because Octavius has been transferred to Benghazi and they use rota systems for everything in the Forces. Then a cloud goes over the sun and Speridakis walks by and smiles wide, removing a Panama hat from his shining crown; at which Dympna jumps up and de-crumbs her tiny lap, and crows, "Oh, Peee-tah, darling, I'm late." And goes.

"Hear ye," says Petronella. And William begins The List.

"From the government of Mother Greece: Ajax and Lysistrata in the outdoor theatre at Paradelphi."

"Ay-as and Lysis-TRA-ta," Megas groans.

"From the government of Mother Turkey, film festival at the Ali Pasha Cinema. Free sweetmeats.

"From the government of Mother England, the Ballet Portobello in the ruins of the abbey of Benevenuto: Pineapple Poll, Les Sylphides, and other ballets to be announced.

"From the government of Mother America: at the American cultural centre, the John Barthleby Dance troup of New York, New York, New York, and the sousaphone band of Flyfoot Berazi.

"From the government of Mother Russia: the Red Army Chorus at the Loucoudi outdoor cinema.

"From the government of Papa Malraux, Bruno de Montherlant, in a concert of Chopin, Rachmaninoff and Marcellus, with recitations from the collected works of Alix de Cahot. At Baffo Castle, north-west tower.

"And of course from our own favourite, the Royal Air Force Dramatic Society and Marching Band, Peter Barnes in *Julius Caesar*."

"Panayiotis has been busy," Aphroulla says. "We shall have a very nice summer."

"I shall build a balcony in your studio," says Megas, "and play Romeo and Juliet by William Shakespeare." Maro, seeing herself an unlikely Juliet, has the grace to blush. She is a fine stocky girl but it is easier to see her in a wrapper in her *monospitos* door, sending the little ones to school, than as fair Juliet.

Or coming home with a mule and cart laden with a harvest of oranges. It is said that her father is rich and powerful, but something in her has never left the land. She is much more than Nora or Juliet.

Aphroulla has been only politely interested. At last she has seen Alexis at the gate. She jumps up, strides towards him. The others rise as well. I wonder who is paying. William and Megas, it turns out. It would be unthinkable for a woman to pay unless she were by herself. Parasitic but convenient.

I am hot, now. The splendour is beginning to droop off the castle walls. Once there were falcons and leopards and bridges, canals; the moat was filled, the kings kept court and exacted tribute from pilgrims, crusaders, foreign emissaries. Now we sit here. We are riff-raff.

"Come on," says William. "*The Four Feathers* is on at the Princess Melina. We'll be late."

Might as well go; Speridakis has laid me off again.

It is not *The Four Feathers* as announced. Rather, ten instalments of *Trader Tom of the Seven Seas* strung end to end, with Dutch, Greek and Arabic subtitles. "Petronella," William whispers, "lives with a Turk and his brother. Roger went to see her once and saw them both having at her in the courtyard."

"What's Roger like?"

"Drunk. Clever. Me in twenty years."

"You think so little of yourself?"

"I don't think of myself at all. Did you use to see these things at home in America when you were a child? I like watching for the bits that link the episodes. The exposition's all so beautifully elementary. Cheap job, not cutting the overlaps out. Must get my Gran to give me a see-in-the-dark watch: amusing to time the exposition."

At five we stagger, drunk with sound and darkness and noon wine, into the gritty street. William steers my elbow with absent-minded politeness. They always mind their manners, public school boys, though they don't always notice who it is they are using the manners on. For a moment I am lost in the circles of the town again. We take a wrong turning and find ourselves in the dingy Turkish square. A Kiplingesque street sign says "Ataturk Maidani". The flat light lays a calloused sole on the detritus of empires, the English cut stone jail, the Venetian column. In every direction there is a minaret and beside each minaret a round tomb with bottle-bottoms stuck in the plaster for lights.

We are half-dead with subtitles. We sink into plastic chairs outside an archway that shows no sign of habitation. William claps his hands. An old man in a head-rag, and a suit and vest, but shirtless, shuffles out. To my surprise, William orders in Turkish.

The cups are chipped, the glasses are smeared; the old man's hands are running with filth. I've never yet on this island felt this kind of *pudeur*, but I shrink from my cup, I feel the edges of my whole self curling, I am after all a sanitised westerner. I've tried to accept everything here, but this is my limit. My head is pounding. William tries to get me to tell him whether he should go home and be apprenticed to the family wine-trade. I am sunk so low in myself I cannot utter. Max savours the *dépaysement* of returning to the world after three hours in a movie, but I do not.

We part at a familiar corner. As soon as I have left William, I regret my rudeness, turn to wave to him. But we are cut off from each other by one of their big, square home-made parrot-gorgeous buses, red and yellow and green enamel, and brown faces hanging out windows waving and laughing; a wave of vitality pushes towards me. It is a restorative. William is sloping across the square far out of reach. He has put on a little white cotton hat and looks like a tiny English child in *Swallows and Amazons*.

&

The air is cooler in the derelict khan, but I am still not very cheerful. Was I born to watch old serials with young Englishmen? Did I come here for that? I go through the archway to the stable . . . a roofless structure that might once have been a chapel, and stare at the sheep tethered there, which is lackadaisically gnawing a discarded palliasse. Its long drooping ears sway lazily. Its fur is filthy and matted and one of its legs is deformed. It moves its rear away from me in case I want to kick it. A month ago it could have dined on the mustard growing through the floor, but that is dead, now. It is a very sluttish sheep. It ought to be up in the mountains.

Laddie is lying in a pool of sunlight on the balcony. "Whose sheep is it, Lad?"

"What sheep?"

"In the shed."

"I don't know. Sometimes somebody ties one up there."

"It's a horrible sheep."

"All sheep are horrible."

"It's very dirty."

"All sheep are, by nature, dirty. And stupid."

"It's eating a mattress."

"Leave it alone, for God's sake. Learn to leave things be."

"It might be thirsty."

"I know, you're going to take it water in my beautiful new plastic dishpan and leave the dishpan there, and it will be stolen, or the sheep will eat it and I'll be accused of poisoning someone's Sunday dinner."

"Do you think it's a Greek sheep or a Turkish sheep?"

"Depends on whether it came in the front door or the back, doesn't it?"

"It's not a proper door, at the back."

"What did you do this afternoon?"

"Went to the movies with William."

"Cradle-robbing, aren't you? What did you see?"

"*Trader Tom of the Seven Seas*. Elevating."

"Ugh. Who paid?"

"Both of us."

"Where do you get all the money, from your fancy man in England?"

"How long have you been here? Five years? Six? How much money have you made? How have you lived?"

"*Touché*."

"Mother used to say I was lazy, but I've never seen anyone like you."

"You haven't been here long enough. How long has Speridakis laid you off for?"

"Until there's something to do. Until Dympna goes on holiday. Oh, I don't know. Maybe I'll look for another job. They've given me a work permit."

"Much good may it do you, slaving in offices."

&

In the cool of my own room, lying on the orange divan Costas built me, I read Max's letter. He has been hunting capercailye in the highlands and thinks it a superior occupation to not looking for the dog-headed saint. He doesn't think he can come quite yet.

Laddie knocks. "Are we going to eat?"

"Is there anything to eat?"

We settle on bread and tea and yoghourt and the first apricots. "Do you remember our lyric imaginary childhood?" he asks.

"Vividly."

"I walking along the beach playing my little prodigy's fiddle, you following from a distance?"

"Your faithful shadow."

"My ambition to be the greatest musician in the world and yours to be the greatest musician's wife?"

"Yeah. My brother Leo's was to own a sports car."

"What's come out of it all?"

"He got smashed up in the winter rally. I'm eating apricots and yogourt."

"Are there any olives?"

"Dried up. I threw them out."

"You could have put more oil on. What kind of oil are you getting."

"Dunno. I just hold out the bottle and yell 'olio'."

"That's not the word."

"It gets the stuff."

"How much do you pay?"

"Two bob, I think."

"Peanut oil. Let me get it from now on. Are you going out tonight?"

"Efy's Pa's picking me up at seven."

"Better dress. You look as if you've been sleeping in your clothes. And . . ."

"Why are you suddenly so friendly?"

"You look as if you're here to stay, so do me two things."

"What?"

"Throw out your jeans, and forget I ever came off a farm."

"They don't mind. Two hundred acres of lakeshore make your father a great landholder."

"By their rules, he was a peasant. Otherwise you'd be shooting with Max in Scotland."

"Maybe I could say my father's store was a department store."

"Shut up about the store, just shut up about the store. There are lies, and there's . . . discretion. You like to keep good company. Don't forget to keep your mouth shut. It doesn't interest them where we come from."

I find myself dawdling as I dress, dawdling, hesitating, wondering. At noon I was happy because I felt I had made some kind of commitment, but now I feel myself sidling away from commitment. Not wanting to betray Max? I don't know. We've done that to each other before, and it's been all right, and he isn't here, isn't likely to be here for a long time. No, the funny feeling has something to do with a commitment not away from Max but towards the island. It's important to know in these things what you're getting into . . . no, that's cold and middle-aged.

Promptly at seven I hear X's motor idling in the street below my slot of a window. When I pass the kitchen to go out, Laddie is slumped at the table. He seems so deeply and unremittingly sad that I put my hand on his head. He jerks away like an angry child.

&

Dear Max, What's all this, you asking me to rite in rime? I haven't thyme. And anyway, in grade seven, in Mr Porter's class, I had to write out rhyme a hundred times. And Byronic stanzas! About the rime on the spreigh? Well, I did try. I got the rhyme all right but I couldn't get the content in. How's this for idleness?

Rime stands against the sky like lovers' legs
Obscuring the view and changing the perspective;
End of line threatens, question begs
Answer, not rime; rime is the Chateau d'If
Beckoning, form dictating all the messages;
Content rebels. If rime is facultative
Pope wins; three cheers for Colly Cibber
And I must go outside and buy a pound of liver.

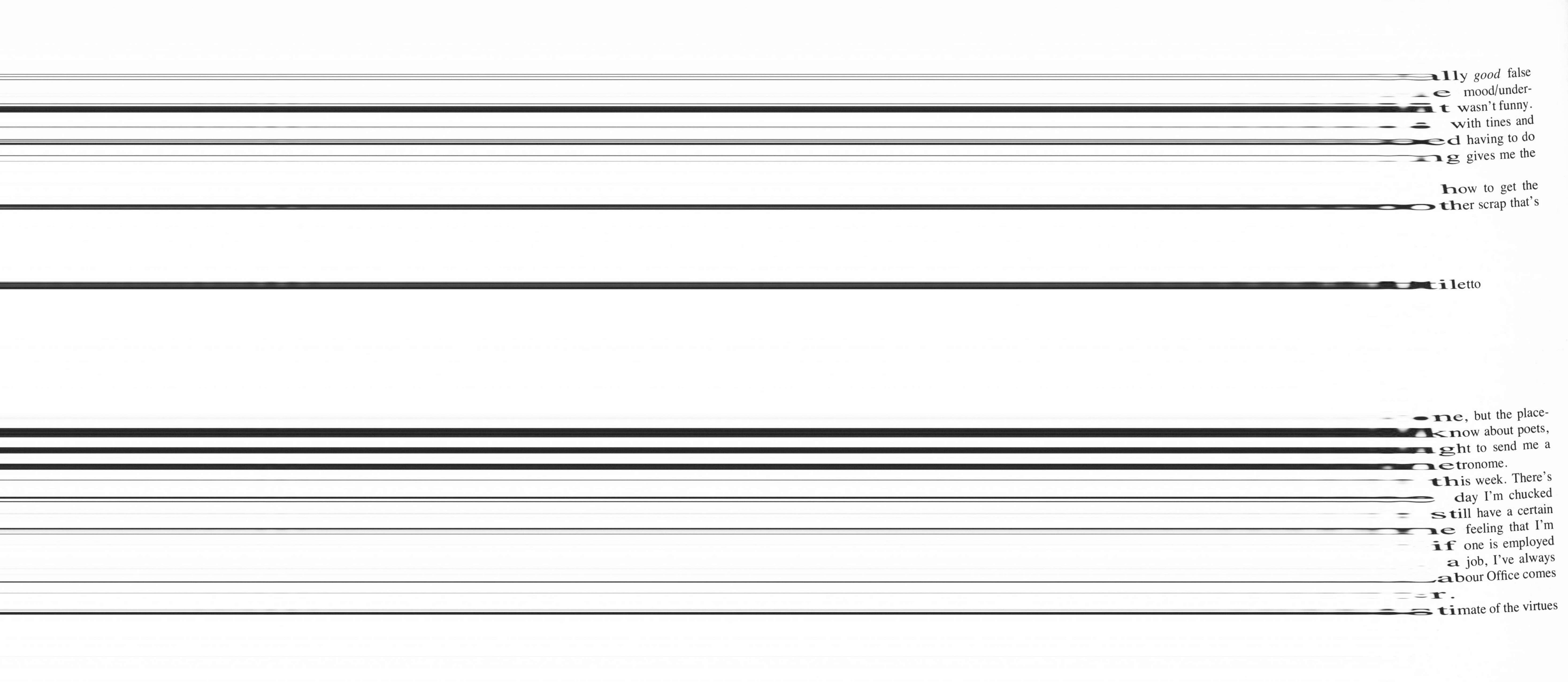

lly *good* false
e mood/under-
t wasn't funny.
with tines and
ed having to do
ng gives me the

how to get the
ther scrap that's

iletto

ne, but the place-
know about poets,
ght to send me a
etronome.
this week. There's
day I'm chucked
still have a certain
e feeling that I'm
if one is employed
a job, I've always
abour Office comes
r.
timate of the virtues

and values of my friend
I am somewhat offended
not First Class People—th
Fifth Class—but did you
into the arms of the High
ers who used to live her
nicely, sir, even if they'r
being upper crust, sir.

It is true that I'm gettin
can't take the cases and c
in school. It was laid on sp
who couldn't get on with
they said there were more c
I failed to insist on my ri
Pambos, who thinks it ve
the picture of the saint wit
yet. I don't think they want
pagan still exists. Yet arou
girls still tie small rags on t
delivery.

So I suppose I am bound
one's friends to live one's p
one available to me. If the
piss off to the pub in the aft

Fish, your letter has m
was happy. I am not learn
enough. I should be sitting
Museum. Instead, having hit
tank of popular misinformati
out the origins of the khan,
it was builded 300 years ago b
conception—it makes me vi
waist-scarves and huge grease
turning like dervishes in the c

I find myself dawdling as I dress, dawdling, hesitating, wondering. At noon I was happy because I felt I had made some kind of commitment, but now I feel myself sidling away from commitment. Not wanting to betray Max? I don't know. We've done that to each other before, and it's been all right, and he isn't here, isn't likely to be here for a long time. No, the funny feeling has something to do with a commitment not away from Max but towards the island. It's important to know in these things what you're getting into . . . no, that's cold and middle-aged.

Promptly at seven I hear X's motor idling in the street below my slot of a window. When I pass the kitchen to go out, Laddie is slumped at the table. He seems so deeply and unremittingly sad that I put my hand on his head. He jerks away like an angry child.

&

Dear Max, What's all this, you asking me to rite in rime? I haven't thyme. And anyway, in grade seven, in Mr Porter's class, I had to write out rhyme a hundred times. And Byronic stanzas! About the rime on the spreigh? Well, I did try. I got the rhyme all right but I couldn't get the content in. How's this for idleness?

> Rime stands against the sky like lovers' legs
> Obscuring the view and changing the perspective;
> End of line threatens, question begs
> Answer, not rime; rime is the Chateau d'If
> Beckoning, form dictating all the messages;
> Content rebels. If rime is facultative
> Pope wins; three cheers for Colly Cibber
> And I must go outside and buy a pound of liver.

"My ambition to be the greatest musician in the world and yours to be the greatest musician's wife?"

"Yeah. My brother Leo's was to own a sports car."

"What's come out of it all?"

"He got smashed up in the winter rally. I'm eating apricots and yogourt."

"Are there any olives?"

"Dried up. I threw them out."

"You could have put more oil on. What kind of oil are you getting."

"Dunno. I just hold out the bottle and yell 'olio'."

"That's not the word."

"It gets the stuff."

"How much do you pay?"

"Two bob, I think."

"Peanut oil. Let me get it from now on. Are you going out tonight?"

"Efy's Pa's picking me up at seven."

"Better dress. You look as if you've been sleeping in your clothes. And . . ."

"Why are you suddenly so friendly?"

"You look as if you're here to stay, so do me two things."

"What?"

"Throw out your jeans, and forget I ever came off a farm."

"They don't mind. Two hundred acres of lakeshore make your father a great landholder."

"By their rules, he was a peasant. Otherwise you'd be shooting with Max in Scotland."

"Maybe I could say my father's store was a department store."

"Shut up about the store, just shut up about the store. There are lies, and there's . . . discretion. You like to keep good company. Don't forget to keep your mouth shut. It doesn't interest them where we come from."

Isn't that beautiful? I tried to do it with really *good* false rimes/rhymes: for another verse I got rime/wine mood/understood (but that's a rhyme-to-the-eye, isn't it?) but it wasn't funny. Three bloody days I've spent riming your rimes with tines and wines and limes. I don't mind Byron but I loathed having to do the 18th century in university and the whole thing gives me the taste of old forks in the mouth.

But I take my hat off to you: who know how to get the content in as well as the rhymes. Oh, here's another scrap that's not too bad:

My friend Loizo's gone, not to Aleppo
Nor on a tiger's back, but to Beirut,
Leaving the post to Mrs Barnes and her stiletto
Who points out smiling that it's truth
Argentina's finished. Nothing to regret-o
To-morrow six hundred Germans in Peru
Will need their palms read, Alexandretta
Request credentials for a hundred Jews
Of Spanish origin in Timbuktu . . .

There's even a little information in that one, but the place-name stuff is pretty cheap, isn't it? So now I know about poets, they work hard. Point taken. Maybe you ought to send me a false-riming dictionary and a false-thyming metronome.

Well, it was fun and I haven't had much this week. There's some odd game going on at the office. One day I'm chucked out, the next brought back by messenger. I still have a certain amount of money in the bank but I hate the feeling that I'm being played with. And not really knowing if one is employed is maddening. And I don't feel *safe* without a job, I've always worked. The next time the chappie from the Labour Office comes around I'll take whatever else he has to offer.

Although I suppose you've made a true estimate of the virtues and values of my friends in what you call the Eating Society, I am somewhat offended by your tone. No, they are probably not First Class People—the White Russian Twins are deliciously Fifth Class—but did you really expect me to walk off the plane into the arms of the High Commissioner? And that gang of writers who used to live here is gone. Aphroulla's bunch suit me nicely, sir, even if they're not important people. Damn you for being upper crust, sir.

It is true that I'm getting on badly with the language. I simply can't take the cases and conjunctions in. I wish I'd done Greek in school. It was laid on specially for certain lads of good family who couldn't get on with Latin. I could do Latin and when they said there were more cases or tenses or whatever they were, I failed to insist on my rights. Ah well, I have learned from Pambos, who thinks it very funny to say "Where, please, is the picture of the saint with the head of the dog?" No results yet. I don't think they want to admit that something so radically pagan still exists. Yet around the shrine of St Catherine young girls still tie small rags on twigs to ask for fertility, lovers, easy delivery.

So I suppose I am bound to disappoint you: one always wants one's friends to live one's pseudo-life; but I am living the only one available to me. If there were anything better to do than piss off to the pub in the afternoon I'd do it.

Fish, your letter has made me dissatisfied where before I was happy. I am not learning enough, using the place well enough. I should be sitting at the feet of the Director of the Museum. Instead, having hit my own level, I swim in the vast tank of popular misinformation available to me. Trying to find out the origins of the khan, I ask Pambos about it and am told it was builded 300 years ago by Turkish monks, a mind-boggling conception—it makes me visualise Orthodox monks with red waist-scarves and huge greased arms, buns stuffed under fezzes, turning like dervishes in the courtyard. Then I find that to Pambos, the word Turkish means "foreign, or not-Greek"—built by somebody he doesn't give a damn about.

Ah, but in the mountains I have seen scarlet pimpernel winking among the gorse and wild lavender (which young men pick to bedizen their bumpers with), not the size of a baby button, but visible yards away, a scarlet staring day-glo eye. And there is asphodel on the plain. And asphodel is tall as mullein. And it smells eerily of skunk. And the blood of Adonis is what anemones are called. And he was anemic, because they are a very pale pink, here. The central plain gives the island a core of loneliness. It seems to me to belong more to the Desert Fathers than to the Psalms, and to the Chronicles of the Crusades. But probably the Holy Land is much more sensational, so don't build your hopes up too much. And come before August. I hear it's unbreathable.

One day I lay dreaming in the remains of Phoenician fishponds and all the poetry that came to mind was yours and Eliot's and Pound's. If I knew Homer perhaps I would have thought of his. It was rough returning to the world of Arsinoe shoe-laces, Othello ice-cream and Aphrodite shoes, but on the way I met a man gathering herbs which he said would be sent to Canada for kidney medicine. And the icicles in my belly are slowly melting. Oh, but I wish you would come, and help me build a composite view of this place.

I append a report—my kind of poetry—with love, affection, and many embraces: A.

–ps: Going back to the subject of disillusion: it is as genuine as the confusion of this letter. The place keeps going in and out of focus on me. As the weather warms, it seems to flatten. The good stone fades, one notices more metal and rusty barbed wire (a little left from every war since Cleopatra's), eons of tastelessness. The islanders don't have the natural ability of the Ibizencans to invest everything they touch with aesthetic glory. Perhaps they had it wiped out of them by too many conquests, quite lost their Cycladic feelings. They seem to have difficult, dark souls. It's all this bloody deux-nationalism, much fostered by mosque and church. And they're as bad as Torontonians about tearing buildings down. Half old Magosa went to build the sides of the Suez Canal. But that's a story for another time, my love, good-bye.

&

THE SUBJECT OF YOUR CONCERN is a meeting held on Wednesday, 30th April, at 8 p.m. at the home of an archaeologist of local origin. He was educated in England, France and Germany and is at present Deputy Assistant Director of the Department of Antiquities. He occupies an eight-roomed villa twenty miles from the capital, has four children, and a good local reputation.

The meeting was called to discuss excavations the Director hopes to carry out at a site near the great ancient city of Paradelphi, where a Roman theatre has recently been restored, and where it has been established from informal peasant digging, aerial photographs and the structure of unnatural tumuli on the site, that a group of tombs at least Mycenaean in origin exists. The entire location is overlaid by a number of shrines sacred to St Timotheus, on the site of the largest of which St Paul is said to have preached the apocryphal Epistle to the Maloundians.

Those present included the Secretary to the Minister of Culture, the Bishop of Maloundia and Archimandrate of the Monastery of SS Timotheus and Pavlos (the first person to have held these offices jointly), two attendant acolytes, Mrs Thekla Nicolaides, assistant to the assistant Deputy Director, the President of Poseidon Diving Equipment Ltd, who is prepared to investigate the harbour near the site, a representative of the British Council, several local businessmen and two foreign observers.

Proceedings began with coffee and a discussion of the weather. Formal remarks were made on the subject of the welfare of families and businesses, these in English. Then the language of the discussion was changed to Greek and the Assistant Director made formal application to the Bishop for permission to excavate the site.

The Bishop stroked his beard, took in the company with large soft hooded eyes. "No, my friends," he said. "The site is a place of pilgrimage to all of Christendom." The company fell respectfully silent and the acolytes crossed themselves, then giggled. The Bishop put his hands on his knees and looked around the company. A servant appeared with refreshments. "To your very good health," said the Assistant Director."

"To yours."

"There is an American expedition which would make the excavation very much worth our good republic's while."

"The bones of St Timotheus are not to be on any condition disturbed."

There was that in the Director's eyes which led one to think that only on important occasions such as this did he believe in saints, but he crossed himself and said, "It could be arranged to work on the periphery of the crypt."

"The site is sacred to all that is dearest to Eastern Christendom."

Another silence. Another tray, containing cheese and stuffed vine-leaves, small fried fish, and bread and little shapely silver forks, was circulated. The bishop held his glass to the light, exhaled, and smiled at Mrs Nikolaides' legs.

"The site is believed to have previously been a landing-place of the Argonauts," the diving man said.

"We are interested in the Christian rather than the ancient pagan world," said the Bishop.

"Surely the Homeric tradition belongs also to our spiritual heritage."

"I have discussed on previous occasions the danger of that point of view, sir. The church is concerned with the religious state of the people."

"So far from the Motherland," said the Director, "it is difficult for them to retain the spirit of Hellensim."

"They are very faithful but they are in need of guidance."

"The Museum is in a position to employ forty workmen on the site."

"The site is the tomb of St Timotheus, whose bones are on no account to be disturbed." The Bishop then produced from under his skirts a bottle of the Monastery's famous rose-coloured brandy. A health was drunk. The discussion continued in the same manner for another hour. Then he took his leave, and the others followed.

One of the businessmen remarked later to an observer that a great deal of progress had been made. "Within one month," he said, "we shall give a grand banquet for the Bishop. The Ethnarch will personally attend. As well as the American archaeologists, who arrive at the end of May."

&

X: You feel used, and I am sorry for it.

A: The sun is leaching the imagery from the stones, and now that it has gone, I cannot make the magic return again.

X: It is difficult to live in ruins if you have not the habit of it. Still, mud walls are good. You will be cool in summer.

A: You have a practical mind.

X: And so have you. Yet I have disappointed you.

A: You have taken your clothing off, but not your dignity. It makes me feel alone.

X: Then I have put you in quite the right frame of mind for reading English poetry when I leave you, which I must do.

A: You aren't comfortable, there is something déclassé, some-

thing low here for you.
X: I have low associations with this quarter. It is very strange for me to come here.
A: So my beautiful orange divan says that odalisque has one meaning for you and one for me? What position have I put myself in?
X: A charming one. I have tickets for the theatre next week, and the day after tomorrow an Israeli is to play the harpsichord in the ruins of an abbey in the mountains. He is quite good, and as there is also a wedding in that village, we shall also be able to hear the old fiddlers scraping not very far away. I think you would like it. Will you come with me?
A: Your wife?
X: She is abroad. It is quite normal for me to seek other company.
A: You are forgiven. Barely.

&

Footsteps descending. I have made a commitment. It doesn't feel right, but it feels good. It's a practicality. Why doesn't morality as I was taught it understand practicality?

Now he's going through the arch, by the closed iron curtains of the shops in the dark, dim street. He's turning the corner, feeling for the big familiar car hidden in an empty archway.

He's good. He looks as if he'd be too refined, but he's good. He isn't ashamed of pleasing a woman.

Now he's getting into the car. There's the thick soft sound of an expensive door closing.

You've got to have someone. I could have had that poet. He didn't look as if he'd be company.

What's that line in Evelyn Waugh that's so useful? "Never apologise, never explain."

Not a night to brood alone. As soon as I hear his car purr

away and admit to myself that I prefer cars that purr to cars that cough and that the temporary company of one rich man will not keep me from getting through the eye of the needle, I hurry out to Aphroulla's. And find, surprisingly, Laddie and Florinda there. Everyone is busy. Aphroulla is packing, she sits surrounded by her own ikons and images, a rich medley of styles from the mediaeval to the cubist. A new hotel is opening on the east coast, a mural has failed to arrive from Israel, we must mend, fold, parcel woollen evil eyes and fat beach-ladies in cloth, cactus patterns in paint, Egyptian-looking animals with human eyes. For the first time, Aphroulla, who has exhibited in Paris and London, is having a show in her own country.

"Where is the ikon of the dog-headed saint, Aphroulla?"

"I don't know. In the museum at Athens, I should think. Help Florinda fix the hem of that tapestry, will you? No, you cannot, you are left-handed, the stitches would go the wrong way. Laddie-mou, you must put those frames in the crate so very carefully, good, ease it in, fine and well done. Oh, the men here, they think it is not masculine to be careful. Florinda, you are *magnifique*. Can you repair this? I did not know so many years had gone by since I took these down. You roll it around the tube. I am glad you have come. There is something nasty going on at Loizos' office, I think I know what, but I cannot tell you yet. I think you ought to stay away from it. My mother is being very wicked again."

"Why?"

"Oh," she shrugs, "who knows, with those foolish people? Here is one you can sew by yourself."

From inside my stunned silence I watch them at their preparations, three now allied who had never admitted to friendship before. I see the broad-based body of Florinda clothed in stained accordion-pleated synthetic of a vicious mauve colour, kneeling and stretching to her good work. Her grizzled head is turned away from me, but I can feel the pins between her lips. Then

she turns her head and her fine accusing blue eyes gloss over Laddie, who is tacking burlap to the back of a tapestry. He raises his head, view A2B, the Moonlight Sonata, and the most fetching kind of aristocratic longing suffuses his expression. Aphroulla says, "I am really extremely sorry to find that Loizos has involved you in such a low intrigue. I do not know what you will think of us on this island." But she does not look sorry. I pour myself some of the brown cirrhosis-seed that did in the White Russian Twins. I have been feeling useless for too long.

"Laddie was telling us about your home," Aphroulla says.

I open my mouth like a fish, but he forestalls me. "She didn't get home for Father's funeral. It was when her husband left her without a bean in England. I was in Corsica, and Barbara was in Australia. I thought I'd better go.

"I took the plane out of Ajaccio in full sunshine. Everybody came with me, there had been a party the night before the telegram came, and it had been much forwarded, so I left in a hurry. I was staying with B, the choreographer, a marvellous man who owns a castle. The piano is in the donjon and in order to get servants he had had to get permission from Rome to have the whole village exorcised; the castle was haunted. But B. could always manage that sort of thing. Edward was there. We had been having a marvellous time. I didn't want to leave, but it seemed obscene to let the old man be buried alone.

"Mother had died about five years before. We went home for that, of course. It was before things started to go badly for us. Since her death he had been living alone, and he seemed all right. I felt pretty terrible I hadn't been home while he was alive, but there was always the problem of money. My reviews had been getting worse and worse and I knew the money was going to run out like the red stuff in a broken thermometer that isn't mercury.

"So, I remember, they all poured me onto the plane in Ajaccio on a sunny day in February. It was early in the morning, the party had never stopped. There was something going on between Eddie and this composer, but I wasn't worried because I had a positive thing going with the choreographer. There were a couple of women. It was a nippy day, even there, but Edward was drunk and wouldn't give me back my camel-hair coat.

"Well, I went from Ajaccio to Nice to Paris to Montreal to Toronto and then I took the train. All I remember is getting colder and colder. I stood outside the train station with my European luggage, freezing in a raincoat. The one taxi driver wasn't sure he could fit me in when I told him I wanted to go out the Lakeshore, so I told him to drop me off at Christina and Lochiel, where the lawyer's office was. I should have told him the undertaker, but I wanted a cup of coffee first.

"I got to the lawyer's office and went in and asked the girl what time it was so I could change my watch—after all, I'd come half-way round the world—and I had a wrangle with her about changing some francs so I could take a taxi: the funeral was to be in half an hour. I went straight home and, blessedness of permanence, the key they gave me when I went away to the Conservatory in Toronto still fitted the lock. I marched in, and, feeling like a thief in the night, put on my father's winter Sunday overcoat and his best galoshes. If I could have found any other sweater than a moth-eaten purple and grey cardigan that he wore in the barn, I'd have taken that too. I kept thinking not, my father's dead, but where did I leave my duffle coat in London?

"I never really liked my father, to tell the truth: he was a dim and aquiescent man. Fortunately for me he had long feet, and I could get into his galoshes to go to his funeral. I went to the bathroom, I opened a window or two—he had been in hospital for a month, the house had an old man's neglected smell—stuck out my tongue at that awful picture of a woman playing a spinet in the dining room, slammed the door, and for the first time—for the first time—I noticed that the house was barely worth the name of a cottage. Did you ever notice that? It's mean and low and incredibly small. When I shut the door the whole house shuddered and shook. The paint was half off the frame siding."

"You'd been staying in a castle. You'd forgotten how we lived."

"But do you mean," Aphroulla asks, "that you have wooden houses as they do in Istanbul?"

"We have wooden houses, as they do in Istanbul, though, because of the need for heat, probably on a smaller scale."

"The danger of fire must be very great."

"Anyway, I got to the funeral home with five minutes to spare and five dollars in my pocket. The taxi cost the boatfare from Ajaccio to Nice. I was cold, stunned: the trip, the change in time, temperature. I was barely human. I had to go onstage and be chief mourner and worry later. They had him all propped up on red satin. Auntie Lena, his sister, had made the arrangements. He looked stuffed. The undertaker had made him up and he was leering. He looked like old Pa Kettle in the movies, not like Father at all. I wanted to be sick.

"Luckily, the United Church isn't given to long funerals. The minister rattled through the 23rd Psalm and we sang 'He Leadeth Me.' I remembered some of the relatives, but goofed on some of my first cousins, who seemed incredibly stout and middle-aged. They were all pale and pasty, covered with winter fat. At least the peasants are tanned here. Stinson the lawyer, I remembered, but the rest—well, I never really knew my father's side of the family. My mother didn't get on with them. I looked at them, strangers in ugly hats and beaded veils and dun-coloured serviceable coats. No furs, Aphroulla, we weren't that class. They frightened me. All I could remember about them was that if they got a chance they'd lynch a person like me. Oh, I suppose they wouldn't but . . . you can't like people if you don't know them, can you? Women with boxers' faces, and tiny shrivelled old men. The organist was terrible.

"I got a tiny thrill out of going in the undertaker's Cadillac behind the hearse, with a little purple flag flying and the lights on, and a cop on a motorcycle to take us through red lights; but other than that I felt totally blank. I kept telling myself, they're your family, they've slaved for you. I didn't care a tap for them. As for poor old Bert, laid into ground that must have been dug with a diamond drill, at five below zero and a wet wind off the lake, all I could remember about him is that I practised the piano instead of helping him with the chores. He was being buried in a forest of pink granite tombstones (they never give themselves away, do they, those people of ours, Audrey? even their tombstones are identical, and they call it democracy), and I was wearing his galoshes.

"After the ashes-to-ashes they all shook my hand and I was charming as ever I could be; too charming for a funeral, I heard later. They said I was 'affected'. They also said I never shed a tear. I was too bloody cold.

"Auntie Lena asked me to the house but I had promised to meet Stinson in the Crystal Grill. Later, at his office, when he showed me my father's papers—mortgages and promissory notes that financed my wonderful musical education—I wished I had gone in one of their enormous pastel motor cars to eat hot roast beef sandwiches with black gravy and biscuits on the side in Auntie Lena's kitchen. I remembered her, all right.

"All those years Mother and I were tugged along by some kind of dream. 'Lafcadio is musical,' she would say, and I, in the hope of being something, not the indeterminate dreamer I was, followed along with it. I mean, if you can't make yourself go in the barn because you're afraid of the bull—though I wouldn't be now, would I, sweets?—you have to follow some other line. And of course I am musical. But when I saw the papers Stinson had, and went through the safety-deposit box and the drawers in the house, and remembered how once Mother laid that great dream on me and I tried to fulfil it and become her little gentleman pianist, I wanted to cry for old Bert, really mourn for him.

"Stinson changed my last francs for me. I took another taxi home. I should have called Lena, but I went to sleep in my own old tin bed and stayed there for a week, shivering. I ate peaches and terrible canned hams from the emergency cupboard. There was also tea and sugar and some honey. It was two miles to the store for bread. Nobody came and nobody phoned. Finally, Auntie Lena came over and said they all thought I should have come before he died. I said I didn't know he was dying; that mollified her. I asked her what she wanted for a memento. She said, to be paid what she was owed, because cousin Cameron's boy was going through for a vet and you know what that costs. You couldn't blame her.

"I might have got more money by taking a taxi into town, or even walking—the buses don't run any more—but who at the Inchcape Trust ever heard of the Credit Lyonnais?

"It was my old music teacher, McTavish, whom I remembered as a fierce old bugger, who rescued me. Phoned very timidly out of his retirement and asked if for the humble sum of a hundred dollars I could bring myself to give a concert on the high school Steinway. They had it tuned for me and I practised in the auditorium. The schoolkids came and listened. McTavish had made a great fuss about me over the years, his own little Glenn Gould (and I was glad I had stayed in Europe, where the crits couldn't get to him). He put up the money for the tickets and the posters. I sent flyers to all the Moores in the phone book because I couldn't remember which ones were my relatives. And free tickets to Auntie Lena. Mrs Morris who ran the Community Concerts told me what to put on the programme. They'd progressed beyond the Turkish March but not very far, I had a terrible argument with her about the Satie.

I froze at bus stops and ate broccoli casserole with gusto and the neighbours. Stinson lent me an old suit of tails that had been his father's.

"I'm impractical, no business man, but not impossible. I got old Erlbach up from Toronto. He got his press people working and booked me in Toronto and Montreal. The notices weren't really bad. I asked him what else he had, he said, the Sault, Swift Current, Port Arthur, Rainy River: it sounded like the weather on TV. I took it. It wasn't the career I had dreamed of, but I had an odd feeling that for the first time I was working for a living. Coming out from the draughty backstage of those high school auditoriums, alone as the Ancient Mariner and sitting down and being something for them—not only playing, but being something. Erlbach must have fixed the tour to see if I could take it, though, because it was rough. I made enough to get back to Europe if the worst came to the worst and the estate was worth nothing, but not enough to decide to stay home.

"When I got back, Stinson had arranged to sell the farm to a real estate outfit for housing. We'd have made a packet if we'd held on for another two years, of course, it's all houses up there now, they say, but we were all in the same ropey financial condition and even split three ways, even taking all the debts out, there was a tidy sum. Enough to come here with Eddie and put plumbing in the khan, anyway.

"Of course the house—do you remember it?—was on an amazing piece of land. There were high cliffs going down to the beach. And I looked out over the lake and I thought it had some of the power of the Mediterranean, if it were only *civilised,* I could stay there. It occurred to me for a fleeting moment to do that; stay there. Then I thought I would only wind up in McTavish's shoes, teaching, and playing organ in some United Church or other. And if it's civilised in one way, it isn't in another, it simply hasn't been lived on long enough—loved. And the government gets in the wine. Did you know there are only two French wines at the local liquor store, at four dollars a bottle? It simply wouldn't have done.

"I left in the spring, just after I had got back from the tour. I was half-sick and exhausted. But the lilacs were out and when I looked back, I saw them towering over the doorway of that little house, standing on either side like bunches of tall, emotional women."

The doves are making their rolling liquid sound. Aphroulla sighs and moves from her knees to her haunches. "I would have stayed," she says. "But you are like me, an artist. You must always be going somewhere else."

Florinda sniffs.

VI

SNAPSHOTS: CLICHES: MAY

Dear Max, I've got the place alone to myself at last. Laddie's gone off with his friends to the seaside for a week. I can go down the stairs without eliciting snide comments about what I'm wearing, I can sit and read in my shorts on the gallery (but not, of course, walk the street in them) without provoking rage; eat what I want; do what I want when I want; see whom I want: glory! It reminds me of first being given a quarter to baby-sit myself. Though I won't dance with scarves today naked in front of Eddie's pierglass. My breasts aren't brand new any more.

Any kind of cohabitation can become oppressive, but since Laddie's major mode is a fit of the sulks it's marvellous to be free of him. If you don't come soon I'll have to move on somewhere—England or Turkey. Perhaps Troy?

The weather is glorious: high summer, clear skies. Beach time, and the north coast is now sprinkled with open-sided bamboo shelters where struggling couples succeed in keeping beer cold and kebab hot for crowds of swimmers and tanners, mostly foreigners and young people. Anyone over forty is too busy, or never learned to swim. There's no bus to the nearest beach and hitchiking is disapproved of, but somehow when one is free someone is always driving, so life is gay as a clutch of little flags.

Except today. I promised I'd go in to the office, so I will, but it's very uncomfortable. Whenever I'm there Mr S.'s mother comes in and stares at me as if I had my fingers into the till. It's very uncomfortable. I don't know quite what I've done, or what he's told her I've done, and I don't like to ask. However, it's payday, so I'll keep my promise.

I can't think of any other special news. Oh, I went and examined Agrotis-from-Agros's perfume factory, a mere shop full of old kerosene cans of flower essences. He puts them up in old Chanel No. 5 bottles as colognes and brilliantines of vile consistency, but the scents are lovely. I'm terrified to wear them, considering the strictures on women who wear cheap scent in literature. He has an alcohol base for cologne, and a Vaseline one for brilliantine, and bottles and a funnel—presto, a factory. Brilliantly simple.

Must dash, it's later than I thought. I'll post this as I pass the P.O. Come soon, my love, I've never seen you with a tan. I'm black already. Cheers, A.

&

That was a lie, we're on summer hours now, with a siesta-break between one and four, which makes a maddening hole in the day. But I don't feel like writing any longer. He seems very far away.

The sun has a sharp edge to it now. In the spring everything seemed more romantic, but there are no shadows now, it seems, and distances are changed. Now that the flowers have dried up, except for the carefully tended geraniums, the place is beginning to look sordid.

I wish X would come. Somebody. Anybody. No: X. I suppose since Efy has no piano lesson he's had to take her to the beach.

I feel like making love, that's what it is. I've felt like that all the time ever since the weather got hot, it's as if someone had put something legendary into my food. Partly summer body-consciousness, I suppose, feeling tanned and warm. I never felt that way in England. It scares Puritan hell out of me.

On the principle that the devil finds work for idle hands, I lock up the kitchen and go out with Max's letter. The stores are shut, but loafing along the street behind the big boring new Orthodox church, I see an English girl called Caroline Williamson in the window of a teashop. I join her, and she talks about her children. Nell's getting along fine at the convent, and her lessons are in French, English and Greek; but little Eric's a chauvinist who'll only speak English, or Turkish to his nanny. They'll have to send him to an English school, which will cost a packet, and Jack's boat business isn't doing very well. It's hard, being a foreigner.

She's putting in time before a dressmaking appointment. Ready-made clothes are hard to find, but there's a little Armenian woman . . . Married women's lives strike me as grossly unreal.

We part at the ramparts and I wander down the street to The Brigadier. There's no one there at all but the White Russian Twins, and I can't bear to hear them cackling "Why are you here?" so I nip into the loo. When I come out, Speridakis' clerk is standing by the door. "Mrs Ladi, Mr Loizos wishes to inform you that the office is closed today."

So it's still the idle hour when I get back home. Ayios Mammas is sitting on our steps. He doesn't look poetic now as he does at night mooning and lalling outside Aphroulla's gate. He's an old ruin in cut-off canvas pants, a dirty shirt and bare feet in peeling sandals. He's sitting crying, rocking his perambulator. "What's wrong, Baba?"

"My kitty, she is sick," he answers in English, holding a flaccid ball of fluff to his sordid beard.

The local taxi driver thinks it ridiculous to take the Canadian lady and mad old Ayios Mammas and his kitten to the vet. "Dirty man, dirty man," he says. I am about to put on my best English manner and commandeer him when Ayios Mammas refuses to be parted from his perambulator, so we decide to walk. Ayios Mammas doesn't know where we're going, but the taxi driver tells me where the Government animal hospital is. I take the old man's ragged arm at corners, and governess him along to the ring-road boulevards the English built outside the walls. Thinking what a sight we must be, and how a man comes to this.

The hospital consists of two cement block buildings with functional tin roofs in a large corral under some palm trees. We join a queue of peasants holding donkeys with their guts hanging out and goats in arrested labour; poor, patient defeated people hanging onto poor, patient defeated animals. This is the side of island life you don't see in pretty articles in the *National Geographic*. Wilted kine and mangled dogs. And everyone standing, standing.

Ayios Mammas hangs back like a shy six-year-old. He is afraid, and certainly the other animal-proprietors are eyeing him without friendliness: a dirty man with a prophet's white beard, warty hands, a soiled white shirt, splayed feet in sandals. We stand uneasily at the edge of the crowd, I holding the limp white dirty kitten. The peasants don't look malevolent in the fields, ploughing and waving at passing cyclists, but here, having walked in from their villages, worried, exhausted and pulling starving and dying animals, reduced to the level of trading their kine for magic beans, now standing in filth and sickness, sweating, waiting, staring at me and Ayios Mammas, they don't look friendly. I don't blame them. Of what value is a sick kitten compared to a beast that once turned a wheel or pulled a plough?

Government white-coats open the surgery and announce that siesta is over. Names are called out. A shepherd carries in an enormous dog with swollen feet. A woman hauls in a half-dead donkey, pulling and beating at him. The sun is overwhelming now. There are flies all around us. One of the goats has a tiny hoof sticking out her behind. Ayios Mammas stands with his eyes to the ground.

"You, lady, you," says the white-coated official.

"No, I must wait my turn."

"You, lady, you. Come now." So I take the poor kitten into the shack, which is a spare but efficient surgery. They wipe off a big enamel table soiled with blood and copper sulphate. "It is Ayios Mammas's kitten, it is sick and he is sad."

The vet laughs. "Kittens are cheap, here."

"It is his child. He cries."

He grins, and twists the kitten to examine it. "Paugh, lice, worms, fleas. Ayios Mammas is a dirty man. Reno!"

Another white-coat comes grinning in with a hypodermic. "For you, lady, anything. For Ayios Mammas . . ." he shrugs, jerks his thumb in the air, hands me a prescription. Through the window I can see lifeblood of landscape pouring out, and I skitter away as fast as I can go.

Ayios Mammas cries and presses his warty nose to my hand. As we pass the Pharmakia I have his prescription filled. He waits, cradling the mewing kitten in his arms. We process home, myself two steps ahead, woman, kitten, madman-sage. I leave him at the foot of my stairs and go and get a basin, soap, water, to wash the cat, thinking, the English have got to me, and their dumb beasts, and beating kids but being kind to animals. As I wash the cat the fleas and nits crawl up my arms. I tell Ayios Mammas to turn out the carriage. He refuses. I make a forbidden fire in a can in the courtyard. "There, throw out the old newspapers, I will give you new." He does, unwillingly, as I stand over him. The sense of power is wonderful: he does what I say. Dangerous. He weeps as he shreds lousy newspaper and lousy rags into the can. Then I find out why. In the bottom of the carriage are pound notes crawling with insects. For one of them I buy a can of insect-spray from Phaedra. He panics: no, lady, no. Must the money be full of worms to satisfy his primitive theology? I am so North American I can't look at a worm without gagging? We must carry this through. "The kitten will get better now," I say, handing him the drops the Pharmakia gave me for its eyes, and its worming powder. I put clean *Observers* and *New Statesmen* on top of the deloused money, and give him a worn teatowel for the kitten's bed.

But from the archway and out of Phaedra's back door, and from the Turkish side, people are watching us.

The kitten is weak and half-blind, but wonderfully clean and white. Ayios Mammas trails uncertainly away, wheeling enough money for Alexis' education down Monodromos. I should have hung one of their blue and white beads over the carriage to ward off the evil eye. What was that book of Forster's where the Englishwoman came to Italy and upset something that was perfectly all right and the baby died?

At least there's not so much of the day to put in now. I go to the Post Office now it's open, and find a parcel of books from Maurice Henshaw: treats. *Eothen,* a mysterious book my grandmother had, which sat on her desk between *Lavengro* and *The Tenant of Wildfell Hall,* and which I never opened. Toye's *History of Fortifications*—now why would he send me that? And a thick one, almost folio size, Cobham's *Excerpta,* a compilation of historical materials about the island, from Strabo on up to the first British Colonial officers. Well sir, an improvement on William and Roger's lavatory jokes. If it wasn't too hot to read.

Funny, I wanted so much to be alone, and now . . . .

Good, there's Michaelis down below blowing his Citroen horn. "We are going to a village to eat stolen meat." It's a kind of dish, it turns out.

&

MONODROMOS

I come in late, too full of wine to sleep. I pick up *Eothen*: it's a travel book. Good God, William Henry Kinglake passed through here on his way to visit Lady Hester Stanhope in the Lebanon. What a terrible chauvinist he is, and what good fun. Lady Hester—old, fierce, solitary, mystical, living on a mountain top with a private army, a maid, and a devoted doctor. There's been no one quite like her since. Those eighteenth century women when they decided to be unconventional . . .

Marvellous to have been born when the world was younger. Would one have survived, been tough enough?

In 600 B.C., Nebuchadnezzar rebuilt the walls of Babylon, giving the outer wall a full thickness of 85 feet 8 inches. At Ur of the Chaldees, he thickened the walls to a depth of 38 feet 4 inches. Fancy that.

The families that built the Palazzos of Venice and Genoa, and the big *hotels particuliers* of the south of France had mansions here. The world tied up in a bow.

Glory to sit reading late, alone, with a bottle of brandy and warmth and warm music drifting in from the nightclub around the corner, picking excellent brains. They should have taught the odalisques to read.

I must have drifted off. There's something funny. Something isn't quite right. Did I leave a cigarette burning? No. The light's out.

I'm not alone. That's what. There's something big in the room, big and breathing. Something like a bear. Cripes, it's getting closer.

"Missus Ladi, Missus Ladi," and who's calling me that? Whose are those big fat . . . ?

"Get off me, get out," I hear myself shrieking. But the shutters are closed, no one will hear. I can't see a line of light. He smells. Who is it?"

"Mrs Ladi, Mrs Ladi . . ." he's on the bed on me, it's the fat bristly taxi driver who took me to meet X at a rendezvous.

I particularly chose him so he wouldn't know who I was, he isn't from this quarter. What does he think I am, a mattress?

"Get out. Get out. Don't paw me. I don't want you. Exo. Exo. Exete, Exeunt, whatever the language is. No. Don't." One of us stinks of brandy. "I don't want you, you fat old thing, get off the bed."

He's drunk, I think, soft and unco-ordinated. But he's working at me like a bear on a honey log, slowly, with determination and his paws back to back. "Shoo. Bugger off. Get out!" It's no good screaming.

Stupid man, he doesn't know how to go about what he's going about, he's too drunk. He gets his head down low and I swing half off the bed, grab Cobham's *Excerpta*, and give him such a clout on the head with it he falls off onto the floor.

He sits there with his pants down and his big dick lolling out like a sausage. "Lady?"

"Get out, Takis, get bloody well out or I'll run for the police."

"Lady, I loves you."

"Get out." I brandish the book again and he lumbers to his feet and runs for the door. Along the gallery. Down the steps. Out. Good. I lean against the door clutching Maurice's precious book. History has its uses.

&

Maundering over the absurdity of lying adrift in intellectual pretensions with my legs open and my door unlocked, I stay awake for the rest of the night. In the morning, Megas comes with tickets for his workshop production of *Death of a Salesman*.

He is courtly and cocky and charming, and subsequently late for work.

Byzantium is a long way from the land where not-fucking was class.

And of course I go to work half-dead, and there's a great deal to do, and I get back and there's X on the balcony because they have this way of being turned on by the smell of another man on you, and he's halfway into the *Excerpta*. "The English," he says, "are not like anyone else. This chap who made this book, he spent his life as some kind of civil servant, but his real life's work was this. How did he find the articles? Why was he interested in this island? Who translated them for him? Where did he find the energy in this climate? You have good friends, to send you books like this. It is worth seventy-five pounds."

"It's a very useful book."

"Yes, I imagine so. Come, I am taking you to lunch with a friend of mine who collects antiquities and has a splendid villa by the sea."

An hour later we are lunching under an umbrella on a terrace. The sea lies simply shining blue below us.

Giles is an Englishman of the managerial class who served with the British in Palestine before he settled here. "I had a little money, I simply couldn't bear to leave the Middle East. It's a bit dodgy living here on a fixed income, but I manage, I manage. One misses, of course, the sophistication of London; but not its stuffiness. I hear you know the Williamsons. Jack's a good chap, I've done some diving with him. Would you like to see some of the things we've found together?"

He has coins, and chunks of mosaic, gold jewellery and terra-cottas. "The figures of course didn't come from the sea. The peasants bring them round. I can't take them off the island, of course. When I die, they'll go to the Museum. Aren't they all splendidly priapic? They know my taste."

Such strange figures in pointed hats, driving chariots, lashing oxen. All with wicked smiles and penises. "They're immensely valuable, of course. I suppose Caroline didn't tell you that last summer in a fit of rage she threw six of the little single ones at Jack and broke them all. It gets jolly hot here."

He is baked brown from his beachcombing. His eyes are astonishingly innocent and blue. Like X, he appears to have an absent wife and a good mind.

&

When Laddie comes back, Peter and Dympna take us to the beach for a picnic. Raging along in Peter's Morris I see a different version of the landscape, hills divided and numbered in whitewash: parachute practice fields, Peter says. A paint-by-numbers world.

On the beach, Dympna and Laddie smooth Ambre Solaire on each other's bodies very carefully. Dympna does not speak. Peter talks endlessly of the difficulties of producing *Julius Caesar* for the Forces. Members of the cast are continually exported to Aden, Gaza and Benghazi.

Dympna decides she would rather cook dinner than eat at the beach. We drink brandy sours on their verandah before the meal. Branches of their palm tree fall off at regular intervals with a sinister swishing sound. "There are rats in that palm tree," Dympna says.

On the way home in the evening, both pleasantly drunk, Laddie and I stand a long time against the cool wall of an outdoor cinema listening to the sound track of *Beat The Devil*.

"God, I miss jokes," he says.

&

X takes me to Florinda's for tea. He is astonished that I know the names of different kinds of cows. She has a flagging Jersey, a caved-in Holstein which she calls a Friesian, and a kind of humped Egyptian brown thing. I order my tea clear.

Florinda joins us at the table and she and X discuss the virtues of the *Excerpta*. She says, "You can say what you like about British rule, but while we were in charge everything ran as smooth as seventeen buttons."

&

That same evening we dine at the house of a friend of his named Giorgios, who used to work at a grand and famous and glassy restaurant in Paris, behind the Palais Royale. He's come home and retired to a lemony coastal village. He cooks for his friends when the spirit moves him, as it has done tonight.

There is time to put in. We take a high road along the mountainscape and drive through a tumbledown village Gunnis has recommended as pure Lusignan in style. I haven't quite got my Royal Houses straight yet, but I think the Lusignans got the island from the Templars who got it from Richard the Lion-Hearted who got it because Isaac Comnenus insulted his wife. The village looks hot and poor and extremely undistinguished.

"Gunnis wrote his book a very long time ago," X says. "I came to this village several years ago when I first read the book. They gave me some quite good carvings from the old church for firewood, and I found a woman with a beautiful dower chest full of old embroidered vests and caps and shirts. My friend Omo bought them from her, and she has built a new house of cement block. You think that's bad, eh? Cement block is hot, but it is also clean. You can't count on stone walls lasting healthily for more than eight hundred years. All this tumbledown business is picturesque, but in one of the most beautiful villages I know—not here, further south and west—there was leprosy not long ago. They slept with their animals. Ox breath is considered good for the health by the oldest peasants. You and I like old things because we have sophisticated modern taste, but time passes, there is disease, it is better to sell your dower chest than to live in a house that has been without a toilet for eight hundred years.''

In the courtyard, under a bougainvillea vine, in the soft, soft summer air, Giorgios serves the dinner he had made. It is seasonal and simple—young lamb and artichokes, tender lettuces from seed he brought from France, peaches in William Pender's grandmother's champagne. He has brought us here because the time for all of this is ripe. He joins us with a strawberry liqueur his wife has made. I call for nightingales and X and Giorgios laugh. ''Procne was the nightingale, wasn't she?'' I ask.

''No,'' says X crossly, as if I have spoiled his supper. ''Philomela. Who ever taught you your history?''

After we have said a sentimental goodbye to old Giorgios, we decide it is too good a night to go home to empty beds. We slide down to the sea and swim naked in a secret cove of his, make love on the sand and then drive to the crest of the mountains to watch the sun shoot rose-coloured up out of Syria, tossing the doge-cap peaks from left to right. Eagles soar below us. The colour of the sea lightens from azure to an unimaginable turquoise. Grouse whirr. He lies on the pine needles and says lazily. ''You wouldn't think there was going to be a war, would you?''

''What? When? What about?''

''Oh, I don't know. But there will be something. When I left you waiting in Ayia Varvara I went into the police station to see about a farmer who has been behaving badly to the bank. On the notice board it said there were fourteen missing Landrovers. They must be arming.''

''That sounds terrible.''

''Oof, it happens all the time. It's very bad for business. Still, it will take them time to get around to it. Don't tell Loizos. I don't know what he is doing these days.''

''Nothing that looks fishy to me.''

''You don't know Greek. It's too hard to learn, with so many people speaking English. Oh, you know, I wish this nationalism was over, I am getting tired of drinking bad brandy instead of whisky. It's time to go."

On the way home he drives me down the mountains as if he were a gorilla swinging down trees. Through the moonscape where the dried-up limekilns are, around the fertile springs, past the brick factory and into town, leaving me at the northern gate.

&

A sheaf of German reports have come in to the office. I take them to the Goethe Institute, where there are good commercial dictionaries, exchanging the baleful eye of Mrs Speridakis, senior, for that of the West White Russian Twin. With luck, I can make them last a fortnight.

&

Aphroulla stands over her Alexis and his homework. She drills, he jerks, squirms, twists, corrects, repeats, and tries again. He is in his penultimate year at the Gymnasium, being prepared for entrance exams to universities in France, England and Greece. For Greece, he must write in three languages, demotic, ancient, and some kind of Byzantine church-and-state Greek, highly difficult and artificial. In French he is tutored by the spinster daughter of a house which has been established here for 400 years.

He also studies trigonometry, calculus, philosophy and many varieties and versions of history. He is hollow-eyed. "Alexi," she says, "if you do not try, you will spend your life in a world that is small, small, small . . ."

Caroline says that Giles knows a family that has been here

at least since the thirteenth century and always sent back to Italy for their wives.

&

What kind of editor sends an alcoholic poet to Ireland?

&

Cleopatra was a Macedonian Greek. The world falls apart, reassembles itself, falls apart again, and you discover that Cleopatra was a Macedonian Greek and the kaleidoscope turns. She wasn't an Egyptian like Nefertiti, she was a Macedonian Greek. They weren't philosophers and pot-makers, they were Empire builders, just like the rest of us. They got away with it.

Well, X it turns out has never heard of the War of 1812.

&

Dear Max, I am heartsick about Ireland, I feel it's all for the worst. I know you're hard up since the BBC didn't buy the play, but dear, why spend time in Scotland getting in shape and then go to Ireland? Couldn't you come here instead? It's all sitting here waiting to be described and the weather it marvellous if you're not wearing hairy tweeds.

I know, I sound like everyone's Mum. I've no right to cajole, persuade. You'll do what you want to do.

But I was so excited to get the proofs of your poems, and upset by them. The Dance of Death is superb, Max, nobody can pull off that kind of long poem now and make it joyful, it's full of words and wit and it puts its dukes up to its subject, it's a marvellous thing . . . but if you go to Ireland for a month will you get those proofs corrected? (Jupiter has one "p".) It's all you on the page and it's wonderful, but behind it I can hear your awful rattling cough and I shudder. I didn't know you knew how sick you were last winter, which is a thing a person can say only if she's never been sick, I guess.

But it was all there, Magill Articulator, Magill Prestigitator, Magill Juggler and I loved it and you, and it made me feel what a goddam waste it was, you going off to Ireland. Suicidal.

Of course maybe you're like the Bloomsberries, who reacted fatally badly to the sun. But where I come from you count on getting two months of heat to dry the winter catarrh out of you and I think you need that.

I keep saying to myself, I won't urge him to come, I won't nag and possess him, but I do, yes, I do. Because I don't think you're bored with me, that's not why you're going to Ireland, I think there's some tide in you, driving you out to places you should not visit. Don't go off to all that green gloom, Max. All your old Irish friends are in terrible trouble with Guinness and unsaleable jokes. It will all end badly, and you hate hospitals and what a waste of a poet that would be.

And you've worried about being *vieux jeu* and the Dance proves you're simply not, oh, come here or get on with the corrections, don't go lolloping off to Ireland, even for the *Sunday Times*. It's not worth it. I have friends who will buy you lunch, here.

You didn't ask for that, you asked for news. Well, Will Pender found a girl to sleep with at last and was jubilant. A nice big Russian girl who married a guy in the Department of Agriculture while he was there on a tour, in order to get an exit visa. She didn't appreciate the life he led her and has gone independent. She's very pretty on a large scale. William was so happy until he ran into two drunk policeman in a bar and they confessed his bed has been bugged in case she's a spy. No one's seen William for three days.

Pambos is well, but impervious to the supplications of his children, who now come every night to the shop and plead for him to come home. "Father, dear father, come home with me now . . ." As the clock in the churchyard strikes, he toddles resolutely to the Spitfire Cafe and his waiting hubble-bubble.

I have had tea with a lady who owns a beautiful collection of Coptic daggers and altar cloths, and I have been driven along precipitous coastal roads to Tylliria. Imagine it. That's it: cliffs along which run high, winding roads, isolated villages of vine-growers and basket makers, little frescoed churches. For a shilling a gypsy girl called Sara showed me the "Fontana Amoroso" of poetic fame. I have also been handed pitchers of water to raise a sheen on newly-excavated mosaics of birds and banquets. And been feasted with pigeons and wine by someone's servant, Ali.

All this is very pleasant, but I don't want to spend the hot weather here without you. The Europeans are already beginning to crack and the less resigned islanders are looking grim at the prospect of summer heat. Mrs Loizos Speridakis, for instance, has been hospitalised for attempting suicide. The office is in chaos. Wish, as the postcard says, you were here.

Ah well, you've gone, and godspeed to you. May it bring you much joy. Tell Maurice his books were a godsend, and I am the envy of the literate community. Don't stay too long, there, now. I can't wait forever, there's a rumour that Edward's been seen in the northern mountains, and the Lad is house-cleaning desperately. All my love, A.

&

What good did beauty ever do anyone? What good has it done the people here? Can you eat it? Can you sleep with it? Why do we kill ourselves to make it? And why are the makers of beauty killed and eaten for bread?

&

''I was passing, and your light was still on,'' says X almost sheepishly.

''I was reading.''

''How are you? You look rather ill.''

''Oh, I was at the Williamsons' too late last night. We all got sobbish on old Billie Holliday records and red wine.''

''You waste yourself. What attracts you to such dissipations?''

''I don't know. It's what people do. What else is there to do?''

He looks somehow disappointed, so I pull myself together and go into the kitchen and make tea. But it is not tea I want and when he leaves at dawn, I bang my head like Laddie against the wall.

VII

HEAT

Heat drips like syrup off the mespila tree in the courtyard. Heat oozes from the crevices of the stone steps, from the armpits of the horned columns of the verandah. A white, nitrous, heat-caused efflorescence stains the walls. Cockroaches the size of Cinderella's coachmen are generated by the heat and tapdance on the stone cell floors at night, clicking their chitin blakies. The shutters to the outside world are closed, the khan stinks of centuries of pee, and the old woman will not stop her crying.

Heat sours the clay breath of the winejars and radiates from the stone. The flat sun invades at six in the morning, pressing down on the rubble of the north wall, flattening the mosque-washhouse hexagon, lightening the filthy alcoves of the camel stalls, unshadowing pretensions. We shelter from the heat as if it were a blizzard in Saskatchewan.

No sea-breezes reach the place where the city squats between the northern and southern mountains; there are, at night, brief exhalations from the burning plain, but it has not rained since April, and it will not rain again until the fall. The people in the street walk slowly, leaning and hunched against the sun, always in headscarves and sunglasses.

At dawn, the last of the night's shallow coolness expires; then, a work crew clatters off a village bus bearing airdrills, shovels, picks and mattocks to continue the destruction of the mud-brick building across the road, which, although it was not beautiful, had a charm in its wide, soft arches and a texture in its sagging surface that no new building will replace. Now, as the bricks are pulped to dust by old women in leather boots, a fine silt fogs across the street to join our lunchhour company. The priest supervising the suppression of the building wraps a white scarf across his face and sends himself into purdah. The old woman squats, a lone Eumenide, beside the two beaded Norman stones that decorate our doorway.

She has been there, ululating, for ten days. She sits scarfed and coifed in dusty black like a nun, raising her eyes to Allah or Ishtar or whoever it is she worships (she is Greek but she belongs to an older and less divided world), lamenting my sins. I am not allowed to pass by her. It appears that I have done something very, very bad. The only way I can get out of the khan is to clamber through the broken Gothic doorway on the north side, and the day after she came someone boarded that up from the outside. If I try to go through Phaedra's shop that monster with her great breasts slung loose in her wrapper sneers and laughs and blocks the way. To call the police in order to leave one's habitation is hopelessly foreign and middle-class but it is also more than I can do to pass the old woman, who throws herself at me, reaching her clawed hands to my eyes. She is little and old, a bundle of cords and straw, scaly. A witch escaped from a fairy tale: one's sleazy conscience come to life.

Laddie can get by her, and the boy with the Butagaz, and the man about the drains. William Pender passes freely in and out, as well as Megas and Ahmed. Pambos will not pass her. He tells me she is someone's Yaya, which appears to mean either grandmother or eye-glasses, and holds his finger to his temple, screwing it around in a gesture of madness. He smiles reproachfully at me. He knows what she is saying. I can only guess.

MONODROMOS

She's not incredible—nothing is incredible once you get off your home ground—but she is very strange. The first time I tried to get through and she launched herself at me I came back and sat on the stairs and shook my head. Then I steeled myself and went back again. There was something I wanted to go out and do, which seemed important then, which I can't now remember. I summoned that dignity I find when I pull up my shoulders and stomp hard on the stones and pretend I'm the Duchess of Barbarossa. Nothing doing. She scrabbled at me like a cat, touched me and pawed me. I saw right down her toothless mouth and yellow throat. To get past her I would have had to hit her. I came away shaking instead.

At first, hearing her all day crying "Bad woman, bad woman," and other imprecations I understand only in my blood, I felt an awful, withering guilt. I have, after all, been dining out with someone else's husband—fouled the nest of Efy's mother, gorged myself on the profits of another household. I have, to put it politely, dallied with Maro's man; my desires have been vast. I have read without close attention to the text, and neglected my share of household duties. I have indulged myself in spiritous liquors, wasted money on cigarettes, committed, in short, the usual thousand sins a day. At first I felt I'd earned her.

She makes the old beggar-women in Sophocles Square look untroubled, unwrinkled, and young. Her tongue wags in her jaws, her head nods spastically and rhythmically, she warbles like a hen. Her headdress is drawn across her corrugated forehead like a nun's coif, her cataracted eyes are milky and malevolent, she is centuries old, and who is she if she isn't Guilt?

After four days of being nerve-wracked and unstable about her, I decided I liked her. I still do. She makes me sweat with nervousness and shame. She takes my worries and embodies them. She takes me off the hot sun-stinging streets and puts me back into the condition I was conceived in: a warm enclosure.

Who is she? Where did she come from? Did the stones breed her?

While she is here, Xanthos will not come again. Good. He has begun to shape my vision, he now stands between me and the island I have come to see. I shall miss him, but I shall be free again.

But who is she who sews on my school tunic the big all-American A?

I don't have to go to work, I can't go to work. I am Rapunzel, shut within my fortress. *The sun shall not smite thee by day*. . . All I have to do is endure the ululations of an insane old woman who yells to the street that I am a bad Frank who has no babies, and I am free. I could do anything. Read a book. Write a book. Paint. Draw. Build. The walls are thick, the doors are thick. I am a prisoner, but I am also safe.

It is the heat that is the enemy, it sits upon you and destroys muscle, impulse, all initiative. Laddie trails limp as a morning-glory vine around his empire, swiping at the little heaps of excremental rubble the place seems to generate. He gives me looks of superior sympathy as he comes down my way. "Poor darling? Can't you send it away?"

Aphroulla has taken herself to the beaches of Paradelphi with a pup-tent and caused a scandal. That the sister of Loizos Speridakis, a lawyer, should be disporting herself in a bikini on the beaches, fucking the fennel: a government committee will be formed to rape her and destroy her. They wouldn't dream of buying her work so she could afford a hotel room. Laddie and I are jealously replacing her as a salonnière, and during siesta we have huge luncheon parties, while the old woman, holding my big A in her lap, vets the customers under L.G. Moore's brass plaque.

Yes, I really think I like her. What's there to do if you do go out in this weather? Sit in the Brigadier and get plastered with her *semblables*, the White Russian twins? Follow Dympna down the way to that pointless office? All my life I've been trying to discover some reason for the surge of activity my birth plunged me into. Love? That was a bust from the beginning. Money? Never made enough to make living worth while. Beauty? It's wonderful, I always get hooked on it, but it's no reason for anything. Why keep getting up in the morning, enduring the days? Why bother to breathe? To bring up the children? I don't have any. I'm forced to go on being for the sake of a straight chair, an ugly table and two bice-lined notebooks with carmine margins. Not that I want to stop, but when there's time for a pause, and I realise that the Industrial Revolution is ruining the world, that the government is bringing television to the villages so they won't make things in the evening any more, that the whorled carpet beaters are imported from Yugoslavia, I wonder why the heck I have to keep plodding through dreary days.

One morning Laddie went and got the police. They were very embarrassed. They said sadly, "She is too old." They tried to get her to go away and she wouldn't. They were very young. They said she wasn't asking for baksheesh. Laddie said she was shouting rude things about his sister. That cheered them up, and they talked to her a long time. They told her not to shout words any more. "She is somebody's grandmother," they said, and shrugged and went away.

What I should do is write a murder-mystery, call it "Death Comes for the Yaya". She could be found by some tourists in an old tomb in the countryside, mummified by heat and lack of air. Who would have done her in? Relatives, for her dower-money? Foreigners, for spying on them? Some woman she camped on and called an adulterous tart? She wouldn't be easy to get rid of, she's too sinewy.

Dympna arrives in a taxi bearing a portable typewriter (white) and some files from Loizos. Would one, please . . .

"How are things?"

"Peter's play is postponed until September, thank God. The

director's been posted to Gaza. He's Brutus, now.'' She doesn't look me quite in the eye.

Laddie returns the completed files to Speridakis. My fingers slip on and off the keys from perspiration. I waste a lot of paper.

I could go to Egypt for eight pounds, but would I, in this heat? Egyptians come here for the cool of the mountains. Worms of perspiration, ants, rather, humiliate my thighs and fertilize my ankles. I could go to Lebanon for the same amount, but Beirut is expensive and I don't need carpets for my dowry. I could go to Anatolia and get rubbed out by my Greek friends when I got back. The old woman is indefatigable in her crying.

Megas sits hunkered like a Mexican against the wall; his head is turned to avoid seeing the minaret. He is arguing about architecture with Michaelis. It is siesta time and we are going to have lunch. He doesn't like modern buildings, good for him. I say that I like the wide, pointed arches I see everywhere here. ''They are Turkish,'' says Megas. ''When we have our way, all the arches like that will be gone.''

''Round arches are Byzantine,'' says Michaelis. ''But pointed arches carry more, they can be stressed from four directions. Even in Greece we have such arches, but not so many as here. We do not consider them to be political arches. When you take them down, what will you replace them with but the modern buildings you dislike?''

''We will devise new modern buildings more suitable to the climate. With air conditioning.''

''Even in the villages where arches make shaded streets and verandahs? What does it matter if an arch is Turkish if it keeps a place cool? Where will you get the water for your air-conditioning?''

''Does it take water?''

''Bah, stupid. You are incredibly stupid, Megas. How did you pass the post office examination? Yes, air-conditioning takes water and you have no water and what you have, you waste.

The only way to save water is to get along with the Turks so where ten peasants have one hundred irrigation canals they can agree to have one for each field. And to get rid of the goats so the plain can be reforested. How many times has the UN told you to get rid of the goats?''

''There have always been goats, and then what would we eat?''

''Tinned meat from Argentina like the rest of the world.''

Megas grimaces. ''Greek forms are pure,'' he says. ''The square, the circle. All the architecture should be Byzantine from now.''

I put in, ''In the Middle East, there's a little bit of everything, Megas: Arab, Turkish, Byzantine, Roman, Ancient Greek, you should be proud of that.''

''The first houses with stairs were Byzantine,'' he says, ''I read that in the book. The arch grew up when the Arabs tried to build stone tents.''

''That is too simple,'' Michaelis says. ''That will make the Gothic a high stone tent. You forget, in those days everyone was travelling about. There were the Crusades, there were the eastern invasions, the journeys of exploration. When the travellers found a form that served, they kept it.''

''Turkish arches no longer serve,'' Megas says stubbornly.

''Neither does Ibsen,'' says Michaelis with a sneer.

Heat brings out cruelty. Ibsen is everything to Megas, his soft face crumples. Michaelis looks at his watch and goes away. Megas is waiting for Maro. He gets up, goes into my room, and sprawls helpless with heat and discouragement on the bed. Rolls over and reaches out for me like an affectionate child. By God I could take him up on that, but do I need another old woman crying on my doorstep? The intolerable drills start up across the street. ''If you want to make a new society,'' I say to him sternly, ''do something about the noise that shuts out the voice of Sophocles.'' Laddie comes in and shouts because the Conservation Authority has shut off the water again, and I haven't filled the kettle. We send him out for cold white wine and cigarettes.

&

"I am very sorry, but she will not come away."

"You should be sorry. Can't you do anything with her?"

"Oh *Panaghia-mou*, not me. You ought to know. She thinks I am worse than you. See these scratches on my arms?"

"In a way, I don't mind her. There's nothing else to do. But she's ruining my reputation in the neighbourhood. Why are people always haunted here?"

"I don't understand."

"Well, you're haunted . . . Ayios Mammas trailing you around."

"Oh, that. You were very kind to him, I hear. She should like you for that. But this is something special. She is convinced, absolutely convinced, that you have stolen Loizos from my mother."

"Not from his wife?"

"Oh, she is so weak. But she wishes to sue him for divorce on the grounds of adultery with you."

"But that's ridiculous."

"Have you been anywhere alone with him?"

"Only paying debts around the quarter."

"Nothing else?"

"Once he took me and Laddie to a nightclub to make up a foursome with a client."

"That might have done it."

"They're all mad as hatters, Aphroulla."

"You and your old Turkish monastiraki. You live here, so they will believe anything of you."

"Can't you get your mother to take her away in a wheelbarrow?''

My mother? Of course not. She has as bad an opinion of me as she has of you. Does my grandmother never leave you?''

''She goes home about nine. Then I go out and walk around for a bit. That's how I found out you were back. Most nights Ayios Mammas was leaning against your gate pretending to play a lute, and yawling like a cat. People were throwing things out of windows at him. He was rather pretty, like an old, crazy Pierrot. But he wasn't there tonight, so I came in.''

''Sometimes I think that everyone who has ever touched my family has gone mad. He is such an ugly old man. You have no idea what it was like to live with him.''

''Don't you think Loizos could do something about her?''

''But I thought you said you liked her?''

''Oh, in a way I don't mind being shut in. It gets me out of wandering around the streets, of going to that office—that's the point of it, isn't it? It's nice and Proustian. But really—I can't even go to the beach.''

''Loizos hasn't the courage to go anywhere near her. It is a great pity we have so many cousins in the police who are also afraid of her.''

We are dining in Aphroulla's courtyard on the carcasses of her pigeons. Ahmed and Michaelis were to join us, but, masculine, have declined to arrive in time. She has set up a primitive barbecue on the ground and is grilling her squabs on the kind of 25 cent metal rack we use for hamburgers at home. But pigeons and wine are superior to hamburgers and pop, and we are both feeling the magnificence of the night. ''Where did you get your column?'' I ask her.

''From an old house my mother owned.''

''Here things are scrambled, but never quite lost.''

''Oh, a great deal has been lost, I can assure you.''

There is a sound of caterwauling outside the wall. ''I must go to London, to New York, to Paris,'' she says. ''Do you understand?''

A month ago I wouldn't have, but now I do. ''You need a patron,'' I tell her.

''Your Xanthos would do. Why does he not buy things from me? His wife is very intelligent. She has bought a lot of paintings from Christoforos.''

''He was a friend of Ayios Mammas.''

''They are cousins, I think. Everyone here is cousins, and takes sides. How can you understand this, coming from where you do?''

''Aphroulla, until I was twenty-two I had never stayed in a hotel. We didn't travel much, but wherever we went we stayed with cousins.''

''But it is such a big country.''

''It's as little as this one in its way.''

''I must go somewhere: London, New York, Paris, anywhere. You must go too. There is no way to be free here, as a woman.''

''I don't mind that so much right now. I have been too free.''

''It will eat into you as acid into copper.''

''How's Alexis doing on his holiday in France?''

''It is unbelievable: I am obliged to send him money for food. They do not provide him with any salads. Perhaps he is lying, and wants money for women. Well, I send him as much as I can. At Paradelphi, I made some drawings for the French Cultural Centre.''

''We all missed you. I had a funny little set-to with Megas. He's very attractive, isn't he?''

''Oh, you should sleep with him. He's very good. Why did you choose that white-haired old Xanthos? Megas is a much better lover.''

''I would have felt awful about Maro.''

''Maro wouldn't mind, she is old-fashioned.''

''I bet she has a grandmother too. Where are Michaelis and

Ahmed?''

''I do not know. Time is nothing here for men. Perhaps they have taken up the art of the nargile and taken their mouthpieces to the Spitfire. Why do you love Xanthos?''

''Love is a very big word.''

''Do not be modest, it does not suit you. Why Xanthos?''

''I like his hands. I like his mind when I can find it. I like the food he shares with me.''

''I am disappointed. You should rather have had a big peasant to subdue you. Xanthos is too refined. He is what the Americans call square. You will never know this island through him. He is just like a Frenchman.''

''That poet came one night, that friend of yours. I was a bit interested, and then I remembered some story of Sartre's where the woman crawls around on her knees and elbows being buggered like a dog. I don't want to be an animal, it seems to me that if one stands for anything, one has to stand for not being an animal.''

She sucks one of those flat cigarettes. ''You are very innocent,'' she says.

The door of the courtyard opens: the two men we have been waiting for burst in. ''But the meat is burning!'' Michaelis cries. ''Useless women, gossipping again.''

Ahmed squats by the fire, picks up a tile and fans the charcoal, puffing slightly. He rocks on his heels and looks as if he is listening to an ancient song. He has a long, serious face. He has been coming to Laddie at night and I wonder if Aphroulla knows. ''What do you do, Ahmed?''

He looks at me half-dreamily, over curls of smoke. ''I am an architect.''

''What do you build?''

''Nothing until I am finished my apprenticeship.''

''What would you build?''

''Oh—lady—palaces.''

&

"The woman is an inconvenience," X says.

"I thought she was your grandmother at first."

"You have a bad conscience."

"She moved aside for you nicely. She almost curtsied."

"She is not my grandmother; therefore she respects me. You must learn to deal with these people as you have dealt with these walls."

"What do you mean?"

"I—here—this place is something else to me than it is to you. You are free to live in it. I could not have done so: to me it is a caravanserai, that is, a rather inferior piece of history not so good as the two historic caravanseraiem which are national monuments. It is a faint memory of tentpost and Doric columns into the north wall of which was incorporated a piece of an old Armenian church. It is an old dog which one kicks every time one passes him. I should have torn it down and built something practical in its place."

"What sort of thing?"

"Oh, something clean and modern with air conditioning."

"Michaelis says there is not enough water for air conditioning."

"The Israelis will soon have invented a good de-salination plant. Then we shall have air-conditioning: everything is possible in this modern world."

"Get rid of the old woman, then."

"Everything is possible except getting rid of that old woman. What have you been doing since she has come?"

"Oh, I go out at night after she has gone and follow Ayios Mammas around the streets."

"I saw him on my way tonight. He is living in an old doorway. The beggars of the neighbourhood steal from him when he sleeps. He is mad. Sometimes I think everyone in this quarter is mad, but rather prettily. Why else would you hang that carpet-banger on the wall?"

"I love it. Have you ever tried to draw one? Follow the withes?"

"You are mad. Come out with me, now."

"Not till I have had a bath. They've just turned the water back on."

"What a thing for a woman to mention. Bring your bathing-suit. First we will cleanse ourselves in the sea."

"I love you, Xanthos, in a funny way."

"Hurry. In the morning I go the office at six, you know."

&

The islanders are slowed down by the heat but it is the foreigners who are really lazy. Michaelis, Megas and Aphroulla sometimes come by at siesta, but they are impatient for work to begin again. Will Pender and Roger Salmon sprawl at leisure. To be an outsider is to waste your life.

&

Laddie has brought another phenomenon into our midst, an obvious descendant of the old woman who lived in the vinegar bottle. Her name is Beatrice Wender, and she teaches archaeology at a mid-Western university in the States. She is an authority on the iconology of pots. I do not like her.

She lives in Edward's room, rises early, puts on a big white hat, and returns bad-tempered at noon complaining about the weather and the lack of real coffee. She has been here many summers before, but she does not like the tapwater, nor the water Lumumba brings in the wagon, nor bottled Mouttoullas from the mountain springs. She wants real chlorinated water from Lake Michigan, and droops, drip-dry, in a blue nylon dress like a crestfallen kingfisher, around the compound. She works at the Museum, which is cool inside, and fails to understand siesta.

There are no piano pupils, since school is out, and Laddie can no longer play. The weather has put the piano morosely out of tune. There is a piano tuner, but he has the talent of the picture framer in Pentedactylos Street, who for two shillings will slap wood and glass on your calendar and smear it with white paint. So music is suspended, and Laddie's income is this incubus.

I have my poets, painters, bankers, he has his old hags. They sit at night and drink coffee in intolerable conspiracy. "Doesn't your sister ever cook?" she asks. He becomes difficult about returning the reports to Speridakis.

I think often of the sea, the sight of the sea from the top of the pass, the vast blueness one still obstinately calls wine-dark, and the castle half pasting the view away, and the goats and the hills; and the womb going flip-flop in the very rich hour. Then I think of my worn dress sticking to the leatherette of a car seat and my thighs patterned by wicker seat-protectors and the sweat running like ants down to my ankles.

&

I have sent out for plates of chick-pea soup to the Turks. It arrives on a bicycle in stacked enamel pots, with garlic and parsley. William Pender is charmed, and whisks off in his car for some of his grandmother's wine. The malty bread goes well with it. . . Laddie has contributed a salad of tomatoes and cucumbers in alternate rows, a real *panaché* that you get in student restaurants in Paris. We squeeze lemon into the soup. Dr Wender complains that the food is heavy for the weather. We have sent out to the store across the way for more Chinese enamel plates. Peter Barnes says you don't get anything like this at the Naafi.

Megas is talking about Ibsen again. He comes alive when he talks, his hair springs from his head, his hands are sea anenomes in a colder, faster sea. His eyes flash. When Maro's father builds his dower house he will have his own theatre. "You live in the future, don't you, son?" says Beatrice Wender.

Flies are heading for the soup plates. Will Pender helps me clear the empty ones away. We put newspaper over them until there is water for washing-up. Laddie is leaning on his elbow. What hair he has left is hanging into what soup he has left. Maro is shiny, immobile, though her knees stay resolutely together.

Everything is suddenly quiet, except for the clatter of plates and spoons. Then the drill starts up across the road, the muezzim turns on his mechanised minaret-cry, and the old woman begins to wail and mourn again. Megas comes out of his drowse. He has been sitting with his thumbs at the top of his pants making faces at Maro. He stands and stretches. "Opa," he says, "Opa. What do we do with our lives here, then?"

I retch, and go to lie on my bed. Later, from far away, I hear someone say, "She liked *Lysistrata* because she understood the word for cucumber."

&

Heat. The old woman ululates from her uvula. Phaedra, the slut, from her rat-eaten grainstore bars the way. Her husband would let me through, but he's scared of her. I have to send a basket down on a string from the window to Pambos' doorway, with florins in it. He goes out and gets me cigarettes if he's there. Beatrice Wender usurps me in the kitchen at night.

I read a lot. Braun says the Gothic arch comes from the Armenians who learned from the Byzantines who learned from the Persians that arches hold up domes. Somebody else evolves the Gothic quite differently. You've got to know more geometry than I do to argue with them. Yesterday Roger Salmon brought someone around called Roderick who had been to Turkey. There's a big lake there called Lake Van, and a special breed of cat called the Van Cat, that has webbed feet and swims. Maybe I should have learned Turkish instead of Greek.

Laddie and Bea Wender are worse than the radio. You can't turn them off. I don't know what they have to talk about. It should be the iconology of pots—I wouldn't mind hearing about that—but it seems to be the smallest kind of gossip they share, who does what and isn't it a shame? I asked Bea Wender what iconology was about and she was short with me. Any idiot, she says, knows that pots have authorship and that the authorship is authenticated by means of deciphering and comparing the patterns on them: birds' wings, bulls' faces. They never made the fine complicated story-drawings the Athenians did, their patterns were cruder, but you can trace every one of them down to their makers if you try. She makes archaeology about as exciting as knitting patterns. That pots have authors just as poems do ruins the Homeric world for me. Everything should be anonymous as the Odyssey now is.

But maybe Max is right: to know the authorship of the dog-headed saint would be to know the island.

Christ, they've gone into the music room, they're singing duets. The piano sounds like an old pump organ. Beatrice and Lafcadio, essence of essence of monkey glands: THOOOOOOOO, I no mooooooooore shall see thee, YEEEEEET is thy name a spell . . . Old Rosa at the clavicle of the clavichord giving off memories of countertenors and intimations of an immortality achieved by selling eggs door to door. How could things have even tried to turn out so . . . ?

Xanthos, God bless him, looking as if he smelled a bad smell. "Goodness, I am always having to rescue you from something. Has the old woman gone? Do they not go out ever? I looked for you last night but you were not here."

"I got discouraged and went out. There's always something unbearable, isn't there, that makes you go out and dissipate yourself in low company?"

"Whose?"

"Roger and the White Russian Twins. I feel terrible today."

"So you should. Shall we go for a drive? Bring your bathing costume."

"Can we go to the umber mines on the way? I've been reading about them."

"What umber mines? Where did you get that book? You have good friends in England; they send you excellent things. What a very old map! It must be Birdie's mine they mean. The old copper mine in the middle of nowhere. It is not worked at the moment. The old women go out and gather umber for pocket money. It lies there on the earth. It occurs with copper pyrites. What a thing to make a fuss in a book about! What a foreigner you still are! No, we cannot go there. It's like Dante's Inferno at this time of the year. I have something else to show you."

It seems to me that tonight there is the barest promise in the air of relief from the heat. Perhaps it is only the speed of the car whipping through the plain towards the sea. Xanthos is quiet. "I have been away, and I am going away again tomorrow. I have to see people almost everywhere. I enjoy that. But first I must visit Aglaia and the children in Switzerland."

"Efy said they were going to the southern mountains."

"Efy always says what she wishes were true. She lives in her imagination."

"She's only a little kid."

"That's what Aglaia says. After the summer you will meet Aglaia. She is Greek, but she was raised in London and in Paris. She always goes away for the hot weather. She is very intelligent. I wonder how you will enjoy her company?"

"Does she know about me?"

"Of course not. Though perhaps. You can't tell with Aglaia."

"I don't think I should like at all to meet her."

"Oh, if you are going to have affairs with people you should be tougher than that. Why does she leave me four months of the year if she expects me to be faithful? Will you be jealous of her when she returns?"

"Only if she has a grandmother who likes to sit in the gateway and make loud noises."

"There is someone you care about in England, isn't there?"

"He's in Ireland, now."

"Will he come to visit you?"

"He was supposed to have come by now, but he had to work."

He reaches out, now. "It is always difficult to love another person and then another. One never quite achieves satisfaction, the emotions are too diffuse. One is forced to live not for one's lovers but for what happiness one can seize and enjoy. Do you know where we are? Have you been here before?"

"I don't know. Yes. But very fast. Florinda wouldn't stop the car."

"Once, for a few years, this was the richest city in the world."

The full moon is out. I can see ruined towers against the sea and the sky like magic lacework. With a shout that is between a laugh and a croak he starts the car again, runs it towards the land gate and turns sharply to the left. We are driving along the ramparts of the old city, close to the fingers of the eucalyptus trees that grow in the moat. The gutted ruins of three hundred and sixty five churches lie below us, and a hundred smoking kebab stands. A lighthouse jerks its beam across our faces. He drives roughly and very fast. "Look, look out to sea." The moon on the water is like a great golden coin. Before I can jerk my head back, we are down again, speeding along the coast road. He pulls down a sandy road and we dress and swim. All you have to do is lie on the thick, stinging sea. He shows me a cove where golden coins have been found. "When you get to know my wife," he said, "I shall have to stop making love to you. But you will be able to come to my house. I will show you things that are not in the Museum. My friend Giles has very good diving gear, and I know many fishermen and old shepherds. It is perhaps unfortunate that I have friends who are also on the staff of the Museum. I think always that they are waiting for my plane to crash so that they can take my treasures. Traditionally, our people have been afraid of the sea: it is the one difference we have from mainland Greeks. But I was educated in England. I will take you diving one day: under those waters there are miracles." His shoulders are phosphorescent in the moonlight. He dives, comes up, blows like a porpoise, grabs me, laughs. "Have you seen the film of Cacoyannis, where the boys have funeral games on the beach? We made such games here, after school once, when we were young. Look, the moon is gone. I will race you to the shore."

After a night like that you wake at dawn feeling clean again, after only one hour's sleep and the drills don't bother you, or the old yowling woman. But in the kitchen Bea Wender in her bright nasty drip-dry dress (why have they invented a dye that doesn't fade and soothe?) raises her voice. "Well, you're up early."

"Felt good. Got up."

"I could swear you only came in an hour ago."

"Could I just have some of that water for coffee?"

"Help yourself. How much longer are you going to stay?"

"How much longer are you going to stay? I'm waiting for a friend."

"I've been here before, you know, and that's one thing I know about this place: they always say they're coming, but they never come."

"What are you doing staying here if you've been here before? You've got American money. The hotels are better."

"Oh my goodness, I wouldn't stay in a hotel. Not on my salary. I like your place. It's charming. And so's Lafcadio, he's a darling. If you looked after him he might do something with himself."

"He doesn't like being looked after, and anyway, it isn't my job."

She looks at me sourly. "You're irresponsible. It's not right, the way you sleep all day and stay out all night. You're a grown woman, not a college girl. Here you come claiming you're only waiting for a friend and stay months without even lifting a finger to help him. Why, he says you won't even wash the kitchen floor."

"He tells a fine story."

"He's one of the most charming men I know. How did he come to have a sister who's a lazy hussy?"

&

The heat goes on stinking. Bea Wender has adopted a very small cat that comes in in the morning and licks the sweat off my back with a very rough tongue. It's an oddly erotic feeling.

Why, coming from where I do, the flat windless tail end of a banal plain, do I choose to summer in the windproof shadow of plutonic schists once part of the African Rift Valleys? Do I not remember the burnt landscape of Mars? There, I could stand on the cliffs challenging summer thunderstorms after days of drought. Here, drought is endless and noisy and debilitating and it is only drinking wine that keeps me from going out and knocking over the old woman. That's what I should do. Just put on my big winter shoes and kick past her, or jump on her and crush her. She's so small you could blow her away. Why not break the taboo and knock her over? She's only a cardboard figure out of Greek theatre.

Out in the street, commerce is sluggish. Fat men sit dozily beside their stacks of pots and pans and blankets. The women do all their work, their voices rise in complaint.

Peter Barnes has taken to coming to lunch with iced German beer from the Naafi. He wants to talk about Dympna but he can't, so he goes on and on about *Julius Caesar* instead. We had it in school. The boys liked it, the girls didn't. No parts for them. It's obvious what's going on, now, but I can't say a thing to him. I guzzle his beer. I want men to pay me when they bore me.

Laddie lies like a dead fish on his bed all day. In her penetrating voice, the Wender tries in the evening to cajole him into practising for a concert. Then he is giggly and coy. But he is also irritable, because she talks to him half the night and he can't go out cruising.

Loizos Speridakis comes, surprisingly. Stepping gingerly round his grandmother, looking white and exhausted. He accepts a glass of wine, and sits down very carefully. "I am very grateful to you for your work."

"I'm not grateful for your grandmother."

"I am desperate. I can do nothing with her."

"She makes a fool of me in the street. I suppose you were going to see someone else and you said it was me."

"I am sincerely sorry."

"You bloody well ought to be. Why don't you tell your mother? I thought you were a grown up. Pye doesn't have baby agents."

"I tried to find a Greek girl for the office, but their English, you understand . . . Bibi can answer the telephone but her letters . . ."

"We're not talking about Bibi. You're a good, kind man, Loizos, and if you had to rope me into all this you can at least take that shaming old woman away. Isn't there a law against public nuisances?"

"From the English days, but... no one will in this case enforce it."

"Have you tried?"

"Yes. With no result. She and my mother are too strong. The women here..."

"Have ingrown matriarchitis. It comes of being in purdah."

"Mr Barnes is becoming difficult."

"Peter? I shouldn't have thought he..."

"He is very jealous, very violent. I wondered if you'd..."

"I'm not a tart, Loizos, I'm not taking Peter off your hands."

"Oh heavens no, not that. Look, tonight..." He hunches forward and becomes conspiratorial and he has just the voice and personality for conspiracy, he is perfect, and I enjoy him. "Look, tonight, I will send a taxi for you and you and Mrs Barnes will go to the seaside. To a very isolated place I have arranged. Her husband is not free. She is on the point of breakdown. If you are with Mrs Barnes, I am not with Mrs Barnes."

"Are you coming to be with Mrs Barnes? I won't be your duenna."

"No, no, none of that. But at the office, everything is impossible, and you are not there, and she is almost ill. It is not possible for you to go in the daytime, the person who takes you bathing has gone away..."

"Shut up about that."

"I will, on certain terms..."

"It will be very nice for me to have a seaside holiday."

"What are those white lilies growing in the sand?"

"Squills," she says.

"Do you want the mask and flippers?"

"No, thanks."

The beach is of fine white sand and we are the only people on it. To get to it, you walk through two fields of Biblical thistles and climb down a bank among lilies: virtue rewarded. The rocks lying off the beach like long white whales are wave-washed raised synclines and anticlines, the things you read about in geology at school: rounded on top, parallel to the coast, with deep crevasses between. Speridakis says the Italians bombed them for English submarines during the war. Between the rocks there are cool frightening depths full of fish.

There is a village nestled up against the mountain, safe from pirates, but the hotel is the only building on the water. It is a shabby cement-block thing, kept alive by a sulphur spring where old Armenian women soak their rheumatism. It has running cold water and an electric generator that shuts off at ten. The rooms have iron twin beds, tacky varnished wardrobes and simple chairs. At dusk every night, a one-handed man throws a stick of dynamite into the sea to bring up tomorrow's fish. The purple one with the miserable face I like to stare at under water—the longer you stare at it the more miserable it gets—tastes like turnip.

We get up early as the sun slants across the incredible mountains, because our room faces east. The sunrise is pink and green, like a bad picture, colouring first the peaks towards Syria and Lebanon, then the hills behind us. Then the castle above us. It's frighteningly violent, the successive slashes of colour, then the threat of the heat. It makes you want to roll back time and create more darkness, but once the temptation to open the shutters has been given into there is the thrashing hot light of day and nothing else.

It's so long since I've shared a room with a woman that I find I'm very shy. But Dympna is as well. She utters many sighs and makes small gestures and spends a lot of time in the bathroom. I go down first in the morning and swim before the proprietor, who is also named Loizos, has made my Nescafe. I can't drink sweet Turkish coffee in the morning. Then I eat bacon and eggs in a wet bathing suit under his arbour. Dympna comes down all perfect in a white eyelet shift and has a cup of clear tea and one piece of dry toast.

I have brought maps and guidebooks from the Henshaw Collection with me and I am working on a sort of index of the island for Max. It is despairing work: there are obviously hundreds of villages one will never see; but it is something to do. Dympna writes letters. ''Who're you writing to?'' I ask.

''Bunty.''

''Who's he?''

''My son.''

''Where is he? England?''

''They say he's incurable, but I don't think so. They say he won't understand but I write to him anyway. Loizos says he can get him out for me. I could bring him here.''

''What would Peter say?''

She tosses her head. ''Shall we go to the other beach?''

Because there is a near beach and a far beach—the white lilied one. It is far away enough that no one goes there but ourselves and a shepherd. If we stay there too long we see him standing miserably above us on the headland, staring, waiting for us to go. He wears baggy pants and a white soiled shirt and a head rag. He and the sheep stand and look patiently uncertain. We pick up our books and magazines and flippers and plastic noseguards and towels and bottles of Ambre Solaire and climb back up to the hotel. Then he descends with his flock, solemnly shooing his bellwether off the lowest rock; she swims the whole flock across a shallow segment of the bay. The shepherd paces the perimeter, making encouraging noises. Then they go away again, the whitest sheep in the Mediterranean.

I was ill in England once. Charlie Meadows had taken me weekending to some rich patrons of his in a grand pink Queen Anne house in Suffolk. I was put in a big room with rich curtains and on the Sunday morning every time I tried to get out of bed I fell down and cried. Maids came and gave me trays and books, doctors came with hypodermics. It was something to do with my liver—not drink, at that stage of my life. That family kept me for weeks. I kept saying, "I'm not really ill," and "I don't usually do this sort of thing," but none of them listened, they brought out more and more beautifully illustrated books and better trays. I felt evil and idle and helpless and tearfully grateful. I wanted to pay up and get out but it wasn't possible. Then one day I was better and they sent me back to London with their chauffeur. I wrote and thanked them and never heard from them again. Charlie said, "Cheer up, they felt noble. Anyway, they're filthy rich, it was only mildly inconvenient. I tipped the butler for you."

Idling on this beach I feel as I did then, rich and overprivileged, but for some outside reason, some unchosen idea. Loizos-the-Hotel cooks very simply. He used to keep a chip-shop in Camden Town. But his English is amusing. He says he knows we are waiting for our lover-boys here. I tell him we are playing a game called fill-in-the-blanks.

"Soon you'll be going back to Peter," I say to Dympna.

"I hate Peter. He's . . ." She can't ever make words come.

"He's a bit dim, but really very nice. I mean, not a *bad* man, Dympna. People've had husbands worse than him."

"I hate him." She tosses back her hair and glares. "I suppose since this is our last morning I ought to confess something."

"Not unless you want to."

"I made up Bunty. I mean, I dreamed him. One night. He was so warm and round. Like one of those toys made out of soft plastic balloons. I tried to tell Peter about him and he laughed. There never was anyone like him, so round and warm."

Down deep under the water there are swarms of little garfish like green fluorescent pens. But no amphorae.

Villages in L: Lagoudera, Lakatami, Lania, Lapathos, Lapithos, Larnaka, Lasa, Laxia, Layia, Lazania, Lefka, Lefkara, Lefkoniko, Lemona, Leonarisso, Limnia, Liopetri, Livadhia, Lephos, Louroujina, Louveras, Lyssi, Lyso, Lythrangomi, Lythrodonda.

The clerk Stelios comes rattling down the mountainside for us on Saturday and Dympna and I are both profoundly glad. The village donkey brays farewell as we leave and we bray back. Beauty is after all not enough.

&

Back, but no one else is. Not a friend to be seen. Even at ten at night, I am sucked through the airless channels of the street like change in the hardware store. Aphroulla is out. The House of a Thousand Bottles has more people in its band than at its tables. Pambos' shop is empty, and in the Brigadier Fivos and an English airman are looking at dirty pictures. Xanthos is in Switzerland, there are no lights in the Villa Williamson, Petronella's in England. I rattle around the town like a pea in a pod. Suddenly, rounding a dark corner, I meet Roger Salmon with his drinking sailor's loping roll. "Come," he says.

Travelling like him is like being in a Western: I need net tights and a gun-belt. We go from dirty cellar to dirty cellar. Landlords cut hunks of ham from hanging blackness. Roger holds up a white palm against my contributions and grandly puts our growing thirst on his tab. Many dark eyes are rolled. I haven't been in these places except to pay Edward's bills. They aren't dangerous, they're only the simple tavernas where the neighbourhood men drink, but they're not used to women, and I have to stick tight to Roger. The music when there is music is from the far-away villages, high and wild, with loosed cadences and voice-clicks. Deep at the back of the cellars they remember how things used to be.

We are in some neutral quarter, a place of chipped plaster where they don't seem to be Greek or Turk: rather, something earlier. I ask Roger which they are, I can't make out their words at all. He laughs. "When the knives come out, you'll know." He isn't treated respectfully, there's none of the catering to foreigners you find in the better watering-places, he's merely tolerated, and here he pays cash. I don't like it, it's too dark and smelly, and I am getting too drunk, I tug his arm to go.

In the street, the air is cooler. The sky, like the ceiling of a primitive church, is plastered with blue paint and very yellow stars. We hold each other up and he finds the way home. A little figure, hunched with shining eyes, comes out of the darkness, "Baksheesh, baksheesh."

"No baksheesh." Automatically, both of us say that.

"I will tell."

"Who will you tell?"

"Your husband, lady."

Roger turns around and picks him up like a cat and tosses him in a doorway.

"Why'd you do that?"

"Know him. Only way to get rid of him."

"Nice people in this quarter."

"Hmm. See that? How's your Greek? What does it say on the door?"

"Family house."

"Know why?"

"No."

"All the others are whorehouses." He laughs like a donkey.

It's a street I haven't noticed before, not far from us either. Running neatly between the backs of a mosque and a church, a row of poor little one-up, one-down houses, the kind they tart up in Pimlico.

We sit on the steps of the khan, sobbing on each other with drink. I tell him the story of my very sorry life. Bea Wender slams her door. I realise I have my arms around Roger, holding him fast to me for dear life. "Where do you live?" I ask.

"Nowhere," he says.

"You can stay here."

"Wouldn't think of putting you out, my dear."

"You've got to go somewhere."

"Oh, I'll go . . . somewhere."

I manage to make him up a bed in one of the empty rooms.

&

Dear Max: Yes, September is better, as far as the weather goes. It'll leave you more time to finish the work on Ireland.

But I grow impatient. Laddie lies all day perspiring on his couch, the Wender woman is still here, and the stupefying richness of the place has palled on me. I can't see anything beyond my own weariness now. I want a brisk wind and a new dress and a raft of green Penguin books. That old woman who sat in our doorway is still sitting in our doorway. I wish Allah would spirit her to Ireland. She could get a job as a banshee. I'm bloody tired of her. I tried to put R. Salmon up here but Laddie and Wender objected and even Pambos who's a fair lush himself. Everyone's rotted sour by the heat. A married friend confessed to me that there was no making up quarrels in bed when they couldn't bear to touch each other. Now when the children are noisy her husband just rows out as far as he can to sea, puts a wet hat on and sits sulking in his boat. Tensions seem to be building up between all the friends and lovers. Even William Pender's good cheer is flagging. I heard some journalists talking of political trouble in a bar the other night and couldn't bring myself to care. The middle classes go to the mountains and sit in the resorts all night and play cards. Mountains without water! I merely endure. It's like waiting out winter, but much, much worse. If no one's around in the evening I put a little water in the tub and sit and read. The Wender says this is unpatriotic. I don't speak to her any more.

So you're forgiven for going to Ireland. Get *wet*. Then come here and dry out. And let me know when you're coming—before I melt on my butter-dish. There's a teaching job going which I would hate to take, but the money's good. I have to know what to do. If you're coming soon, I won't; late, I will. I haven't looked at the landscape lately, so I don't know what it looks like. For heaven's sake write and cheer me up.

"You say I am not a nationalist," X says, drawing lines on the table with the condensation from his glass, "but I am very deeply so. Not of course in the sense your friend Loizos is, I am not political. He is a Hellenist and wishes to be united with Greece, the mother country. But when I go to Athens I am depressed by the way they speak my language, it sounds so soft and effete that I miss the harsh consonants of my native land; and when Efy returns from school with a book that has the Greek word for 'comb' in it and not the island word, I get very angry. Even you are picking up a 'bad' island accent, you would be laughed at for even the little you know because of your accent. There are those who try to reject the fact that we are so far to the east, but to me, that is part of our richness."

"Do you belong to any kind of political party that stands for that?"

"Good God, no; what do you think I am, a fool?"

"Isn't this a democracy?"

"I vote, I support my government, I cross myself whenever I see a priest. You know, today I saw a priest first thing in the morning, I almost ran him down in my car. It is very bad luck.''

''But heavens, Xanthos, if you can't work in politics . . .''

''Oh, you can, but why would you? I don't want power. I want to be left in peace.''

''So work in politics. That's what it's about.''

''You are very naive. You come from a country that is very innocent. Where shall we eat tonight?''

''All you think about's your stomach.''

''Don't sulk at me when I won't talk about politics, woman. You go out with Roger, you get drunk, the first thing you say in a bar is Xanthos says . . . they all nod, they have seen you in my car, crack . . .'' He takes his head off with his forefinger. ''Besides, food is one of the gifts of God, and a very great one. It should be prepared with care, eaten with respect, and not while smoking mentholated cigarettes, and discussed in detail. To eat well is to be at one with the gods. The old and the new. There is something I think you have not eaten yet, a sweet called honey-balls . . .''

I can't resist a giggle. Fortunately, his vocabulary is wide, and he laughs too. We drive to the seaside and swim and eat grilled mullet and enormous salads under a bamboo shade. Without talking politics.

&

Now I sleep naked with the door open. Nobody comes, and I wouldn't care if they did.

This morning at six the regular ululations start, but the air-drills don't. Maybe they've finished that part of the building, or it's the day of their patron saint. I open the shutters to the same powdered air, however, and in the kitchen, the same high querulous voice is talking to Laddie. I put on a nylon wrapper like the ones the other hausfraus of the street wear in the morning and go to the bathroom. Then get coffee, silently, padding the stones in cheap sticky rubber sandals. The kitten gets the scrapings of their frying pan: that's enough of the kitchen for me.

Wish I had a morning paper to hide behind. The author of *Eothen* made a few *bon mots* about the island (in one village they slaughtered him a "low-church-looking hen"), but behind the beautiful English sense of humour he has a tedious English opaqueness about the humanity of other races; and the Holy Land always was a bore. I can't settle to anything good, anything the slightest bit heavy, and there's no junk left to read except for my own notes for the unwritten detective novel in which the Yaya is found dead in a neolithic tomb and Bea Wender in a taverna and Dympna in a stone sheepfold that looks like a church, all strangled presumably by the same hand. The suspects are Speridakis, who turns out to be a dope smuggler, Peter Barnes, because he's too nice, and a guy I've invented called Bill Mavrovouni, whom Xanthos informs me must correctly be called Bill Mavrovouniotis, too long a name even for a murderer. Already it sounds dismally like the rash of novels British journalists turned out after the Troubles, violently melodramatic. And there's too much landscape, too much architecture. And I don't like plots, so . . .

"Mrs Ladi, Mrs Ladi." Hoarse cries in the street. Pambos, Mr Flores, Costas Costakis, Costas-Carpenter, Aristides: "Mrs Ladi, Mrs Ladi."

"What is it?"

"Come down, Mrs Ladi, and meet us at the door."

"Why?"

"Come down and see."

They are grinning, insistent, they stand under the window like a group of clay figures in the Museum, with their pointed chins and odd jolly hieratic smiles. "Mrs Ladi, Mrs Ladi, come down, come down."

"Okay. *Endaxi*, I'll come down."

What are they up to? Xanthos says I'm sentimental about

them, they're a bunch of hicks and mugs, it's condescending to be so friendly. But I don't know, I like them. I don't think they're anything special, they just accept me. More than a lot of other people do. I put on a dress and hurry down the steps, slip, pick myself up, hobble to the gate. The old woman is there, ready to lunge. "Mrs Ladi, Mrs Ladi." There is something mocking about them, for a moment I think of kids at school rubbing crossed fingers, "Audie lu-uvs Laddie, Audie lu-uvs Laddie," but that's not what they are up to at all. "Come through," says Pambos. "Come. Pass through."

I look uncertainly at them, at the old woman. She still sits hunched with her tongue lolling in her empty mouth. A hen's mouth with no beak. She's sinister as a German soldier in hen-face armour. She'll tear my eyes out. No doubt I need that. I have sinned, father, I have sinned. But so has she. I don't want to go out into that hot street, the dust. Why should I leave my geraniums, my *Eothen*? I'm a Turkish monk, now, boys. Except at night.

"No, I don't want to."

"Come," says Pambos softly. "You must sleep no more all day. It is bad for you."

I look at the old woman hard. She meets my eyes and shifts away. "Excuse me, please," I say, and turn sideways to step past her. "Excuse me, please, very much, old woman, if you please." I. Kykkotis, Grammarian, to the life.

She looks up again. She curves her lips, opens her toothless mouth, closes it again. She looks down. She mumbles something.

"Pass," says Pambos. "Pass. Pass from your monastiraki, Mrs Ladi."

I pass.

From the street, there is a scattered cheering. I look around half dazzled by the sun. The cadaiffi-maker waves, and the sulkiest silversmith, and the perfumier leaves his brilliantine stand to come and shake my hand. Mrs Phaedra wipes her hands on her apron and pats me on the back. She shakes her whole body with laughter. The besom vendor and the chairmaker wave and laugh. A kebab maker I do not know comes out of an alley and shouts, "Bravo, Mrs Ladi." Pambos and Flores and Aristides and Costas Costakis and Costas all raise their arms in glee.

The old woman scuttles away like a crab.

This is not an hour for Coca-Cola and propriety. We all go into the taverna. "Wine," says Pambos, "much wine for Mrs Ladi." Throwing an old brown crumpled pound note down. I have a note in my pocket too. I throw it down and they accept it. It doesn't do to count out money in music lessons.

I think I understand their newmade song:

Mrs Ladi has come out of her khan
Out of the old Turkish monastiraki,
The sun is high and we shall drink much wine,
And Stelios shall make for us a *souvla*,
Today we eat well, today we drink wine and brandy
And here are fine cucumbers from the market.
Mrs Ladi has come down among us once again.

I run out of the taverna to look and see if the yaya has really gone away. She has. "Goodbye, old woman," everybody yells after her. She does not turn around to wave.

"Evil old woman," Pambos says. "Dirty old woman." Leaning back and beginning to whiffle another song in his nose. Costas Costakis excuses himself. "Pambos drinks too much," he says. "Very too much." Pambos gets up and runs after a blue and white dress in the street, comes triumphantly back with Laddie and Mrs Wender. The Armenian pizza vendor passes innocently by and is mobbed. Pound notes fly out. A spirit is loose. The old woman is gone.

Pambos and Costas-Carpenter and Aristides sing with their

heads back, they sing far back in their throats a song that belongs to the high mountains, to the sun of Africa, that intermittently descends in round Shakespearean hugs and caperings, Falstaffian boluses of conviviality. The sound is high and harsh and far away, the sound of sex in the making, ritual in the conniving, the cock seeking prey. They sit with their eyes sunk together in eldertime, antic, frantic, Attic; with a fearful intensity, a stiffness of stylisation they sing so low in their throats, so harshly, that the body wants to burst.

There are those on the sidelines who left their villages longer ago, who remember the vibration, but no longer how to make those sounds. They hang embarrassed against the wall listening.

Then in a low voice Pambos says, "Go home, now", so the foreigners leave. The sun is like a thunderbolt.

&

And this morning someone left on Dympna's doorstep the brown beeswax ex voto-figure of a baby, full size, one of the things you buy in the oldest candle-shops: this one with new finishing nails stuck in the eyes, ears, nose, mouth, breasts and private parts.

&

And last night Roger Salmon took a bottle to the house of the White Russian Twins and they danced and sang, and the East German Twin fell down dead. The West German twin had a fit of hysterics, and Roger, unaware that he had removed his clothes in order to seduce the White Russian Twins' landlady, rushed naked into the street and was arrested. Neither of the German embassies has a doorman now, and it is safe but sad to go into The Brigadier.

&

Villages in M: Malounda, Mathiatis, Mandria, Mansoura,

MONODROMOS

Margo, Mari, Maronia, Melandra, Monagri, Mosphiliti, Mousoulita, Moutoullas, Myrtou . . . Will it never end, this heat? Old men sit like dead figureheads on café chairs, and there is no air. The land lies slack and the landscape withers in the mind.

VIII

THE FALL

Max is dead.

I come out of the post office and stand on the highest pavement of the GRV concrete stair, holding Maurice's letter in my hand, staring at a nameless faceless cafe across the road, and some tatty boughs, and a taxi stand, and Mrs Speridakis, junior, Ellada Speridakis, takes my elbow and explains me down the steps, "You see, I was right, he has very much mistreated me, come, I will tell you, we will sit in the *zacharonoplasteion* of Leandros who has fourteen varieties of new ice cream, and I will tell you . . .

"The watermelon is really very good. He went to prostitutes, he went to nightclubs, he went to chorus girls, he neglected me, he laughed at me and told me I was foolish and had no education when really I have a very good education, I went to the convent, I am no ordinary girl, I had a large dowry, his mother never left me alone . . ."

"But didn't you expect that? Aren't you from here?"

"Oh, but I loved him, I married him for love, I wanted to be a good wife to him, don't you see?"

I see the white body of Dympna Barnes rising like a lily from the sand.

MONODROMOS

Max is dead. Max has been dead for four whole days. Henshaw addressed the letter to the wrong box number. Ellada Speridakis looks dead as well. She has purple fingernails and dead varnished hair. She wanted love; she didn't get it, now she's eating watermelon sherbet, dying.

Max is dead. The same sun clangs brass shields over our heads in the street. "What will become of me?" she wails. "Only last year I had a Hollywood kitchen installed in the house. What will happen to me?"

Max is dead. The inside of the telephone booth smells of pee. They are really very bad about telephone booths, surely they could hold it in inside the ones in the telephone office itself. God damn heathen foreigners take half an hour to make the connection to London. Nothing to do but lean on the letter, smoking. "I am sorry to inform you," in queer italic handwriting, "that Max did not recover from our expedition to Ireland. At the most I was an inadequate gooseberry. Although Dublin went surprisingly well, a sordid expedition to Derry followed by an excursion to the dampest nether regions of Wicklow where we were housed in a leaky cottage by a rich garrulous well-provisioned thesis-maker, produced the pneumonia you had warned me might be fatal. I thought I might spirit him off to London in time—in fact I ditched our accompanying photographer in a manner picaresque and alien to my character in order to do so—but the Fates were against us, London was fogged, and the fatal chill had set in. Sir David made himself busy, but between the cup and the lip he took it upon himself to go out in a rainstorm shopping for tropical outfit . . . ran into a friend . . ."

"Both Elizabeth and I were with him. He refused to go to hospital. He said that death was not easeful, but when one was drenched in it, unexpectedly lovable. When Elizabeth was weeping in the loo, he sent you his love. He said . . ."

A rattle on the glass. My call is through. The number rings.

Elizabeth answers. The funeral was yesterday. Now he is gone there is so much to do.

Lady, now he is gone there is so much to *be*.

His papers, what should she do with his papers, and ought Maurice Henshaw after the Irish affair to be relied upon?

Yes.

The flat, his things, his clothes. Why did he want to be buried by the gasworks in Kensal Green? So utterly depressing?

"Would you give Maurice Henshaw what you find of mine, please?"

"Peculiar though it sounds, he asked me particularly to give his old woolen pullovers to you. Could he have been serious? And some books. I'll pack them off. Shall you be coming back?"

Old Max, luminous, numinous Max Magill. Elizabeth chats while a clerk stands by the glass waving pound notes at me.

"Shall I come and help you?" I ask Elizabeth.

"Oh, no. There's nothing . . . I need the time . . . the shock. How very odd to be talking to you, when I said I never would. He went so quickly, went out into the rain that day and that was that, it was as if he wished . . . oh I must let you go. Come for tea when you return. He was so looking forward to your sunshine . . ."

That's Elizabeth: Catholic, divorceless, uxorious, twinsetted and pearled and upper class: Mary Queen of Scots turned inside out. Hope to God she doesn't give my winter coat to the rag and bone man. "Maurice will help you if you won't let me," I tell her.

"But I don't *like* Maurice," she says. And the operator cuts us off.

Old yellow dog of an island snoozing in the sun, tail rucking the armpit of Asia Minor. Max is dead, island. Listen, Max is dead. You don't give a fart, do you?

Sun like a searchlight. What would he have liked? The walls, yes, of course the walls. Never looked at them from here before.

Those sane stone blocks of butter-coloured light. Blasted Elizabeth, twinset and pearls and Max, you musn't, money pieced out. At least she hasn't carted him up to her own Scotch heath to get lichen in his boxed lungs. He would have liked the walls, and the moat, and the rows of men outside the Spitfire, lazing in the sun, oh I couldn't face Pambos, no . . . no, he's not there. And the cotton gin and the halvah factory, guys in undershirts dropping their sweat into the big kettles as they turn their wooden paddles around. The little bars. Ouzo. He liked ouzo.

People hustling along the street with their bags of being over their shoulders, shaking the dried seeds of their selves. What's the use of getting to know all these people? They're just like me, trying to find a place to live, hoping to send their kids to Athens and London. He said to me once, "Don't you know, people don't last . . . only poems?" It wasn't like him. It was in a low moment, after an article by an old friend that said he was running down.

I didn't buy the papers yesterday to get the obits. I don't think I want them. I'd just run him in some kind of senior achievement race. Then there'll be the reviews to bear all alone. What if they don't like the new poems? They were always saying he never fulfilled his promise, as if anybody ever fulfilled a reviewer's concept of promise: to be someone who had been before. That's the reviewer's trade, loading poets down with concepts that can't belong to them. "Died after his time," maybe they'll say. Though I feel him flinging and flinging himself against a wall of words.

Pambos is quietly stitching. He looks up over a pair of old hornrimmed glasses. "Yasu."

"Yasu, Baba."

"Come and sit down."

I stand and watch him shape a shoulder. He whistles between his teeth.

Beatrice Wender is sitting on the gallery on my chair. I go out again, reading Maurice's letter as I walk.

"He said things I cannot reconstruct, having none of his gift for words. But he left the world with the kind of benevolent grace that affected all his moods, half-penitent (he allowed Elizabeth's priest to confess him, but with a terrifying grin on his face), but joyful as well. You know his combination of laughter and seriousness as well as I do. I would like to say that his last grimace was a wink, but he groaned as he died."

Street. Street. Phaedra with her drool. I should beat my breasts, I should ululate in a doorway, tear my garments, I . . .

Will Pender: "You're none too chipper, luv. And me so long gone and now returned and where's the fatted . . . ?"

"William, another time, another time."

The woman with the cart. Bananas are in again and still one shilling. If she put her prices up she'd spoil the rhythm. The rotten bananas are one shilling; the putrifying bananas are one shilling. The pussy bananas are one shilling . . .

Aphroulla: "Oh, it's you. Can you hold this for a moment? I got it from Achilleas, I wonder if the dye is any good. Your hand is shaking. You've been drinking too much. Ahmed is coming in a moment, he will do it for me."

The town is round and everyone in it is mad.

Fivos is discussing a new English woman with Michaelis. "It is a pity she came so late, it is the heat that makes them ready, you will have to work fast or wait until next year."

Megas, playing backgammon in the street, "Oh, good to see you. I have decided to make a theatre in your old monastiraki."

Only the very old and the very young and the very drunk know anything. The rest of us are moles. Roger is trying to spoon up soup outside the Lift Place. Yesterday he got out of jail. "Max Magill is dead," I say.

He puts down his head and cries.

The people in the streets straighten their bodies and assume dignity; the sun shreds itself finely into the moat, the passing pudding-seller sheds his dry warts for a new skin. Roger pulls a necktie out of his pocket and knots it on. "Come," he says, "we must do him the greatest honour." The minarets dance and the orthodox belltowers jangle. We cross the moat to the most dignified suburb and stand Max's memory a drink in the bar of the very best hotel, and pay cash.

You can't stop the earth in its swing, you can't go around like a dope in a Mary Webb novel and tell it to the bees, you get home, hoping they'll be in the shop to sing him a threnody and you find Megas waiting for you in a rented car with the rest of the Eating Society loaded into it. It's the night of *Julius Caesar*. "You're late, there's no more room, you'll have to go with Laddie and Mrs Wender in Florinda's car."

The parched landscape hums for forty miles. The early night slides down. I pretend the others are not there, and they disappear. Did he have a gold coin for Charon in his hand when they buried him in the lugubrious Hanoverian splendour of Kensal Green? We used to walk there on rainy Sundays, reading the epitaphs of minor descendants of the Electress Sophia. Sometimes we took a narrow boat past it, along the Paddington Canal. He liked the combination of cemetery and slum and gas and slime, the true dead industrial gloom.

The stars are like big shining tears.

How did the Romans come to build a theatre here? How long were they here? I don't remember. What did they put on in this part of the provinces? Terence? Plautus? Lions eating Christians? It was excavated from the sand. If only, at home, there had been something along the beach to excavate, some grandeur, to give our lives pretension. Oh, in time, there will be: the sea builds.

All of the English community which finds military Shakespeare bearable is here, hatted, gloved, white-shawled. The smart ones have brought cushions for the stone seats. The proceeds of this benefit are for the Red Cross. Aphroulla and Michaelis and Ahmed have bags of peanuts. The weather is clear, and there is a faint breeze from the sea. Dympna looks frozen, miserable.

I never liked *Julius Caesar* in school. It's all men and fortunetellers and set speeches. Politics and male bonding. Suppose the Air Force chose it so there wouldn't be too many servicemen in drag.

Something can be got out of anything, even this: suck this whelk dry. Don't think of Max. Max is dead, you never saw him again, that's the way the ball bounces, look. Listen.

A glorious big Luddite-looking Caesar with a north-country accent; an underfed Cassius who can't pronounce his t's. The poor new Brutus has a stammer, but he knows his lines. They say the Islanders are lower-class because they don't speak Ancient Greek. Crikey, listen to these men. P. Barnes sends them in on the double like taloned messengers to spout their mispronunciations. What a clever thing, though, a class system where everyone can be placed by the way he speaks the language: Calpurnia's an officer with a mellifluous falsetto accent, purest BBC. If only one could laugh.

Laddie is scanning the crowd earnestly: shopping. Florinda applauds patriotically every time someone gets through a line B. Wender dozes. The key to the quotation is *willing* suspension of disbelief: all I can see is disjointed junior birdmen upside down.

The interval comes at last. The people come and go between ruined basalt columns and faceless statues. There's a Coca-Cola stand in one niche of a gloriously mosaiced Roman bath. I go towards the sea, to the edge of the littoral pine forest, having no stomach now for company. Near here X and I once imitated funeral games—though he said he grew up on quite a different shore. How would I feel if he were here tonight? Roger wouldn't come.

Just where the forest advances on the sea, where, chin-on-hand, I can watch the ripples gleaming, I lie down on pine needles. It is no good to sit watching, rumpled with revolving thoughts, a bad production of a power play. Here, with air above and sea below, in the Brit-planted pines beside Teucer's beach . . . he should have written poems here. Though he wasn't fond of place as subject-matter, he said it was a cop-out. He wanted to get above himself, out of his skin into ideas. He succeeded in the death-dance, but look at the price he paid.

All these disorganised islands and their warring tribes. Wonder about Edward and the snail-factors: that must have been a myth. Though you could believe it on a night like this.

The sea just lies there, thick, half-killed with salt, fishless, harbouring buried coins and amphorae, the colour of blackwine, they say, but tonight gleaming. Lithe boys should spear-toss on the beach for him tonight, or men and women make love in shallow rituals, breeding webbed children.

Far, far away is the sound of the ludicrous recital. Are the actors enjoying it or are they co-opted, given an extra booze ration for every unfluffed line? Oh, surely the world would be better without such foolishness. I can't bear to go back and be polite, pretend not to be bored. Better to lie here and invest an innocent and urbane stretch of headland with imaginative ramblings. You can't look at the shore here and not put words to it. The moon's slanting . . .

Hush now. Low voices. In the next clearing. No, closer.

Hey nonny: not six feet away Dympna Barnes and the balloon form of Loizos Speridakis settle onto the ground, she falling forward into his arms with a little moan. What should I do, announce my presence so we can sit comfortably together?

The cry's going up from the Forum. Funny, you'd always swear the death of Caesar came much earlier on. I mustn't snort, or wiggle on the pine needles: they're very near, I can see their outlines just behind those bushes. They are squatting opposite each other in some kind of confrontation. Oop-la, my goodness, she leaps him. The way they say the Arabs . . . joining giblets, by God.

Is it very English not to want to know that much about one's friends, Max? Dare yourself, look, no, look: try on every new role, it's educational, be a voyeur: look, big hands on gleaming thighs. They make panting noises and little squiffs of moans. There's a wet piston onomatopoetic sound, time's stretching out for them. God, he's good at it, too. Thought he might be. They take it as one of Nature's God-given jobs here, and do it not shame-facedly, but dutifully well. No Saxon pretence there's nothing under underpants. A soft schlupping, a fierce grip, two little stifled cries. Then they lie panting. So do I.

No words between them now. He lies with his hand on her back and fills it. Then they get up and do some tidying. Giggling softly, she pulls the pine needles off his trousers. They go away half-stumbling, brushing their hips together.

What does she want, that wife of his?

Max, you got your funeral games.

And now they're gone I shed my dress and shoes and run fast as I can into the shallow sea, and swim out far, into the star-domed loneliness of the night; and the loneliness makes me think of being sixteen and strong, racing the boys as far out as they can swim, the point where the Legion flagpole no longer can be seen. The sea is cool and stinging now, and this far out I can see the round rim of the theatre. I could float forever. Where've they gone? She to her car (Peter, I suddenly felt so *ill*, darling, and I had to leave your play . . .), he down the lonely sandy road. The bastard, he's giving it back to the British, however much he thinks he's in love with her. He'd have her even if she were Ethiopian, but it gives him pleasure to set his rich jewel in Britannia during the military silly season. Much good may it do him.

Back-floating. Staring at the starred hoop of the sky, far enough out now to see the fishing village up the coast where the dance-cafes are. But by the theatre, car lights are coming up. Time to go home. My body slides through heat-thickened water to the shore.

Florinda and Laddie and Mrs Wender are gone without me. Here are the Williamsons, though. "Couldn't stick it, eh?"

"Had a marvellous swim."

"Thought of it myself."

"Can you give me a lift home?"

They let me off at the eastern gate. I pass through its tunnel by the Antiquity Department stores, and go around the wooden water towers I always used to lose, past a school and four churches and a mosque, up Monodromos. It is a normal process in which no tourist police now intervene. There is nothing to show that I am a person who has had a leg and an arm lopped off. "Death," said Max, "is no strange visitor. Rather an aging friend who hobbles in to tea."

&

My dear (Laddie has shoved the morning post underneath my door), there's been some ghastly mistake. I told my Maker, I have my ticket here in this yellow folder, look, you must believe me. Ticket, seat reservation, baggage fobs. I've no appointment with You, I'm wanted there. He smiled in that Deist way they have.

You said you thought from the poems that I was in a hurry to be off. Ah, but the death-dance was from another country in the mind, a bad patch years ago. I was a death-lover when I rounded forty; now, I'm too old for that.

But Elizabeth and Sir David hover over me, humming like fourteen angels. I don't want no chubes, I scream. I kick my little feet at them. I've this ere ticket to Sunshine Villas under my pillow, I say, you're not pushing me off the wrong way. Maurice Carrion-Fly wrings his hands, "It's all my fault," he says.

But it was mine, of course, and whiskey's, and the weather's in that place: so it will be a while before I manage to wave Excalibur and come to pique you out of the Slough of Despond.

Rage gives me strength. Elizabeth is nursing me with her own kind of Jamesian enthusiasm; her gloomy look makes my life pass depressingly before my rheumy eyes. To get even with her I've sent her to hunt for the George V pennies that closed my mother's eyes. I shall outwit the vultures and come to you before you come to me. I know vultures, and my keepers don't: there's my advantage.

Love and good cess to you. I come, I come. Yea, even in a winged bath chair, Max.

&

"What happened to you last night?"

"Got sick of it, went walking on the beach, missed you."

"You missed a fine scene afterwards. Peter couldn't find Dympna, she'd bogged off somewhere, and when he did find her, he slapped her face."

"Marriage is obscene."

"She could have supported him in his finest hour."

"If amateur theatricals are a finest hour for anyone, God help them, Laddie."

"You're late for work, aren't you? Or are you going in now in the afternoons?"

"Oh, I just wander in and see if there's anything to be done for petty cash. He's not in a very good mood these days."

"What's he up to?"

"I dunno."

"Nice news from England? When's your lover coming? You

could have a party and introduce him to your other lover. Don't look so down in the mouth, it's only 93 today."

"Bye, Laddie."

"Cheerie-bye."

It is Mrs Speridakis, senior, who now sits behind the great desk under the equestrian king. "You are very late," she says.

"Your son does not pay me for hours when I am not here."

"Good. It is pleasant to hear that he is not entirely a fool."

How old is she? Not more than sixty-five, but her face is pouched and lined, you could flip fish into the bags under her eyes. A lifetime of turning life into theatre has been too much for the sack of skin that holds her head together. Only the green watchful eyes show energy. "My son has gone to Athens. He will be away for some time. Mrs Barnes is ill and will not be coming here. I shall rely on you for the English correspondence. You know the files?"

"Not the legal work. He does that himself, with Mrs Barnes."

"There are only a few cases, they can wait. You will work eight till one, four till six, and be on time, until summer hours are over."

"I shall expect a large increase in wages on those terms."

"We shall see."

I am about to get very angry when I realise that her managerial experience has been gained managing children and housemaids. She taps her pencil on the desk impatiently, waiting for me to go obediently to my place. "Seventeen pounds a month for an untrained village girl to do domestic work," she says, "and you, how much do you want? Wages on this island have gone crazy."

"If you don't like what I say, I suppose you'll set your old mother on me again."

"What is your usual arrangement with my son?"

"For six pounds per week I will come in every morning

and do the necessary.''

''What company do you keep? You do not speak proper English any more. Perhaps I can find someone else. My son has been very kind to you, you should repay him better.''

''I will also keep an eye on Bibi and answer the telephone.''

''And not run away with my daughter to the seashore.''

''By all means, if it suits you.''

Her pale weary eyes take the room to pieces. ''All right,'' she says, ''I shall come in every day to make sure that you are here.'' She begins ripping away at the morning mail. ''Help me sort it. Here. No, not that way, this way . . . what's this about? I am left in charge and he tells me nothing. What kind of son is this?''

''Loizos is all right.'' And the funny thing is, at that moment I am sure he is.

&

Outside the villa Barnes, silence is rank.

&

I don't understand it. People die. It's a going further away, an absence. ''An invitation to Byzantium,'' he said, having received one himself. Now he won't answer letters, that's all. He left a blank. There's no drama. It's all very unsatisfactory.

The selfishness of what they call grief.

&

It's only 89 today. In August, it was sometimes 112 in the kitchen, 116 on the balcony. Finally, we smashed the thermometer. Mrs Wender bought the new one. The fat calms of heavy air and heat at home were followed by big symphonic thunderstorms. One ran to stand on the cliffs and watch the big roll from the west. Here, one waits in suspended animation for five months. Still there's no promised rain.

&

Bea Wender is packing and I like her better for it. Two weeks from now she will stand not a hundred miles as the crow flies from Rosa Trethewey Moore's ex-chicken house preaching the iconography of Late Minoan birds to sons of potato farmers from Petosky and daughters of car dealers on the Big Two-Hearted River. Her voice will ring over my inland sea with news of Syrian and Mycaenean prototypes, of the wilful experimental bird-painter who did not sign his name and gave her her summer at the Museum. On the edge of the Laurentian shield, on the shores of its pocked lakes, she will speak of Cretan and Attic bird-types taking wing over Oak Acres, of tripod cauldrons like maple sugar pots, Phrygian bowls with vertical lugs, and the agate mace-heads of Amathus. She will sing the rise of Tyre, the migration of itinerant craftsmen, the plunder-love of ancientness. The notes she took as faun-faces smiled at her from the ground she will pass among serious old soldiers: the perverse sun-lipped smile that gleamed at her from the yellow earth will be described in a language so technical that it seems one of a new religion. The idea enchants me, that bag of bones a link between my two shores.

"What's the matter with you?" Laddie asks. "You're smiling."

"The weather's cooler."

"Roger was looking for you. He's all soft and full of sympathy, sober, almost human."

"Oh, Roger's always human and full of sympathy . . . but sober, that's something, isn't it?"

"Pambos says he wants you to come and see his wife."

"Who else came by?"

"Aphroulla. Looking stern and strange."

"The family fortunes have declined. Loizos' to Aleppo gone and probably with Dympna."

"I get the feeling that everyone has some intimate concern around here except me."

"You could go looking for Edward." Then I suck in my breath because I think, with my kind of luck he'll find Edward dead; dead is a beautiful word and it's my word this week, but if any more deaths happen the neighbours will know I have the evil eye, and the jig will be up for us. So I don't know what to say to him until I notice that he's gone. Into the music room to pound on the old Pleyel.

&

Dear Max, I know the post office doesn't work where you are, the woman was a slob, she let the stamps curl up in the rain and then she went away and was never replaced; the government was never any good there anyway.

Late Minoan III was a washout: the city-states couldn't get it together and the pirates came as usual. The people, used to living on promontories, had to settle on the plain, but it did something to them, having their young men taken as slaves, having to build in malarial swamps and undomesticated mountains. Where snow was not manna, but another kind of fever. Whenever the strangers came they killed the leopards and stole the jewels and the hawks. Because they could no longer live on those tongues of land that jut into the mother sea, they began to bend. The messages from the gods began not to suffice. Anyway, new strangers were always coming with other gods.

The gods they liked best had that strange honey smile on their lips—

&

MONODROMOS

Big soft Speridakis, a man made of felt, labours up the steps in the evening, sits at the balcony table, spreads his hands open and flat before him. "My dear, my whole house has come down."

"Your mother has asked me to take charge of your office. She won't pay me as much as she pays a domestic."

"I see you thinking, he has money, he has money. In fact, I have no money. Law cases—who pays for those in less than two years? The detective certificate is a joke. Ayios Mammas has retained me for two pounds to spy on my sister. The profit on my chemical importing business goes to my mother because she owns the house."

"You're over-extended."

"We're over-extended."

"So you are going away with Mrs Barnes?"

"What else can I do? I cannot give her up. I love her. She is too beautiful."

"So you are having a big tragic love affair."

"So we are having a big tragic love affair."

"What will happen to your wife, your children?"

"I shall have to give the dowry back, and I have spent it. Never mind. Is there not a play in English entitled 'All for Love'?"

"I suppose so. Megas would know. You should ask for money from your wicked old grandmother: surely she owes you something. And she has the face of a woman who can count."

"You are very tough."

"As tough as you've taught me to be, Loizos."

"It would be more discreet if Dympna and I went rather far away. I am counting on your help in the office."

"For how long?"

"I do not know. Until my wife's lawyer has drawn up the agreement. Until I must come back, until the air is clear."

"Where are you going?"

"I have business to do in Tel-Aviv. Then we will go perhaps to Cairo. Not too far away."

"I'll help you out as long as I can." He is twisting his hands.

"That would be very good of you."

"I wish you much happiness, Loizos."

He breaks into a radiant, charming smile. "Thank you." I still don't know whether he's an honest man or some kind of charlatan, he's full of play-acting. He goes down the stairs restored, almost swaggering. But how can you dislike someone you have come to know?

&

Megas arrives cradling a big red Shakespeare in his arms. He paces the balcony. Ibsen is for the proscenium stage, the old Turkish khan is perfect for the Elizabethans, his company know a little English, Shakespeare will be good for them. No, he won't repeat *Julius Caesar,* he wants something with simple people in it. We go over the canon and I am surprised at how many of the plays I do not know. I wonder how Maro would summon up the wickedness of Lady MacBeth. *Othello* is performed every other year by the British, he says. I suggest *The Tempest,* which could be set in the wilds of the west country. I can see Prospero in a priestly stove-pipe hat. We flip the pages. What he wants, he says, is something with meadows in it, and stocky country people.

"Why not *Peer Gynt*?" I ask, because at last I understand what has drawn him to Ibsen; and I have been to Norway with Max and seen where Grieg has his body sealed up in a rock so he could talk to the trolls.

"Hello, Pambos."

"Hello, Mrs Ladi."

"How goes it?"

"Etsi-ketsi . . ." with a wobble of the open fingers, an expression of the littleness of life: so-so.

"Sing, Pambos."

"No, I do not want to sing. Aristides has gone away. His wife is sick."

"He has a wife? I thought he lived around here."

"He has a room near here. His wife has a house. He is there with her and their five children, in her village."

"How do they live on the money that he gives them?"

"Ho, he has no money to give them. They have a garden, and they eat much macaroni."

"How do they pay for the school?"

"She brings her cheese and tomatoes and tomato paste and dried laurel to the market. You have bought these things from her."

And I am ashamed; I have made it such a point to shop as cheaply as an island woman that I have a separate changepurse with a bargaining half-shilling in it, which I hold out, saying "I have only this". How many times has she said "Never mind" and given me what I wanted at that price?

"Why do you look so sad? Why do you want to hear me sing?"

"My *philos* in England is dead—*necros*—*thanatos*—" all the endings are wrong but he knows what I mean and he turns all soft and his eyes well tears. He makes signs with his forefingers of tears running down cheeks. "Sing, you," he says.

The only thing I know: "A mighty-fooortress is our GOD . . ." Belly up on the plate. Only I can't get it out.

&

In the morning, Bea Wender hangs like a dead kingfisher from the mespila tree. The blue of her dress is as electric as ever. I take a look and try not to memorise it and wake up Laddie.

"Shit," he says.

"Quite."

"The rotten old bitch. She was leaving today."

"I guess she decided she didn't want to."

He staggers into the sunlight. The banana woman passes on another round, her early voice quavering, sweet. Bananas are up to three and one half shillings.

He leans over the balcony, peers, and looks away. From the dead bluejay lady. "Bitch. She owed me six pounds."

"You are awful, Laddie."

"Don't notice you down on your knees weeping. Why did you think I spent my whole summer talking to her, because I liked her? This goddam place gets into them, they do damn stupid things. Like that. Like Edward. You and the old woman. That . . . ruin."

"I was thinking yesterday she'd be lecturing not far from home."

"Christ, you would, wouldn't you? Always synthesising tea parties. What do we do about her? Who cuts her down?" With his back firmly turned.

I try to feel superior by looking at her. Poor limp hands, swollen purple, sickening . . .

"Suicide's bloody selfish," he says. "Ever tried it? Lots of my friends do it. Cosimo . . . Brian. Doesn't make people happy, being bent."

"She wasn't, was she?"

"Lord knows. She never said anything about it."

"Why would she do a thing like that?"

"Hell, I don't know. Maybe she'd lost her job, maybe she was carrying on some great romance. The most unlikely people . . . Look, I'll pop into my pants and phone from around the corner, get the police. You'd better lop over to the American embassy. Wear your good dress, make an impression. I don't want to lose my residence permit. Have to do things properly.''

Within seconds we are both more or less dressed. ''Look,'' he says, ''I'll phone the Embassy, you go to the police, that's fairer. Make sure they get a move on, eh? And don't tell anyone what happened: we'll be mobbed.''

The police station is built into the wall down where the palace used to be, between the fire hall and the Spitfire Cafe. Not far. I don't walk too flying fast, I don't want to make a stir in the neighbourhood. What's the word for a female, dead, *necra*? Hardly. Why have I never sat down methodically with my dictionaries so I could talk decently? She was right, I'm lazy, a bad influence. What a beastly way to end. You'd think someone like that who *knew* something, even the iconology of pots, would have that to hold on to.

No, there's really no need to hurry. She'll wait. She has nothing to do now, but wait. In life she was impatient.

In the police station, I play Englishwoman, serious but distraught: excuse me, at the counter, excuse me, but something rather bad has happened at our house. Zap, a battalion of khaki shirts and elegant moustaches is mobilised. All is courtesy and alertness. For the second time I am delivered to my destination in a jeep. Laddie already has to hold back the crowds.

In an hour, during which time I stay in my room, she is gone. A man in a brown suit comes from the American Embassy. We give him statements, coffee, her packed suitcases. She left no note. He gives us a receipt and says he will go through her papers for the name of a next-of-kin and accepts a cup of tea. Phaedra shuffles out to stare at the tree, and waves and smiles. Cicadas buzz. ''I'm frightfully sorry,'' Laddie says.

''You're sure there wasn't some kind of note?''

''Good heavens, no.''

''Was she depressed? Why would she do a thing like that?''

''No, she was all dithery about not missing her plane.''

''Did you ever notice her with a coil of new rope?'' Wincing, he rubs his neck under his button-down collar.

''She got the rope for a fire-escape when she first came. Tied it to a ring on her windowsill.''

''She must have been a girl-scout, clambering up that tree.''

''Archaeologists tend to be pretty spry.''

''Are you sure there's nothing she told you?''

''Look, I'm sure she told me everything. She was that kind of old bird. Night after night after night she blethered away . . . but there wasn't anything to indicate—this—unless . . .''

''Unless what?''

''Well, she was a pretty depressing sort of person, I found. Maybe nobody liked her.''

''And you, Mrs Moore?''

''I hardly talked to her at all. It's my brother's place, not mine. I had nothing to do with her.''

''What was she paying you?''

''Ten pounds a week, all in,'' he says, who told me four.

''Well, I'll get a message through to Michigan and see what they want done. Can you make an official identification if we need one? Or perhaps her supervisor at the Museum would be the appropriate official. You'll have a hard time getting a new tenant after this, won't you?''

And he goes.

''I suppose the neighbourhood would think it indecent if I went to work,'' I say.

''I would.''

''Best thing to do when someone dies, is keep busy'' I say.

He stalks into the kitchen, throws open the shutter, and calls down the stairs. ''Mrs Phaedra, send someone to Mr Speridakis' house to say my sister will not come to work today.''

One by one our friends come to stare at the tree that has borne a birdwoman for fruit. We pay no attention to them. We sit on the gallery on either side of one of their small ugly square tables, a bottle of Othello wine between us, eating fresh koullouri and new goat's cheese. He has much to say. "When you first came, I was out of my mind with grief. I didn't know where to turn. You know I hadn't meant to send for you, but Florinda knew who you were, and where, and she said she'd wire and I didn't stop her. When I saw you, I was angry, repelled. When you aren't here I think, she's the only one who knows about it, how things were at home, what made me."

"I didn't, really, when I was younger. I think I do now."

"Poor Pa straggling along behind Ma's big dream."

"There weren't any dreams in our house: I envied you."

"The fathers were overlooked, the way we lived. I should have listened to yours. He was more than he pretended to be. I came to pick you up for a dance one summer when I was home from the Conservatory and you were upstairs doing something to your hair—you don't bother any more, and somehow you look better, the 'fifties were odd, weren't they?—and your mother was out at the church. Leo was minding the store. Your father put down the paper and looked over his glasses at me and said, 'Lafcadio . . .'—he always called me my full name and made me feel a fool—'before you take her away from her studies and marry her, do you know who and what you are?' "

"You couldn't have, could you? I mean, you wouldn't have? Or did you hate me so much even then?"

"Why would I hate you?"

"I exist, therefore I am detestable. Oh, for hanging around, for being me, being a girl, that's the way things were there. Being smart in school."

"You weren't as smart as you thought you were. But I liked you, I liked the store. I liked your father and mother and Leo. You were all so beautifully normal."

"I loved Rosa because she seemed a character."

"I should have listened to him. 'Do you know who and what you are?' I meant to listen, but that night on the beach you were walking in a long yellow dress on the sand and talking again about getting married, about our having children. I was dead scared of going to England, I thought somehow it would be all right if I could hold on to you."

We go over the old story again, how it was for him, how it was for me. It is the first time we have put it together face to face, but that does not make it new. It is a tired, chipped story, an old third-rate play: two people out for the main chance thinking they can take it by holding on to each other. And behind them, generations on a treadmill, hoping to work their progeny out of the series.

"You should be a great pianist, and I should iron your shirts," I say.

He pushes his hair back and arranges the seeds that have fallen from the koullouri bread in a pattern on the table. "Well, we've grown out of that now. We've even survived it. What I've been wanting to tell you is that Edward is definitely coming back."

"You've heard from him, then?"

"Indirectly, You've had your pound of flesh, now. How long are you going to hang around waiting for your Max?"

"Max is dead, Laddie."

He sweeps the seeds irritably off the table onto the floor. He stares up at me. I can't tell any more than I used to whether his look means irritation or affection. "Where did you get that kind of luck?" he asks.

Then, Pambos, with some expression on his face I have not seen before, hustles into the courtyard. "Come, Mrs Ladi, come with me: there is a lady in the street who looks to see you."

"I've got to go," I say to Laddie. "Something's up. He's never urgent about anything. I'll clear out as soon as I can."

"Where to?"

"Somewhere, I dunno, never mind, 'bye."

&

I keep staring at her as she drives. There is something tragic about her. Something bad will happen to her, I know.

She is nice: cool, fine-boned, friendly, without ceremony. "I have wanted so much to meet you for a very long time; to talk to you. There are never enough intelligent people to talk to here. It was not until I heard the news that I dared.

"Xanthos has a way of finding interesting women. Then I feel forbidden to know them. But you know, this island is very little, one dares many things because one is in need of friends. And Xanthos is in Greece." She flips the wheel as she drives. She wears her black hair in braids around her head. "I know you are friends with him . . . very good friends. You have nothing to fear from me. I have no old grandmother to set on you—in its way, that was rather comical, was it not? at least, a thing that had never happened here before in the history of memory—I simply came to see you because I wanted to talk to you. I have no close friends here. I am too often away, I was educated abroad."

Tragic, the face; yes, tragic.

"What do you do?"

"Oh, I make films."

Small O of remembrance. Then the wheels turn and I know why she is tragic: she has the face of that Spanish woman in the Montand-Signoret film, the girl they scared to death, with him in the bathtub pretending to be dead: *Diabolique* it was called. I laugh, then, and tell her. She laughs, and we are friends.

Their house is less magnificent than I might have expected. It lacks the silken dower-carpets of the big apartments I have been in. It's a big, rather ordinary villa in a nondescript suburb, surrounded by lemon trees and a few attempts at rose bushes. It's set apart from the other places I've been in by its comfort. Usually, people like this huddle a great many objects together to prove that they own them. Things like sofas are prestige items because they have to be imported, they can't be taken for granted. One never has a feeling living goes on in the livingroom. But it's good to sink down in a—yes—European setting, in a room with bookshelves and paintings (but none of Aphroulla's) and a cabinet of antiquities: horned clay tomb-groups with the usual wicked expressions, very witty and good, Museum stuff. "Xanthos is well known by the peasants," she laughs. "Some day the bottom will fall out of the bank because he has bought one more antiquity."

Oof, books on tables, ashtrays, bouquets of flowers. The shabbiness of my whole existence is borne in on me. How funny our setup must have looked to Xanthos! She offers me not tea or nescafe but a long Scotch. Suddenly, I am relieved of pioneering. "Tell me about Max," she says. "I worked with him long ago on a script in Norway, and it is very many years since I have seen him."

"What do you want to know?"

"Everything. I was half in love with him, I think now. I can't think of the world without him. He was such a good person that he has been with me always since I met him. Oh, I knew him a fortnight—it was a documentary for the United Nations we were doing, twenty years ago. Ever since that time I have been swimming in his poems. Tell me about him."

In the end, we are both crying.

&

She lets me off in the square outside the walls. I am hungry. Down in the kebab place in the moat Roger Salmon is lolling on a table. He is at the point of drunkenness where words can only emerge if he taps them out with his forefinger. "Your friends," he says, "your friends. Bad luck with your friends. Mine aren't any better. Did you hear about the Barnes's?"

"No," I lie.

He finds more words. "Rich one, that. Good as that old archaeological bod a-hanging from your tree. Heard that one today, too, I heard. Mr and Mrs P. Barnes: yesterday morning she found one of those wax dolls they hang up in churches at her door. Nails in its privies, nails in its eyes. Gone off to the bloody booby hatch, she has."

"She's in Athens with her fancy man, Roger."

"Mmm. 'Pon my soul. Pete's going home. Requested transfer. Rum chap, Pete. No stomach for liquor."

"The world can't always be charged with the glory of God, now, can it, Roger?"

VIII

THE GRAND HOTEL AND SEVERAL OTHERS

Though it is still warm, the weather is turning autumnal. The members of the Eating Society are buzzing like bees—Aphroulla weaving and mosaicking against Ayios Mammas' quavering serenades, Michaelis fathoming empty wells and railing against empty dams, Petronella pushing William through his first weeks as a schoolmaster—because it is possible to be busy and active again. But there is a terminal sadness in the air.

Almost every day there is a letter from Maurice Henshaw. I wonder that someone who seemed middle-aged and self-contained can become my dependant. Where shall he put my suitcases? Have I asked Elizabeth for any of Max's books? Do I know she is cheating me out of objects Max and I bought equally in the Portobello junk markets, a two shilling plate, a sixpenny lead teapot? Can I advise him what a literary executor actually does?

Elizabeth writes, too, though officially we still do not know each other. On thick, cream, crested paper the Hon. Elizabeth Magill requests the return of personal letters from Max Magill, now the property of his estate.

I spend four days in the dead quiet of Speridakis' office composing replies of an eloquence I did not know I possessed.

Then I go out and buy thick cream paper, a broad-nibbed pen and a bottle of real ink with a cork in it. I write in round imitation Bishop Strachan School characters: "Dear Mrs Magill, with regard to letters of Max Magill in my possession, they are personal and intimate rather than of a literary nature. I do not think they would be of any use to his publisher or his Executors. That such a correspondence should be made public so soon after his death is not in keeping with my memory of his Life. Yours very sincerely . . ."

Gotcha, Lady E.

The office is a tomb. Mrs Speridakis senior has taken her delicate constitution to a spa in Germany. The clerk Stelios is simply not around. Bibi and I hold the fort. Pye writes that the reports I send are out of date. The credit business has perhaps its moral limitations, but there is no bank manager who will give me information only Loizos is qualified to acquire. I continue to send out old reports and wonder who Pye cross-checks with. Bibi experiments with hairdos and talks to her boyfriends on the phone. I hear that Loizos and Dympna have been seen in Beirut, Athens, Addis Ababa. I see Peter Barnes retching outside one of the loud bars where tarts in nylon leopard skins entertain the customers.

The piano pupils are back, shy black-eyed smocked things scooting along the balcony with music cases and hair ribbons. Edward has not yet returned, but Laddie is turning his room out with a domestic efficiency that leaves me cold.

Summer hours are over. The kiosks on the beaches are closing down. There's nothing much to do. I suppose I could spend more time at the Museum, but I'm always having to decide between the entrance fee and lunch.

I haven't seen X for ages. In a way I miss him, in a way I don't. A lot of things have been sheared away, he doesn't matter as much to me as he did before. When a lad comes from his office with a note for me I don't feel like opening it. I tell the boy to go away, he doesn't, I am about to be irritable with him when I realise that he is waiting for a reply. "Could you meet me for lunch at the Grand Hotel at one?" X asks. I could. I don't want to. I couldn't care less. It's ten and I'm already through at the office. It's all nonsense, traipsing around with other people's husbands, sitting discussing the condition of one's soul. "Yes," I write.

Then regret it.

I'm in a black, snappish mood. I have been for days. I don't want to talk to anyone, I don't want to have to be nice to anyone. I want to sit and chew my calloused hangnails. Or pack. Sloppily.

On the way to the hotel I buy a pair of leather shoes and throw my worn rubber thongs into the garbage can in the moat. I sit in the Public Garden for a moment listening to the tinny noise of the traffic up above me. Nothing is any good.

I have to force myself to go in the front door of the hotel. I'm early. I almost turn on my heel and leave, I don't want to wait for him in the big formal silk and satin lounge with the pastel ladies and the elderly colonels. But there's an Australian journalist I like in the bar who makes little cheerful jokes with me. How many days has it been since I last smiled?

I sit opposite X in a kind of Palm Court dining room, the sort of place you see in Noel Coward plays. My hands lie tanned black on the white napery. X seems shy and fussy. "Aglaia sends her regards," he says, looking at his soup plate.

"I liked her."

"I knew you would." He is smooth as always, but his feathers are ruffled underneath.

Around us, waiters in elegant epaulettes are scudding to clapped commands. "The Empiah too, what does it mean to you?" I trill under my breath. He looks uncomfortable. "I hate the way the waiters bow and scrape," I say.

"They are pleased with these jobs when they get them. Their wages are good. It doesn't hurt them to make one's life orderly and pleasant. Have you been well? It is a very long time since I last saw you. I have found a new restaurant in Marseilles that you would enjoy. I hear there has been trouble at your house."

"Dear Mrs Wender strung herself up from our tree. It was so hot that nobody gave a tinker's damn. The neighbours stared, the police measured, and the American Embassy took her suitcases away. Then nothing."

"Oh, when an ugly woman with a bad disposition does away with herself no one cares. She was well known here. She has worked with the museum many summers. She has always complained about everything."

"They might have given her some kind of funeral. It seemed . . . brutal."

"But life is brutal, my dear. Only spoiled children do not recognise that. She was here, she was unpleasant; she is gone, no one misses her. What have you been doing with yourself?"

"Nothing."

"Oh, you're very happy and gay today."

"I could eat tacks. Everything's turned from coloured to grey for me. I'm haunted by the idea that I've done something that will make everything turn out badly for everyone I know. That I've done—no, seen—the wrong things, or been the wrong person. That I haven't noticed enough. Or noticed the right things. That I have to hold the world together with my eyes, and that I can't."

Here, in this grand light salon, he cannot touch me, and I need badly to be touched. "The sauce is rather good," he says, "but the summer is over. One eats with less relish now. I have seen Loizos in Athens looking embarrassed to be happy. Men are really rather simple at heart, are they not? You are still working for him?"

"I go there, but there's nothing to do."

"You have decided to go away. That is what makes you so sad."

"How did you know? Oh, I guess it's obvious. I have to go, Xanthos. There's nothing for me here. I can't make enough money to live decently on my own. I can't stay in the old monastiraki any longer."

"Why not?"

"I irritate him. I always have. And it's hard to live with a consistent reminder of one's failure, of the past . . . of that particularly idiotic, hopeful marriage. I suppose I set him askew with his own present world. I don't know. It's just impossible. He's paid his debt to me. Anyway, Edward's coming back."

He whistles, and a waiter turns. He waves him away. "That's bad," he says, "the man is . . . what is it, one of those creatures that attaches itself to one when one swims in muddy water?"

"A bloodsucker."

"What an ugly word. No, it is not that."

"A leech, then, if you're determined to be English English."

"A leech, yes. He was not liked when he was here. One shuddered always when one met him in the street. From far away he was young and innocent-looking, but close to, there was something corrupted about him. His eyes were one hundred years old. He was an apple with a good skin that is brown inside. Your brother will lose all his pupils if that man comes back."

"He doesn't seem to care."

"Where will you go?"

"England."

"Not to your own village, as we say?"

"Oh, perhaps like your friend Giorgios to retire. Now, I wouldn't know anyone there, except my mother. And I can get a job more easily in England than I can there. The last time I was home you had to fill in cards with personal information, your religion, what diseases you had had, and everyone had to be a specialist, they didn't need general office dogsbodies. And they don't speak enough languages to need translators. It's a rigid world. I don't fit in. My brother Leo writes me every three months I should marry, it's the only way I'll ever get a pension. England is easier to take."

"Until they make new rules for working permits, yes. If you wish to stay here, I think I could find you a job that would be better than working for Loizos."

"What would become of me, though? What is there for me here? I can't belong by birth and I won't do the sort of genteel things Florinda and Petronella do to make themselves belong. I'm a hopeless case, Xanthos. I've a fixation I'm as good as any queen."

"But in England you will be snubbed by little clerks and called a colonial if not a wog by the bosses."

"And go to the theatre every night, and get books from the London Library: that compensates."

"Well, London is big enough to lose oneself."

"Something like that."

"Have you bought your ticket?"

"No, that's the awful thing. I can't make myself."

He grins widely. "I think you are right to go away, but I do not want you to go. This island is too small, there are few sophisticated persons to talk to. If we have you for another week, I shall be very happy."

"Do you think I'm doing the right thing?"

"How should I know? Each person is responsible for his life only. There is nothing I can offer you except help with finding a situation. If I were free to marry you, that would be different: then I would have grounds for persuading you. But there are so many foreigners who come here. Some dislike it—why should that surprise you? It is still very primitive, the community is restricted for poeple like you and me—and some do not. It is rare that a person comes and enjoys it as much as you do, however. You are one who has not complained."

"Thank you."

"But the art of being a foreigner is a difficult one. I know that. Aglaia wanted us to settle in England. After two years I knew I was too arrogant to accept the treatment they gave me. You see, she is more European than I am. They accepted her. Here I am a banker, there, I was always a wog. To the same extent you will not be accepted here. And I know you well enough to say that if you married one of us you would not be happy. You are used to a different sort of freedom."

"I'm not a free person, really, Xanthos. You always say that about me. I'm as tied as you are. I simply live as I was taught to live, by feelings and instincts and accidents. Now my feelings and instincts tell me to go back to England."

"Go you must, then, if that is the way you live. Though I recommend thinking as a cure for feeling, from time to time. But I warn you also, it is a difficult place to leave, this island. Buy a ticket, set a date. If not, you will linger. For many of the people you know, the time to go has come too late."

Then there are also things I have to tell him, pieces of information I can now retrieve from my bundle of feelings: the blond boy down the street who tinkers with cars is building a home-made tank; the bishop of Maloundia, encountered in the street, states that he is the possessor of the ikon of the dog-headed saint, it is at his monastery.

"Bishops do not have monasteries. How he lingers, that one: he returns every moment he can to the monastery he was trained in. It is a very political monastery, and he is a very political man. The Ethnarch does not like him to be there so much. You must go to visit him, you will find him interesting."

"I was thinking of going up there on Petronella's Velo-Solex. Have you ever ridden one? It's the simplest kind of motor-bike."

"Oh yes, in one's youth . . . I must go, I have a meeting. It is a good idea for you to go up to the mountains. Some people say it is dangerous to travel, but in this country the peasants though they are sometimes rude are not brigands. You will be quite safe if you don't take too much money. I would like to come with you, but I am an old man, not suited to rough travel. And I have been seen too much with you this summer.''

Sometimes when I'm talking with him I have a feeling I've been eating and sleeping with a right-wing nut. Other times, he seems like an unreasonably democratic French count, if there are any. You'd have to know him for twenty years to get to know him. Lunch is over, summer is gone. ''Good-bye, Xanthos. Thank you.''

''Oh, I will come to your house tonight with my boyscout water-bottle. And I have a sleeping bag and an oiled tarpaulin.''

&

''But we shall never see you again!'' Aphroulla laughs.

''He will eat you up, schlup, schlup, schlup,'' says Michaelis, munching mightily.

Megas and Maro, who retain some remnant of the faith, are mortified. She is silent and very pregnant-looking. ''But he is a good Byzantine man,'' says Megas.

''Xanthos, he knows nothing about country life. He is up to no good, Maloundia. Did you know his name is Dionysios? What does he do at the monastery when there is already a perfectly good abbot?''

''Ha, have you heard about the abbot?'' Michaelis sniggers.

''It all sounds to me like nasty stories from Protestants about priests,'' I say.

''With a swish of his blue-purple skirts he will sweep you up and we will never see you again.''

''Priests are very bad luck, especially first thing in the morning,'' says Aphroulla with a pious smile.

''Xanthos says he is all right.''

''Pooh, Xanthos, what does he know but the state of one's pocket? But you will be safe when you are travelling: the country people are good. And where the monasteries are is very beautiful landscape. Good journey."

&

Laddie is delighted. He praises my enterprise with unexpected hyperbole. He examines Petronella's motorbike and its little motor, like a cheese-grater on the front. He tries to make it go. It will not go. "Never mind," he says, and goes to fetch one of the street mechanics.

I am as impatient as a child. I want to go, therefore I must go, therefore I am going. Laddie wants me to go. Everything has been arranged. The street mechanic calls his friend. They both tinker. Still the bike will not go. They shake their heads. I try to make it go, with the tricks that Petronella has shown me. No luck. The mechanics say it is a very old machine.

"You could take the bus," Laddie says.

"I don't know why Takis is complaining about its being old. He drives a 1949 Austin tied together with binder twine."

"This time of night there are lots of buses going in that direction."

"I don't want to take the bus. I want to wander around the little roads by myself. I'm always stuck with someone else with something else in mind. I never see what I want to."

"Well, maybe they can fix it."

But they have already thrown in the sponge. The only thing to do now is get it to Petronella's mechanic, but I don't know who he is. And she has moved to a villa out in the country, she'll be somewhere between here and there in her new little car. I slump down in disappointment. Laddie goes out talking to the mechanics. Everything is spoiled for me here, now, nothing ever works. All I want to do is puddle round the countryside for a fortnight, before I go to England. Have one last draught of country air, one final wander.

I'm as disappointed as a child. I want to sulk and whine.

I look away from my little stack of camping gear—rubber poncho, sleeping bag, X's water bottle, folding cup and stick-together knives and forks. I've made a fool of myself again. The one more thing I do is going to be waiting around for the ship.

I consider going on foot. I've borrowed Laddie's hiking boots. But no, I know myself too well. I'd be discouraged before I got out of the suburbs. I could take the bus into the mountains and then . . . but I don't have a proper rucksack. Who'd have a rucksack, now? William? Certainly not Roger. Megas, perhaps. But where does he live?

Suddenly Laddie's calling: "Hey, look, here's your new motorbike."

I run down to him. "You goof, you wonderful goof."

"It doesn't need petrol and it never needs oiling and it's guaranteed not to go too fast. It goes 25 years before it wears out."

The man who owns it explains that it is very gentle and stronger than it looks. To accelerate it, you say "Sho," and hit it with a stick. It brays, and it has long ears and a white-haired muzzle. Lovely gentle eyes. When I get on it, with difficulty because I was never taught to mount, let alone ride, any kind of critter, it turns in circles. "Beat it," says the man, handing me a stout stick.

"Oh, never."

"Very gentle donkey," he says. "Very nice donkey. One pound per day."

"What's its name? What does it eat?"

Its name is Lina, it eats oats and grass and if you want to ride like a woman you hook your knee on the edge of the saddle-bag. Laddie helps me load it.

&

"Sho. Sho." I am in the middle of the ex-Government House Roundabout. "Sho." Gravel trucks behind me, jeeps and cars around me. "Sho, Lina. Sho." She just stands there and blinks. When I hit her what I think is a resounding thwack, she turns and stands facing one of the gravel trucks. The driver laughs. I get off her and pull her to the side of the road. I drag her to a culvert and use the curbside to mount her again. She turns around and heads home. I get down again, turn her around by her bridle, and start pulling her south.

The suburbs are unending, the traffic is heavy. I decide to wait until we get into the real country before I mount her again. I can't get my leg over her without standing on some sort of stone, Laddie's boots are too big. I don't want to make an ass of myself in the traffic. So we slop along nonchalantly, both on foot past villas and schools and churches and blacksmiths' shops. They're like suburbs anywhere in the world, these villages, they have no heart, and leave a mechanical stamp on their people. To the outsider at least.

Both houses and countryside are at their worst in this season. Everything looks chipped and dirty after the heat. Once we're beyond the last dormitory village the road branches into what I call the real country, where there are orchards and olive groves. Lina lets me get on her, actually lets me ride a couple of hundred yards, then carries me into someone's grove of olive trees. She hasn't got proper reins, just a knotted string bridle. She seems to know I don't like to use the stick. I have to get off her to change direction, and the country is flat and level here, it's hard to find anything to stand on to mount her. She knows it's suppertime back home. "Come on, Lina."

I haven't walked so far in years. In the distance, a five-domed church humps the horizon. Grace is beginning. There are clouds in the sky and lengthening shadows pattern the burning plain. The mountains are so close you'd think you could touch them. Olympus is still snow-capped, even after the heat.

Get along with you, Lina. We're obviously going to have to kip outdoors tonight, but I'll have to get you water, since you can't drink out of a canteen. Have a handful of nice chaffy oats. How do you say, "where can I get water for my donkey?" I know where, can, I, water and for... but I didn't think to ask about the word for donkey. Isn't that stupid? I'll have to listen hard to the next person who speaks to me.

Come on, now. Sho. If you won't come, I'll have to hit you. You're a heavy darned thing trailing behind me like a stubborn kid, though your little feet make elegant clopping noises. Come, Lady Lina, time's a-wasting.

Five miles out the city, complain of the suburbs as you may, you're in the middle of nowhere. But here's a neat little house with a stone foundation, plastered walls, a tile roof, and a garden. "Where, so please you, missus, can I find water for my ... beast?" I ask. The little old woman bows and giggles and calls out to the little old man who runs, goggles, raises his arms from the elbows like a puppet king. "Come in, come in, share with us. I will give water to your beast."

The little old woman pulls a chair out for me in the front hall, and bustles into the nether regions of the house to bring me a glass of cold water with a sticky sweet on a silver spoon across it. Candied green walnuts. She stares at me with round-eyed goodwill. "Where are you going?"

"*Peripato*." This is the word Pambos taught me. I wander around, like Socrates and Aristotle.

"Where is your husband? Where are your children? Where is your house?" And a lot I can't understand.

"I am wandering around. I have no husband. I wish to see much of this island."

The husband comes in beaming. She tells him about me with much use of *peripato*. He finds this as funny as she does. "Where do you go tonight?"

"I go to the next village."

"It is a very old donkey. Stay with us."

But I think, they are old and very poor. I will eat a week of their rations. I say that I must go. I thank them. "Wait," she says and goes to her kitchen. She comes out with bread, hard salty home-made cheese and wizened black olives. "Good journey."

"Stay away from the Turks," he says. "They're not good people."

Though one of my guilts about this place is that I have made hardly any Turkish friends, I am able to assure him truthfully that the road I am following passes through no Turkish villages. He gives me an avuncular smile and helps me up on Lina with a firm, hard forearm, in a kind of fireman's grip. "Good journey," he says. "Good journey," she says. And they stand like benevolent grandparents smiling me away. Who were the kind old people in Ovid and what were they changed into? "Good-bye," I tell them, "Good-bye. Thank you." My voice echoes against the lonely hills.

The air is soft. There is moisture in it, definitely. One of these days it will rain. Sho. Sho. No? Well, I'll get off and walk. It isn't much of a village but it's probably politer to walk through it. Look how scruffy it is, tin roofs held on with broken cement blocks. A crumbling church. The corners of all the buildings have been knocked off. The cafe is a hole in the wall where two infinitely old priests are drinking coffee.

But beside the café a signpost tells me my road branches off, and I turn to find a watering-trough made of the bottoms of huge clay wine-jars. Lina goes to it enthusiastically and we are joined presently by a man with a string of mules, who says hello in English.

Lina drinks, and I mount her again, and she stands stock still. She can see that with this turn we are getting into the foothills, the road begins to wind mysteriously, the landscape is less burnt umber than green. I tap her ineffectually with my stick. "Sho," I say firmly. Big fool beating little donkey. She turns around and heads home.

"Where are you going?" the muleteer asks.

I tell him, to the next village, where I have heard there is an inn.

He seems to find this very funny. He takes my donkey by the bridle, turns her around, gives her one awful clout with his stout stick, and heads her down the road. She trots a few steps until she comes to a bridge over a dry riverbed: not her sort of thing. When the muleteer catches up with us, he ties Lina firmly to the end of his pack train, clucks to his mules, and carries us off. "I live in that village," he says. "Now she will have to go."

It's getting dark now, and the road goes down and up and around. The valleys are lovely, they feel almost damp and bosky. Lina goes roughly downhill, I lunge forward on her uncomfortably, and think enviously of a mule, and correct myself, because you have to really ride mules and I've never ridden anything in my life but Bert Moore's old plough horse Molly, who wouldn't do anything for you either, but also did not kick. Laddie's pony bit.

The muleteer's name is Leandros. He speaks good English. He has a cousin in town who's a stringer for the *New York Times*. He likes the country himself, he says. Mules are a good living. He makes four pounds a week.

He's a good-looking middle-aged fellow with a stubble of beard and a farmer's collarless shirt; baggy pants and a sash, and high boots. He sits comfortably side saddle calling back to me about his children (seven of them), his work, the neighbourhood. The land is rough, he says, hauling me uphill and down dale through shadowy gulches over which pine trees hang as if the picture were Japanese. He used to work in the copper mines, he said, but he likes being a farmer and muleteer better. He works for himself, and for other people. He can turn his hand to almost anything.

Lina doesn't like going downhill; she can't help following the mules she's tied to, so she rebels by means of a stomach-twitching sashay with her hips. It scares the liver out of me and I think I must look to Leandros very funny, clinging for dear life to her. Until we met Leandros I figured we were making a mile and a half an hour; now he's pulling us up and down and around and through olive groves at an unsettling clip. Then we move up to a bland wooded plateau, and the next thing I know he's saying good-bye, untying Lina, and taking his mules through a courtyard gate. Children are running to meet him. I call him back and thank him with a pound. He calls his wife, who come out and waves; then he gives Lina a last resounding thwack on the behind. "The village is very near," he says with a comforting smile.

As usual, Lina doesn't want to carry me more than a hundred yards, but encouraged by his example I use the traditional method of making her move. It's dark now, time to find a stable and a bed.

It's a big village, and quite different from the one I passed on the way. It's set on the hillside and the houses are big and have balconies with rubblestone columns. There are lights in the centre square. The church is set on a raised terraces, the cafés lie below it, and they are swarming with men. Old women with candles and kerchiefs are handing out boiled wheat and pomegranate seeds for the honour of the dead. "Take, take," they say.

I ask a kid where the inn is, he points to the butcher shop. A man with blood on his hands unlocks a wooden door on a cobbled courtyard. There is a stable, there are stairs.

"Three shillings," he says, hurriedly unsaddling Lina. "The room is upstairs."

By now a number of people are following me. I take the saddle bags and my bundles up a staircase that has come away from its stone wall. In a rickety room I find a rickety bed with clean sheets on. It looks delicious, and there is a water-jug with water in it on the landing.

But the people who were watching me, who have been following me, have also come into my room. "Exo," I say, longing to take off my big boots, undress and wash, "Exo, exete, exeunt, whatever they say . . ." They have unlined loony faces, there are six of them between nine and ninety; a whole tribe, they are. "Get out! Exo!" The youngest is fingering my wallet, now. I grab it away and make threatening motions. They laugh.

"Come on, then," I tell them. I take them out, and lock my room with the great iron key the butcher gave me, and we process to the square. "I want to eat," I tell them. "*Na fame*, *na fame* or whatever it is. Kebab. *Souvlakia*. Baaaaa."

The penny drops and they take me around the corner to the kebab shop. He lets me in, but he won't let them. "They came in my room," I say to him.

He already knows I'm at the inn, I'm not wrong to presume that. He also speaks English. "They are bad people," he says. "How much do you want? Four sticks? Three sticks?" The meat sizzles and I feel faint with hunger. I sit down, and am unsure I will ever get up again. He has cold beer on ice, this man, cold island beer, good beer, a cross between English and German, much better than French or Greek. I drink thirstily and eat like a horse. We have come seventeen miles today, Lina and I.

The café man walks me back to the inn, to make sure the bad people have gone away. I stumble half dead into the courtyard, lock the door, and pee in the hole in the corner where they told me to. Then I go up and sleep the sleep of the dead.

In the morning, I am stiff and slightly mouldy, like an old piece of Masonite. Hungry. My watch has stopped. I have no idea what time it is. I have slept with my clothes on and I feel indescribably dirty. I wash in cold water, attempt to brush my teeth, and go out looking for breakfast. Lina nickers as I pass her.

In the café they tell me I forgot to tie her by the foot and she ran away in the night, it took six of them to bring her back. I didn't hear them.

The kebab man turns up and says yes, it's a big village, they have water here, and a mill, and an agricultural co-op. He himself is also an insurance and commission agent. He has five daughters, five houses to build.

When we start out again both Lina and I are dead tired, but I buy her good oats at the store—Leandros told me to do this—and at the edge of the village where the road turns I pass a big new Massey-Harris tractor sitting in a mud-brick shed of great antiquity and it bucks me up. I pull her past the crossroads, remembering I forgot to look the village up in Gunnis, and not caring much, for the earth is red here, the olive trees creep up to the mountain pines, the roads are beginning to be switch-backs, we're getting high.

I don't know what's so good about poking along. It's ridiculous to enjoy it so much. Lina's pace makes it possible to notice the shape of every bough and pebble. There's copper slag on the side of the road, Phoenician slag, they say, purer than the stuff they can get now. It reminds me of souvenir ash-trays someone sent us from British Columbia: hard black and orange moons and stars, hearts, clubs, spades.

A grouse whirrs and veers away. We startle a hare. I feel like singing, but old summer camp songs don't come out right. Hymns do, but I don't feel religious, only sloppily pleased.

We eat our lunch at an empty forest station when the sun is overhead. I spread her oats on a picnic table, and get water for her from a clay jar tied to a tree with a metal spigot on it. Lina eats my orange peels. She likes them better than oats.

I study the map. I had planned to get to Maloundia's monastery this night if I took the Velo. It's clearly too far. But on a lesser track not far away there's a monastery marked on the map "aban." where I think I came on a picnic with the Williamsons. If I can't stay there, there's another forest station further on. But today I don't want to push too much. There's no Leandros to pull us.

Down, up, along, across the dry streambeds through the unending gentle trees. No sign of habitation here at all, only the faraway whistle of a shepherd, once. The mountains are getting seriously steep, but the little road has been well engineered, and Lina and I lounge along it effortlessly. She's in a good mood today, resigned, perhaps, to her fate.

I'm glad I came. There's a quiet, infantile joy available to woods-walkers, beach-combers, a joy you forget when you've been living the squirrel's life in the city. Max was always good when you could get him out walking in the country, noticed everything, talked to everyone, but also walked silently when the fit was on him, leaving his punning persona behind. Something falls off you when you have the woods to be your cloak, you don't need wit against the world.

So we walk along, making cheap philosophy and stubborn clopping noises. I try reading, but Lina's gait is too uneven, and it's a shame to spoil the experience of sitting vague and idle and staring dumbly at the trees.

The road is deserted. I passed a Forest Service truck early in the morning. I've heard a couple of shepherds and feinted throwing a stone at a wandering, snarling dog, but I haven't met anyone since. There are no towns on my route. The only names on the map are mountain peaks and monasteries. Mine should be near here.

Aphroulla thought me very odd to come this way. Nobody goes to that part of the mountains, she says, there's nothing to see, only peasants and shepherds and ruined villages. But in the middle of nowhere you can hear, not the small pound of your own thoughts, but the small sounds the world makes in its whirling. And feel oddly superior to a jet trail over the capital a world away. Twenty hard-won miles away.

Yes, there's a sign for the monastery, a very dim one, rather on a slant. The road has become a stony track. We go up a hummock, down a hollow—okay, I'll walk, Lina, if you come without protest—and find one decayed tier of a familiar quadrangle, and a tiny domed church. Let's not just admire the terracing, let's sit down on it.

Lina, tied to a tree, doesn't have the energy to crop oats off the ground in front of her. I don't dare look at the view. I need to find water for her, and if I sit down I'll never get up again. It strikes me that if it had water the place would never have been abandoned, but no, I'm in luck, just down below the church there's a kind of spring: a pipe dribbling out of the earth. Not the sort of place Lina would like to stagger down to. I go back to my pack, get a plastic bag, fill it for her. She drinks lazily. She would. I have three maps with me, an old administrative one, a guidebook one, and the official tourist map. I study them while I eat my chocolate and oranges and bread. Lina loves orange peels, she'll stoop to the ground for them.

Michaelis has given me an agricultural monograph to read. It says the island's donkeys are the finest in the world, but underfed. I get up and with some difficulty move Lina down by the spring where there's grazing. If she eats those scrubby bushes. Remembering to tie her by the foot, hoping the knot is tight enough but not too tight. Her sides are all rough from the saddle and I feel sorry for her, but she's not used to conversation, she doesn't have anything you'd call a cuddly personality, she just stands there, so I leave her staring dumbly at the spring.

I suppose I could light a fire, but I don't want to. It's a forest reserve, and a curl of smoke would bring me company. There are no signs anyone's done anything but picnic here—there are pop bottles and empty cans about—for years. The church is locked, and so are the rooms that still have doors on them.

It doesn't matter, I've never felt less curious, though when I finally decide on where to go to the bathroom I have the old morbid fear of being discovered, interrupted. Fine time to start wondering if it's safe to camp out.

Dark falls fast and early. I sleep out on the balcony, I suppose because it's most like home. It's chilly and clear and the stars make a map on the sky. Somebody taught me the constellations as the Big P and the Big W and the Big C, so I couldn't tell you if the Pleiades are out. Skipping through Michaelis' book on water rights and land tenure I read of a village where the division of water rights was dependent on appearances of the Pleiades; another where 179 people had a hereditary stake in one olive tree. No law of primogeniture, no enclosed land, spooks in the bushes and priests in the mountains, no wonder they drove the British administrators crazy. Boys, we built you all these good roads, drove the mosquitoes away, rationalised your land tenure and rescued you from the hands of the usurers, what's all this shouting about independence?

Nobody loves a mother country.

I couldn't care less now if 24 gypsies and a marching band came down at me out of the bowl of the hills. The stone's hard, the night's cold, I . . .

Morning. Stiff as a . . . second night I've slept in my clothes, stink like a . . . where's Lina? There. Good.

Morning. The sky is a bowl, grey-pink. Lots of cloud. They said it's too early for rain, but I'm damp. Ouch. But the peace of it all, the freedom. Bells far away, and birds twittering. And Lina brays. Best donkeys in the world, Lina, make that indescribable sound again: rusty hinges, old iron bars, crows, old broken legs. My old bones rising. Saddle my charger before the bright day. She doesn't like the strap that goes under her tail.

I could do with a village on this route. They say there are no isolated farms and you don't believe it. You could starve up here. Well, not really: without Lina I could get down to the nearest village in an hour or so, and buy. Come on, Lina. Not that road, this one. You're not going home yet.

How long did I say I'd pull this creature over the world? Ten days? My God.

The air is a-tinkle with bells. A shepherd with a flock of white goats appears. Good day. Where are you going? Over the mountain to the monastery? It's very far. That is an old donkey. Of course she does not like to be ridden. There is an old proverb: there are donkeys who carry you, and donkeys you carry. You know which kind you have. Ho. Ho. Would you like some bread and some olives?

We sit down by a culvert and he shares his food with me. I drink water out of my canteen. I say I hope the water from the old monastiraki is good water. Very good water, he says. Nice way to travel, eh?

He is young, not the heraldic-looking shepherd of the plains. He has been to the city. He doesn't like the city. He likes to be free, with his animals. In the winter he lives in a village about ten miles away. In the summer he sleeps in the fields with his beasts, or in a little hut high up. It is a good life. He looks healthy. Instead of black baggy pants he wears blue-jeans, but he carries a crook and a traditional goatskin bag. He helps me onto Lina, and gooses me. I make as if to hit him and he laughs. Whistles to his flock eerily between his front teeth, waves, goes the other way.

The air is heavenly. It smells of pine and something I can't identify, something Proustian, half-remembered. English poetry. *There lies the dearest sweetness deep down things . . .*

What I am doing is cutting across two watersheds, ridges. There are dry streams below me, and red earth. Around me, solid pine forest: trees all the same age. British reforestation, good. You can't hate them for everything. Never seen a forest so dry and clean under foot. The road is narrow, barely a track, but properly engineered. Somebody's project in 1931, maybe. There must be other tracks the British knew nothing about that were used in the Troubles, when they got their independence. Mountains aren't usually so . . . domestic.

Fairly high up, though: the peak above me is 4200 feet. It looks smoky and gentle. Up, down, up down we go, alternately riding and walking. It's easy to get on her now, I can just stand on the edge of the road because it's a cliff, and sling my leg over; when I can pull her close to. She's smart, and she's heavy. Well, if you won't go any faster than that, I'll read, then.

Without primogeniture, the land is infinitely divided. Why, Laddie's father's farm would have been in eighteen parcels by now, with all of them fighting over the well and the apple trees, because ownership of trees is separate from that of land. If you graft a wild tree you gain ownership. The pistachio tree gives a cash crop. I don't know what it looks like but it grows as scrub around here. Apples are subject to the codling moth—what's new?—bananas to frost, almonds do well, one village is celebrated for cherries . . .

But what's that smell, now? It's unearthly, gold, frankincense ambergris . . .

My God, rain.

Wet earth.

Why did the Psalmist talk about spring when he ought to have been hymning rain? We should sink on our knees, Lina.

Lina is not impressed. She balks. I don't think it will rain much, but we've got another ridge to cross, so I give her a good unhumanitarian whack and she shifts her ass. I'm so sore between the legs that if the Emir of Aberystwyth attacked me with a diamond dildo I wouldn't feel anything. I want to get to that monastery and sleep on a bed in pyjamas. Megas has stayed there. He says the food is good.

It's only the first rain. It isn't even very wet.

I have put the agricultural monographs away in the bottom

of my bag, so I can't look up what the soil is here, but I can easily tell it's clay. It's slippery now, and the rain's coming down in big drops, plashing out of the sky. I should be more grateful than I am. Wet chocolate tastes funny. I bought chocolate because kids in English adventure books were always eating it.

Whatever gave me the idea I could walk this island? You want something the size of the smallest Scilly for a walking tour. Laddie's boxing-glove leather boots are full of water. He'll never forgive me.

Hours. Hours. Come on Lina, it's on the map, we'll get there sooner or later, it's not as if it could fly away. It's only five miles, though that must be not counting switchbacks. We've got to go more than a mile an hour, girl. Shall I check your shoes for stones? You won't let me. Look, I've got blisters, you don't know anything about the blisters I've got, but the thing about boots is that after your feet give out the boots go on walking. Just make an effort. I know you're wet but so am I. X's waterproof poncho has been stored away for years.

Below us, I see the tiled whorls of a little church. I hope it is a village the mapmaker forgot. An hour and a half later, we reach it. It seems to be an old one restored. There's new Frost fence around it, but the gate is unlocked, thank God. I tie Lina to the portico, lug the saddlebags into the miraculously open church, and sink into a high-backed narrow-seated Orthodox pew.

Christos Pantocrator gleams at me from the ceiling. He's been repainted with poster paint. It's heartbreakingly obvious that this is an old church restored with a fine brush, bright new paint and a hard edge. Religion and aesthetics always in conflict, but no varnish, Mr Gunnis, on the iconostasis.

It's funny, I have no emotional response to Orthodoxy, only a deep feeling that politics is imbedded in it. If this were a Catholic or a Protestant church I'd have some canned feelings.

Now I'm only glad to be out of the rain, and appalled that new frescos look so awful. I should say some prayers. I guess they pray standing up, there are no kneelers. The last time I was in a church it was Easter, and they were all milling around talking while the priests chanted.

Dear Father God, Charon, Jupiter, et al, Moses, Aaron, Paul, Barnabas and Aphrodite: take care of Max.

It's cold, though. Stone walls do not a hot house make. I don't know what saint this place is to but it's well kept up. New tiled floors, new plaster, and lots of candles. I'll stay here till the rain lets up.

The rain doesn't let up. It's still pissing down two hours later. I've read about gabbro and serpentine and terra rossa, camels, market-gardening, the madder-market, wheat cultivation, phylloxera, and co-operatives, and know off by heart the differences between mules and jennets, and it's still pouring. I'm shivering now, and goodness knows what Lina is doing. I've been thinking for a long time about this, I who was too goody-goody to light a fire in the national forest. Finally, after smothering three cigarettes with my boot very carefully and wiping the floor with Kleenex and spit and pocketing the butts, I go over and light a holy candle. Then I pour some of my can of Nescafe into X's tin Scout cup, and add water from his canteen, and hold it jerkily, with a tired arm, over a brown holy candle under a wide-eyed Trinity.

Goodness, God exists indeed: a blast from a horn comes out of nowhere. I drop the coffee all over the floor. The horn blasts again. I take off my pullover, wipe the floor with it, and rush outside into the rain.

Four stove-pipe priests are sitting out on the road in a black Mercedes. "What is that donkey doing tied up to the church? You must move him."

"He'll get too wet, he must have shelter."

"Move him, move him. It is impiety. Are you coming to

the monastery?''

''Yes, later.''

''When the rain clears? Good, we shall be expecting you. Move your donkey. He will dirty the church.''

I untie poor old sad Lina and take her over to the fence, choosing a place where she cannot gnaw new-planted trees. ''It'll be over soon,'' I tell her. With a stick I move her manure off the floor of the portico.

But it not over and I am cold, and as wet as she is, having run out without the poncho, and wiped the floor with my sweater.

Unless you lay out in the full sun in high summer, it would be impossible to die of exposure in this country and this climate. It's ridiculous to complain of the chill. Nevertheless, the chill is sepulchral. It will take sixty holy candles to warm up some coffee. After two more hours, finding the rain not ended, but increased, and thunder in the air, I saddle up Lina. ''Come on, girl, we'll get up the mountain. It's only two miles.''

As the crow flies.

It's sheer mud, now. I have to pull her and beat her every step. I can't see, the rain is in my eyes, Laddie's boots are so wet my toes are swimming, the road is a pool of red plasticine. The sky grumbles at us, the clouds suddenly gush like a woman peeing in a pub, I am hauling this goddam animal straight up a mountain and a tree comes crashing in front of us. Right down across the road. Lina sits down. It is easy to decide to give in to her. Hard to decide to spend the night back in that church. Because if it were old and unrestored it might have some kind of magical overtones . . . and be locked. Ah well. We plod through the water downhill. Unsaddle. Sigh. The rain is coming from all directions. The portico of the church is already clean of donkey shit.

I am just opening the door when the car horn sounds again and a monk calls out. ''Get in, get in, give this man your raincoat, he will ride your donkey.''

&

In the monastery, there is a stove, a kitchen stove. Two laymen are boiling up little copper pots of Turkish coffee. Two acolytes are working bread and oil into fishroe with big wooden pestles and staring at me, and giggling. My boots are steaming. I am speechless. I stink. The one who speaks English says, "It is a very bad storm. The telephone lines are already carried down. If you had listened to the wireless last night you would have gone back to the village. Drink up your coffee, here is bread and honey, now it is time for church."

I am put, dripping, in the very back pew of the church, which is not a pew, but a row of seats with very high arms and a sort of misericorde to brace your bum against while you lean on your elbows. You don't sit down. It's a very dim, damp church, large, newly painted: it could be a big Baptist church built in 1911 at home.

There are two rows of chairs facing each other in a sort of choir. Two very old monks, two middle-aged ones, three apple-cheeked acolytes if that's what they're called, and three laymen in Marks and Spencers' pullovers are leaning on their elbows while above them my friend the Bishop of Maloundia intones from the highest seat what I take to be the whole of the Synoptic Gospels. Then each of them chants from the scriptures in turn. When they're not singing, the acolytes chat and giggle. No one pays attention to them.

The ikons at the front of the church are plastered with silver and gold. On painted scrolls familiar surnames are written on the pillars—donors or supplicants, perhaps. The monks sing a million Kyria Eleisons, the Bishop's voice like an organ rises over theirs. Then suddenly, the tone changes briefly and they turn on their heels and process out, the Bishop, and the Abbot, who has fine flashing eyes, the old monks and the young ones. Pandelis, the layman who came up with me in the car, takes my arm and says that now is supper.

I am ravenous and half unconscious. I shall become legendary as the foreign women who ates her beans and garlic like a pig. I don't care. We're at a long table in a plain little room. Halfway through the meal, which is eaten in hungry silence, the man who rode my donkey comes in. "That is some donkey," he says, filling his plate. "Next time you travel to the mountains, you will get a donkey from the mountains. Take the bus back."

At the end of the meal, everybody stands up. I take my purse and turn to leave. The Bishop holds my shoulder firmly. I have forgotten grace. I am really very badly read.

Now, I think, dry clothes, a warm bed. But the Bishop invites me to the Abbot's office for coffee and sweet walnuts and the monastery's famous red cognac brought in by the acolytes who giggle at the sight of me again. The Abbot excuses himself. I don't mind. I am mesmerised by the fact that in the fireplace there is a blazing fire.

What Greek I have learned is now lost to me. I can't think of anything to say. The Bishop's English is made up largely of serviceable pieces of rhetoric. We don't talk to each other. I just sit back in an armchair by the fire watching the steam coming out of Laddie's ex-beautiful boots and smelling the donkey and pee and woman and coffee and no-washing smells that are coming off my clothes. I ask for another coffee, for I have now no pride and no shame. They have to take me in, I am a pilgrim, and if they just warm me up I will put all the few cents I own in the poorbox. But I have to say something, so I say, "This monastery is a very old Byzantine institution."

He likes that. He says it has existed for many centuries and been burnt down and rebuilt many times.

I smell the dirt cooking in my matted hair, now. The fire is wonderful. I spread my hands to it. "I understand you have many beautiful ikons and treasures."

That takes him another half hour, during which time I get

warmer, accept another coffee, become a little stronger. He pulls off his bookshelves a collection of plainly bound Byzantine music manuscripts which look marvellously old, and use a notation that looks like Arabic shorthand. They are on parchment, and someone who knows about such things would be very excited, but I can only nod and say, very good, very good, *para*-very good. He looks very pleased, either with me or with himself or with Byzantine notation.

The main thing is, I am beside a fire. I must enjoy it. In a moment they will put me in a room where it is cold and monastic.

We are sitting in expensive royal blue armchairs on either size of the blaze. "Your hair is very wet," he says.

"Yes. Very wet indeed."

He looks me straight in the eye. "Comb it out."

"Oh, no thanks. It will dry as it is."

"Comb it out."

I am about to argue with him, then I look up at him and I see that with him there is no argument. My arm rises of its own accord, I pull the elastic out of my hair. Where do they get their fat authority, these men?

So I am leaning over the fire and combing my hair and thinking of an ikon I saw somewhere of a virgin and child, and she suckling, and the breast joined to her body by only an isthmus, a string of flesh, as if the painter had never seen a breast, and now he is here, in my lap that smells of donkey and woman and wet wool, turning my breasts as if they'll screw off if he tries enough. He has big hard thumbs. *"Koukla mou,"* he says.

What is there to say to him? "There must be some mistake"? That would hardly do. I am so tired I am detached from myself, I don't quite care what is happening to me; but I smell so bad: maybe it's the smell that turns him on. "Dolly," he says in English.

I hate those endearments that turn women into toys. I'm

not fond of beards, I've never developed a taste for unsolicited tongues. He's not unattractive, but he's rough, and I feel terrible. This wasn't what I wanted. I wanted to get dry. I push him backwards and he nearly falls on the floor. "Oh, creeps, let me alone," I say.

He thinks this is very nice and funny and he sits in the chair across from me grinning, and says, "I love you," and "You are very beautiful," and the wet smell rises from my pullover. And I tell myself I'm a dope, what kind of nut goes to a monastery anyway, he thinks I'm a gift from God. And he goes on talking, and the thunder and lightning shake the building.

I feel very far away from myself, I don't know what to do. "Dolly mou," he says, and leaps onto my lap again, and begins getting intimate around the waist. I defend myself with the thought that a pilgrim is entitled to three nights' free stay in this establishment. I push him back into his chair again. He sits knees akimbo with his cassock hanging down between his knees, staring, no, gloating over at me. "Dolly mou," he says again. Staring, as if he can hypnotise me. Is he circumcised? I catch myself thinking. So he's having some effect. Well, why not let him? He's dying to do it. Little boys are to be indulged. No. No, damn him.

"You are a holy man," I say. "You should not be doing this."

This ought to make him laugh, but it does not. He stares at me solemnly. His chest heaves. He holds out his shaking hands. "I am a monk," he says. "But I am also a man."

Then he leaps again. I'm too tired to put up much of a fight, I'm not connecting. I feel that I've asked for his fanatical attentions by coming here. I think again, the quickest way is to give in and get it over with.

No, that's tart's thinking: you've done enough of it here, girl.

I've never seen a man in such a foment. He pants, he flies

around and pulls curtains, tries the locks on doors. There are three doors, one we came in, another to some kind of corridor outside the window, presumably a balcony, because the rain is flooding against the window, the other to another room. There's a big new Danish modern desk with a swivel chair and a telephone, a nice little sofa, and these two chairs. They spend money, these guys. The locks are Yale locks, I could get one of them open.

But isn't there a civilised way of getting out of this? Look, it's late, I've come a hundred miles today. It wasn't far by your Mercedes reckoning, but at mine, it was a hundred miles. These big boots are steaming, I'm saddle-sore, I've got cramps now. It may be mental cruelty to deny you, you might even be good at it, but you look like a guy who'd go green for a tuppenny upright. I'm better than that. I guess I have my price, I guess I'm a snob, but you look as if you have sheepdip disease.

I get up and try to just saunter out of the room, but he's not having that. The time he gave me to catch my breath he used for plotting too. When I get to the door he simply bends me backwards across the arm of the sofa and starts fumbling around with my slacks.

This makes me really angry. There's something low about being pushed backwards over a sofa. I give him a push with a big damp boot. He doesn't like that. He is angry, too, now. You're apparently supposed to protest politely and then feel honoured.

He's angry, I'm angry. I get up from the sofa and grab my purse, clutch it to my bosom. I move behind the desk, he comes after me. It reminds me absurdly of a South American who was at university, who chased girls around the stacks at night, swearing there was a pill he could take so you couldn't get pregnant. He didn't catch me.

I have sore legs, I tell Maloundia in my head. My feet are all blistered. I'm so matted together you wouldn't find the place.

He bends me over the sofa again. I swing my leg just wide and high enough to make him move thoughtfully backwards. You old goat, I want to tell him, in the latest French books they don't screw women, they screw hummocks of grass. And besides, you have your own flock of sheep.

He doesn't want me to unlock that door, or that one. Maybe the acolytes are outside, listening, like a bunch of long-haired *putti*. Maybe he sold tickets. He keeps panting his one sticky endearment, "Dolly." Where did he learn that? What a stupid, pitiful man.

But persevering. Look, I say to him, fast, so he doesn't understand it, or just in my head, I've nothing to lose by all this, you'll get donkey-crotch-rot.

"Dolly-mou," he says, his eyes gleaming. Pushing me into a chair again. I push him back into the facing one. The fire is going out. The wind is howling. It should be romantic. It's not.

"Stay with me," he pants as I head for the door. "Stay with me."

But what I can see in his pleading eyes is not desire but the firmest will-to-power. And the chase has warmed me. My head is beginning to function again, I'm not just inventing new vulgarities to throw at him. I look at him and his lovely violet cassock, his touching dark eyes, his aristocratic nose, the smirk on his face. He is relaxing a little, but still clutching and unclutching his fists. Things haven't worked out the way he expected, either. Then I know what to say. It pops into my head. I stand up, face him, and with all dignity and courtesy say, "Sir, I am your guest. Please let me go."

He stands across from me, a dignitary again. "Madame, I shall show you to your room."

&

In a four-bed dormitory cell along the balcony, one bed is

made up. My saddle bags are set on a chair by a blazing fire.

"Thank you, sir," I say.

"My pleasure. Sleep well." Not without taking my chin between a vise-like thumb and knuckle.

I throw my purse on the bed, I go back and lock the door. I unlace Laddie's boots. There is a knock. I tremble. *"Pios ine*?" I ask, knowing I have the words half wrong, but he'll understand. Another knock. I go to the door, open it an inch. A shy acolyte bears an armful of logs.

I make a fearfully extravagant fire in a land which is perpetually short of wood. I feel it owes me this. I set my tin cup on its edge to heat water. I take off my wet clothes and spread them generously over the empty beds. Then I open the balcony door and stand over some dark abyss in my underwear in the rain. A flash of lighting colours the sky. If there are monks on the other balconies I can't see them, and I don't care. My door is locked and a chair is wedged under the thumb-latch. Welcome weather. I attack myself with a bar of soap and dance lathered in the beating rain.

I lie in bed, so tired my body twitches. The room is cold, but the air, in spite of the woodsmoke, is miraculously fresh and clear.

These places in winter: coughs, eagles, five or six monks pacing. The roads impassable. Deprivations. Visions.

I lie in bed, still smelling my own stink. I'm getting the curse. Early. Never thought to bring Tampax. That tears it. What do they use in the villages?

I lie twitching. Outside my door, feet are pacing. Someone is padding the corridor, up, down. Thunder and lightning: what dramatics. I came, I saw, I asked for it. Now I do not feel good.

Funny man, though. The stink turned him on. Shepherds' wives can get divorces on the grounds of incurably smelly feet, Loizos said. Michaelis had a Dutch girlfriend whom he sent away to get a smell. He was offended because she was too clean. He said she shouldn't bathe or shave for three whole days.

Lady Hester Stanhope travelled with a retinue. Sometimes two servants, sometimes five, sometimes a whole private army. You tend to forget that.

Feet pacing. Never met a man so rough with his hands. Thunder. Lightning. Crackling fire. I fall asleep holding tight to the edge of the bed so I won't get up and let the inconsolable pleader in.

&

In the morning, the mountainside is miraculously red and green and clear. I lean over the balcony and smell the perfumed air. In the distance, a pair of eagles are soaring over a village which looks near, which my feet tell me is very far away. I put my clothes and boots on painfully and go out to look for the loo. The Bishop appears as if on roller skates. "Do you wish to shit?" he asks solicitously. "The lavatory for women is at the foot of the stairs to the right."

When I return he is standing outside my door with a steaming electric kettle. I feel sorry for him, but not very.

When I finish my coffee and several cigarettes, I peep out again. He is still by my door. He holds his arm out like the father of the bride. We are hours late for service, I suppose, but he's not letting me get out of it. He leaves me at the back of the church, climbs up into his chair and raises his magnificent voice above the mumble of the others. I look around, astounded. Last night I thought there was some kind of musical instrument in the church, a harmonium or an organ, but no, it is his intoning alone that makes the music.

After church, he takes me to the treasure room to see the dog-headed saint. It's only a small ikon, a Christopher who prayed to the Virgin because he was excessively attractive to women. She endowed him with an endearing long hound's head with a flaring nose like a crocodile. It's lovely, quite early, I suppose, and not mucked up with silver plate. Max would have loved it.

"I did not sleep all night," the bishop hisses, passing a benedictory hand around the glass cases in the room. Reliquaries aren't my style, so I continue to stare at the Christopher. "Women loved him too much," he says. "They also love me. And I love you. What is to be done about this? I must return to town today. I would take you in my car, but what will happen to your donkey? Perhaps you will meet me in my very private apartment in town. When will you be back? On Thursday? And wear not trousers and men's boots, but a lovely gown."

"Sure," I say and go on staring at Christopher-Crocodile as he furtively scrawls on a card he gets out of his pocket. I decide it is plain unaesthetic for people to have breastpockets in violet cassocks.

"You will come, then?"

"If I can. Can you tell me where my donkey is?"

"Oh, that I do not know. I am a bishop, after all. The old men will tell you in the kitchen. Thursday, at eight, in a lovely gown?"

"In as lovely a gown as I have."

Two of the laymen I met last night are cooking little pots of coffee in the kitchen. The one called Pandelis begins at once to chew me out for not having looked after my donkey. "Why are you here? What is a woman doing here, coming up the mountain in the rain with a useless animal?" He sounds like the White Russian Twins.

"I came to see an ikon, and I would like some coffee," I tell him.

"Good, good. Share mine. The Bishop is a fine fellow, is he not? He is not supposed to be at the monastery, but Maloundia is bad for his lungs, he spends all his time here."

"That's nice."

"You must pay Panos for riding your donkey. He shivered all night."

"I will."

"Everyone is very curious about you. You travel so strangely."

"The donkey is the traditional animal of this island."

"Oh, but for many years we have motorcars. Have some bread and honey. Then Christakis and I will show you your donkey. Do you wish to meet an old monk of 102 who was 95 before he gave up women?"

"No, thank you."

Lina is well-stabled and bursting with feed: she has ripped open a bag of oats from the next stall. Instead of meeting the old monk I take my map to the Abbot, who is said to know the country, and ask him about the road to the upper villages. He looks at it and shakes his head sadly. "Your donkey will go no higher. You will need much help. Those are poor villages. There is no place to stay in them. The peasants will give what they have, but they have nothing. But if you go west along this pass, you could spend the night with the boys in the Forest Station at the top of the mountain. Then if your donkey collapses they will come and look after you."

"No, thank you."

So before lunch I saddle Lina and wave goodbye to the laymen and the Abbot and the acolytes. The Bishop has gone ahead in his limousine. And I head Lina out through their big wooden gates, past the monastery farm looking all poetic and Shangri-La, through the air that smells again of thyme and gorse and pine. And I look above me to the village I wanted to go to nestled against the next watershed, and to the peaks that lie beyond that, leading to the cherry-tree valleys on the slopes of Olympus, and I am angry and sad and humiliated. My feet sting in stiff socks, I can hardly sit on Lina, and I know that if I had any courage I would go up against the Abbot's advice, and the villagers would be good to me: because over in the next valley everything is always all right.

But Lina is trotting down through the forest like a lamb. She is going home, and the world is green and red and white chalk mesas, flattening out to a satisfying kind of plain. It's her world and she carries me cheerfully, hee-hawing to donkeys in distant fields as she passes. I eat my honey sandwiches and flip orange peels in front of her, and then I get off at a spring by a carob tree to water her, and she stays untethered beside me. The soil isn't even damp. When the rain came, it went schlup, schlup, schlup.

I'm tired, now, and disgusted with myself. I could have arranged this better, thought it out beforehand. Looked at the weather forecast, listened to Aphroulla. Brought more than two pairs of socks. Got a different donkey. Refused to undo my hair. Never come to this place.

The bells are ringing for vespers when I reach the convent of St Heraclides. A moustached nun lets me in after telling me which tree to tie the donkey to. I sit three hours in church and am reprimanded for crossing my legs. The nuns prostrate themselves entirely and repeatedly with a devotion the monks forgot long ago. I came here once last year with Petronella to watch the Reverend Mother painting uninteresting ikons. She is ill, I am told, but Sister Maria will make me some supper in the kitchen.

It's a lovely place, almost French in its grace and tidiness. In the spring, I remember, they were laying out grain on sheets, to clean and dry it for some kind of Lenten food. And their herb garden was built among old Roman mosaics because before the place met St Heraclides, it was the capital of a Roman City State.

Sister Maria is small and neat and only eighteen. She was educated at an American school on the coast, and sent here because she is an orphan. She likes it, because she is the goat girl. The others sew, or make shell souvenirs, or marzipan from their own almond trees, but they are very sad because the Reverend Mother is in town, in hospital, and she is the last of the ikon painters.

I am put to bed in a clean white room with a bedspread like a French catalogne from home.

I rise long after the holy ladies have made their orisons and spend a long time tending to the blisters on my feet. They ask if I won't stay longer, but I'm firm, I don't want to corrupt them with cigarettes and donkeys and the world. And if I stay I'll get to know them, and they won't be perfect: and I need the memory of one perfect thing.

Lina and I clip right along home. She fords a trickle of water in a wide dry-bouldered river without complaint. She doesn't need to be beaten, she bobs along as if I am a cork. She clatters cheerfully through villages Mr Gunnis assures me are ripe with wonderful iconostases. She doesn't care and I don't either. I look at my feet and I think of the Bishop and I look at the land around me and I think, to hell with beauty. Until the 'thirties the villagers never got more than ten miles away from home in their lifetime and God bless 'em.

You want to take that road, Lina, I tell her, you take it. You know the way home. And it's time we all stopped trailing nosily around the world soiling it.

So Lina takes her road and it's a long time before I realise she knows where she's going, but I don't, and it's getting dark again. So I rein her towards the city and she starts playing her starting and stopping game again. I am cursing her out in the twilight when I hear voices I know. I take her across a vacant lot and arrive at the edge of X and Aglaia's garden, where Giles and they are sitting on the last warm evening. We are greeted with hoots of laughter. I tie Lina to a telephone pole and sink into a plastic chaise longue to the lee of them. X brings me a very large Scotch. I tell them about the Bishop. They laugh like drains. He says he worried aloud about me during the storm but his chief teller said, "Don't worry, Maloundia will come down in his big black Mercedes, and you will never see her again." He apologises for giving me bad advice.

To be sitting in a garden with a drink in a cold aluminum glass seems a tremendous victory. But somehow the story has gone sour in the telling, it has given me and the Bishop less than we are due, it seems cruel and scornful of us both.

Giles says that he thinks Maloundia is instinctively carrying on a fine ancient tradition, that he harks back to obscene tomb-figures, the ritual prostitution of Aphrodite-worship, reviving the ancient link between sex and the gods. "Perhaps," he says, "he is Pan."

I hear myself saying, "Oh, no," in a little half-swallowed voice.

Aglaia winces sympathetically. X says he thinks Pan was more skilful, more practised, more a goat than an ox. The men laugh coarsely again. I get up to go and find I can hardly stand.

I beat Lina past big white villas on stilts and little peasant houses under palm trees, past the English Cemetery, the British Council, the School for the Blind, and the Royal Greek Embassy. I have lost embarrassment at taking a stick to her, that is what donkeys are for. Thank God, here's the outer boulevard. Then the inner boulevard, then the bridge over the moat. Aristides is sitting by the newspaper kiosk with his lottery tickets. "Hi, Mrs Ladi. *Peripatis*?"

"Hi, Mr Aristides. *Peripato*."

The city fumes with warmth and light. I hobble down the narrow streets and Lina comes along with me meekly. There is music in the cafes, and the perpetual quarrelling noise of street conversation. Everyone I pass waves and laughs.

Laddie isn't home. I tie Lina in one of our many stalls, hobble her, rub her down, give her a big plastic bucket of water.

Then run the biggest bath in the world and throw my jeans in the garbage.

I lie back staring at the skin peeling off my feet. Five days I lasted. I intended to travel a fortnight at least. The route I travelled you could cover in a car in two hours.

When I get into bed I am still too tired to sleep. I think of going over to Aphroulla's to tell my story before it is too old and sour, dismiss the idea. I am too tired to dress. I lie listening to the sounds of the night: Lina munching and stamping, cars gunning around. Otherwise, silence. Pambos must be at the Spitfire. The city is beginning to close up early again.

I think, at the convent I was afraid the nuns would smell the Bishop on me.

I think, how much I want to go to sleep, but I just lie twitching.

I think, how I have twitched in this building, how I have twitched and flinched and shrunk away.

He wanted me. I was disgusted and flattered by it. I was dirty, I did not want to be wanted. I was tired. I was also, even a little, respectful of his blue-purple cloth. Why did I go there, how did I get into that?

How did I get to be so dumb?

The countryside was beautiful. Beauty doesn't matter a crumb. You can't eat it. They know that. That's why they cut down trees, build oil wells and car factories.

He wanted me. I was dirty and wet and stuck-together and stinking, he didn't think of that. He said he loved me. He could have looked out his window and seen lightning against a crag, a better thing to love.

Caroline Williamson hates these people. She says of them, everything is money and food and sex, everything is greed. I don't see how you can hate a people, and I don't know what there is but coins in your hem and food in your plate and a man in your bed. Beauty? Art? Bourgeois luxuries, like intellectual theories, toys.

I don't understand anything, not here, not anywhere. There has to be more than greed, even the peasants know there is more than greed, they cling to their old ways, but I don't know where it is or what it is and here I have heard the bellowing of the blood enough to know it is real, more real than I was taught to think.

I lie in bed thinking, I don't understand anything. Not sex, not religion, not art, not beauty, not even Foreign Debt. There has to be more to that big abstraction we call life for want of a better word than food on a plate, cash in the till, legs in a bed, there is more, the people here know it. But I don't know what is. I'm one of those opaque lady travellers after all, who sees, but does not understand.

I don't understand anything. Except that two days ago, slopping along a lonely dirt road with a sullen animal, I was for a moment seven years old and free.

&

In the middle of the night, I wake to strange music. Not the clamour of Pambos and Aristides, but something from wild hills far away. I open my door and peer out. At the far end of the gallery, Laddie and a very young boy are dancing by candlelight. Another person is clapping, another is banging softly on a tambourine. The music is more piercing than the music they usually make here, it exists even in the intervals of their minor scale. Laddie is trying to imitate the boy's sinuous dance, and half succeeding in the coquettishness of his hips, but not at all in his look of concentration, not the boy's half-mocking smile.

"Good, good!" the tambourine player cries.

"Sssh, Eddie. I told you, she's back. You'll wake her."

"Balls on you. Dance," says Eddie.

I pull my comforter into the doorway and lie for a long time watching them. The dancing boy moves with an enticement women cannot hope to imitate. Not after they are eleven, anyway. He's beautiful. He's out of Gide. I watch him. Beside him, Laddie looks like me when I try to sing.

I have to go back to England. Maybe I even have to go back home. I have travelled and seen nothing, listened, and heard nothing. The lenses and membranes are fitted wrong, they're the wrong brand, no . . .

Ah, so: it's not that one doesn't understand. It is that one does not want to understand.

Laddie, get out. Quick.

Laddie does not hear because I do not say those words except in my head. I have no right to. His life is his life. Herewith I give it back to him. He sinks to the ground.

One boy pipes, and one boy dances. The notes are eery Even more complicated than the intervals of Max's a capella Irish songs. More savage than Pambos' *chatistas*, and softer. The dancer's hips are graceful beyond knowing. The smile is the smile on the face of an idol.

We grew up singing a scale with too few notes. A long time ago someone decided the fractured intervals were not good for us. They remembered the disasters. They thought simplification was a virtue. They invented trinities and dichotomies to ease the strain of multiplicity. This boy has been taught to remember the old—not wholeness, but chaos. He will be Laddie's final disaster.

This is the image finally summoned from the remembered, innocent shore. Where apple trees bloomed and lilacs stood elegantly by, and Indians fished with little nets and the eyes could rest and swim in sky and space. This is the old, remembered thing: a boy with the smile of a snake.

I crawl back to bed feeling hollow, hollow, hollow. I have been insolent in my innocence, I think, I have shaken a hand

I ought to have kissed, I have fussed about with the surface of things, I have behaved badly, I have been wrong. That has nothing to do with anything.

There is nothing to understand. There is no understanding. There was a dancing boy. In him I saw heresies and visions and infinite, mocking subtlety beyond the realm of the Bishop and of me, beyond all the people I have ever known, beyond the twos and threes any of us have been taught to think and sing in.

This boy was a child fulfilling a combination of instincts and lessons. This boy was a cannibal dream. We also were taught to fulfil instincts and lessons. Have our lives also shimmered against the night like stranded, silver fish?

These thoughts bring no comfort. My body throbs even after the strange music ceases. I do not sleep. I lie twitching until dawn.

And then I hear a cry I understand, and it makes me weep and retch.

X
LEAVING

Max, when Mustafa Pasha landed on this island with 58,000 men, the fortifications of the city were still unfinished. Desperate messages were sent to the Pope, but he would not provide soldiers or reinforcements or money. Venice sent Martinengo with two thousand men, but he died on the voyage, and they were all sick when they arrived.

It was 1570. The gentry had lost interest in breeding horses. Only five thousand regular soldiers could be raised, and command of the garrison was given to a gentleman without military experience. Roccas took three hundred horse and a hundred dragomen down to Scala to prevent the landing, where he met Baglioni with three hundred dragoons and a hundred and fifty *stradioti*. They saw three hundred sail on the horizon and retreated.

The gentlemen soldiers were not Greeks: they were Venetians, and Franks who had lingered after the Crusading period was over. The Greeks retreated to the mountains, or to the walled cities. Certain of them treated privately with Mustafa Pasha when he arrived, hoping in their hearts that after the inevitable conquest Islam would be kinder to them than Rome had been.

When the Infidel came, the city was not yet provisioned. There were no parapets on the walls to hide behind. The Turks erected pavilions on suburban hills and built ramparts out from them to equal the height of the city walls. In the Cathedral, the Roman Bishop of Baffo preached his last sermon. "Selino Ottoman," he said, "is a no lesse wicked and cruel persecutor of the faithfull than was that antient Pharoah."

The Turks sapped and mined under penthouse roofs, drove the defenders from the walls with hails of arrows and artificial fire. The defenders were equipped with spontoons and halberts only.

On the ninth of September Mustafa's troops crossed the walls before the garrison was awake. Rich matrons were raped, babes were torn from their mothers' breasts, treasure-stores were ripped open. Twenty thousand died in a day. Those who were spared were marched over carcasses to the galleys. Rich booty was forwarded to Istanbul.

And I who was never at any siege, who know nothing of these things, have a ticket for a ship with a classical name that sails tomorrow.

Edward, who in daylight looks pleasant and normal and is unfailingly polite, has helped me pack my belongings in a crate built by Costas the Carpenter. I have stood among friends of the bride at Megas and Maro's wedding and turned down an offer of work in the teashop from Florinda. I have dined ceremonially with Xanthos and Aglaia at a strange outdoor restaurant which was in fact an entire village, for when the figpeckers make their fall migration to Africa and roost in the trees near Paralimni, they are caught with limed sticks by little boys and delivered over to the women of the village. Every garden is crowded with tables and chairs. Kettles are boiled in courtyards. Old women sit in sheds blanching and plucking and tying the birds in dozens. The naked things are boiled with rice in enormous cauldrons. You open them up, take out the gall-bladder, and crunch the little skeletons between your teeth, vying with your friends and relations to eat a mythical number of dozen.

It is festive and grisly and all the island, for that week of migration, goes there.

So I am finally leaving this place, and Aphroulla is leaving also. Her American friends have been fruitful contacts, she has earned enough to go to Paris. Alexis will live with his fierce grandmother. We are booked on the same ship.

I have been for a last look at the mosque-cathedral, quietly, shoelessly treading the worn handsome carpets and staring up at the gypsum-patterned Gothic windows. I have noticed for the first time that the Women's Gallery has reed carpets only. But as always the whitewashed interior sets the architecture aglow, the painted ogival shrines and pulpits canted to Mecca skew my sense of history, and I feel new. I would like to put in this church the lapis-lazuli throne they found in the tomb of St Timotheus, the ikon of the dog-headed saint, a British postman's uniform and one of Giles's phallic tomb-figures. It would be a memorial to all mixtures, to Max.

I have been to the northern mountains in a car with William Pender, and met his monumental Gran, and agreed with him that liver-marked giantesses who carry blackthorn sticks would be difficult people to work for. I have refused to marry William when he proposed in his cups, and had a last swim in the sea, which knocked me hard against the stones in a cold farewell.

I have sung a final dirge with Pambos and Aristides in the company of two policemen, for when I came down to say a formal goodbye to him, he was sitting in the rear of a civic Landrover, bowing to his neighbours grandly. He had been arrested for failing to pay his taxes. He was waving his hat to the crowd, saying last words to Aristides, when his eldest son came down the street. He called him to him, told him his epic story. With a look of great disgust the boy took a brown pay-packet out of his pocket, handed it to his father. Gravely, Pambos paid out to the cops what was owing, pocketing some of the rest, handing some back to his son. "If you have a tree," he said, "You have a shadow."

There was great rejoicing except on the part of the son, who slunk bitterly away. Aristides and Pambos invited me and the policeman and Costas into the shop for a drink. Many songs were sung. Then the policemen re-arrested Pambos for possessing raw spirits, and drove him away again. This time he went glumly. "Where is your shadow now, old wicked man?" the policemen asked.

Now the survivors of the Eating Society are dining for the last time together, and for the first in Theo's new restaurant, a bald cement and linoleum rectangle four times the size of the old place and containing a very loud juke box. The surviving White Russian Twin and Roger are already doing their dormouse act, William and Petronella are being silly, and Laddie and Edward are making sheep's eyes at each other about getting back to their boys.

"Tell them they will get in trouble with those boys," Aphroulla hisses. "The police are very much interested in them. It is forbidden for such purposes to import foreign boys."

I have not had time to talk to him about the boys because the day after I returned from the mountains, I moved in with Aphroulla, and I know, now, if I speak about the boys, how he will react. But I suppose I ought to say something to him. I have known him longer than I have known anyone else in my life, except my mother and my brother. Old friends are a kind of serial story, that is why you keep up with them even after they've turned into enemies. "Take care of yourself, Laddie," I say to him.

"God go with you, darling. *Kalon Taxidi,* as we say."

"Take care of those boys. The police are interested in them."

"Oh, I intend to."

"How will you live, without any piano lessons?"

"How will you live, without your friends? One finds a way."

"They're only little kids. They should be trotting around

with bookbags on their backs."

"Are you still on that? How provincial. Still, it *is* a far cry from being Lord Fauntleroy or the little sugar bride and groom. I suppose one can't expect more of you." He is physically and vocally arched away from me.

"Don't throw your life down the drain, Laddie."

"Me? Down the drain? Little me? Whatever would I do that for? Get on with you, child."

"I won't see you again. If you wire, I won't answer."

"I can't wire if I don't have your address, can I?

"Why are you being serious and bitter?" Roger asks. "There's never any need to be serious and bitter. The past is done. We could discuss English literature."

"Shut up, Roger," says Laddie. "I'm saying goodbye to Audrey. Goodbye."

"Goodbye, Laddie."

"Give my love to your mother and Leo when you write."

"Whose mother?" Roger growls.

"Come off it, Roger." Laddie stands up and signals to Edward. He's spruced up in a white shirt and tie, he looks prosperous. "I hope you marry, or find the pot of gold at the end of the rainbow, or another job, whatever you want."

"I hope you get to Morocco, or some place they won't shoot you for having boys."

"You found flight in my tea-leaves only yesterday, didn't you, Eddie? Yes, we must be going somewhere soon. Bon voyage, sister mine. Adios."

"Ciao."

"Say goodbye to Eddie."

"Au 'voir, Eddie."

"Cheery-bye."

We've learned so many foreign words.

&

It is Loizos who drives us to the ship. He is hectically cheerful, talking about how they have taken over the lease of the villa from Peter, how she is a wonderful woman, wonderful. How he is happy at last. It is the first time I have seen Aphroulla and Loizos together: theirs are two versions of the same face, his horizontal, hers vertical. She sits tall beside him with an enigmatic smile on her face when she isn't checking again for her passport, asking fussy questions about her baggage and saying, "My God, we must go back, I have forgotten to tell Alexis . . ." and giving in easily to Loizos' assurances. I stare at them, trying not to see how the main road branches off into the mesa'd foothills where a few days ago I rode Lina and felt, temporarily, freer than I had since I was seven. Landscape is meaningless, I tell myself, it doesn't matter where you live, it matters how.

But my eyes fly out of my head and I always know where I am in relation to the mountains, and I know I won't lose this land, it is forever stamped in my head.

The port town is ugly, commercial, full of dying palms and scabby apartment buildings, neon bars and rubbishy parking lots. I seem already to have gone away.

Speridakis and Aphroulla are still negotiating her luggage through to the ship when I take the bum-boat with William Pender and Roger Salmon, who have come down to see us off. The ship we're going on is listed as a cruise-ship. It sits offshore looking white and dramatic and posh. I'm going last class in a women's dormitory by the galley doorway, feet in the hors d'oeuvres. I shove my suitcases on a top bunk and go up on deck to have a last drink with William and Roger. Peter Barnes is also on board, already drunk, standing at the bar with two big blondes. He nods, but doesn't speak.

Roger and William and I take our drinks and hang over the railing, staring at the island. "It's like an old yellow dog," I say.

"You could have stayed, you know," Roger says.

"There wouldn't have been anything for me to do."

"You're an enterprising gel, you'd have found something."

"I just look enterprising, Roger."

"Well, you've set our Laddie on his feet again, that's what you came to do."

"Lot of good it did, now they have those two boys."

"Handsome is as handsome does, eh? People do what they want, that's the secret of the old beldame Sphinx. They'll get rid of them or someone else'll do it for them. Not respectable, Arab boys: sully the neighbourhood. Ratepayers won't have it, eh? Should stick to the traditional vices. Drink, women. Give my love to old England."

"How many years since you've been there, Roger?"

"Centuries, love, centuries. Take care of yourself."

"You too."

"I do, I always do."

"William, you should try working for your Gran."

"Good God, no. Here's Aphroulla looking all grand and glorious. Trouble with islands is people are always leaving them. There'll be no place to go in the evenings now except bloody bars. Hi, Aphra!"

Aphroulla is all tears and grandeur, like a movie star. When we got into the car in the morning, I didn't notice how smart she was. She cuts a swath through the other passengers. "Ah, there you are, come and have a drink with me, a toast to that provincial shore. Loizos has stayed on land, he takes the sea badly. Roger! William! Be my guests on this sad occasion."

We laugh and chatter, but already we are other people.

Soon the last lighter brings the tourists who have spent the morning on shore. William and Roger make their escape on it. Aphroulla goes to her cabin. The ship's motors churn. Half a mile offshore and already a lifetime away, the island lies yellow and skinny and underfed in the weakening sun, resigned and lazy. Aphrodite fetched up along the coast there on her seashell, just beyond the NATO base. I think despairingly of all the things I will never understand.

"Rum place," says Peter Barnes at my shoulder.

"Going home?"

"Thirty-eight days' leave, then Aden."

"You aren't looking nostalgic."

"She was a strange one. Tedious woman. Like living with a stone. Wish him joy of her."

A steward tells me I must now go down to the second-class deck. While I am doing so, the island slides away from me.

&

Rhodes: restored ruins, peasant women in high yellow boots, a carved wooden spoon.

Athens: dandelions in the stone floor of the Acropolis. Terrifying traffic. They laugh at my accent.

Genoa: Aphroulla and I trying and failing to speak Italian. Good food in the old quarter; a smart new art gallery full of ghastly 19th century Old Masters.

&

Getting off the ship at Marseilles I am looking around for Aphroulla when I meet a fat man with a raddled, pockmarked face who says, "Yes, you are the lady who rode the donkey through my uncle's village and made everyone very glad."

"Someone said I was a laughing-stock."

"But no . . . Everyone was very pleased with you. It has been many years since one has travelled with the traditional means of transportation. Did you not see, they have written a *satiri* about you in the newspaper?"

"No; what's a *satiri*?"

"You have it in English, too, I think: a funny poem. It is a very old kind of poem, very nice. It was about a lady who wished to see everything and chose the most appropriate means of transportation, one which did not consume petrol and gave off no exhaust but exhaustion."

"That is nice. I didn't last very long."

"But of course not, it is much too difficult to take a donkey so far from its home. Next time you will order one from the mountains to go there. Are you going on the Paris train?"

"I'm looking for my friend."

"Mrs Aphroulla? She has gone to dine with that German fellow, she sent me with a note to you. Here it is: you will look her up in Paris the day after tomorrow."

"Thanks."

"Come, now, no more long faces. It is only a little island. Here, the world is large. I will show you something that will last you all your life. How to sleep very cheaply in a French train."

In the big, cluttered Marseilles station, which is foreign, but still pleasantly Mediterranean, he buys a big bunch of bananas and six bottles of pop labelled Beaujolais. "French wine, very good;" he says, "hurry, bring your suitcases. Follow me."

He sweeps me into an empty compartment. It's at least an hour before it's time to go. I'd like to go out and wander around, I've been in Marseilles with Max."No, no," he says."No farther than the magazine stand. Buy us some very smelly cheap cigarettes."

He's a big man, fat as a toad, and warted with acne. When I come back he's lying back in a mess of banana peels drinking the pop-bottled Beaujolais. "Eat, drink, be merry," he says, "Tonight we shall sleep well. You'll see."

The Beaujolais tastes like melted lifesavers. He's been throwing banana peels on the floor. The carriage already smells nauseating. He laughs, throws another peel down, adds a newspaper and sprinkles it with wine. "Yes," he says, "it is a good place. I love my island. The climate is beautiful even though too hot in summer, the food is excellent. I love my island so much they pay me to stay away. We are very rich. My family name is Precious Blood. My aunts own orange groves, my uncles bottle Upsi-Cola, mineral water, orange squash, my cousins are in the motor trade, it is worth five hundred pounds per year to them to have me stay away. Women love me too much, boys love me too much. In London I am a gigolo, in Paris a pederast. You are not eating bananas fast enough. They are very good for one."

The night train picks up speed. There is pounding along the corridors. The compartment doors are opened, slam again. "Seats here? Seats here? Only two people . . . pew!" The smell of bananas and wine and wet overcoats is overwhelming. "Don't open the window," he warns from his pew across from me. "And do not fear me. I cannot touch you, at the moment I am diseased. Sleep well."

I sleep like a baby until dawn, when the train is sliding through the grainy suburbs of Paris.

I've always had good luck in Paris, it has kept its magic for me. This morning there is a good sense of the city's gearing itself for the day. My big friend gets his bags and mine together and passes them to me through the window. We share a taxi to check them at the Gare du Nord. Then he says, "Breakfast," and we walk in the November dawn down to the river to a cafe he likes near the Louvre. He orders two double milky coffees and a dozen new croissants.

"You did not like to leave. I saw you at the railing crying."

"Oh, I wasn't crying, but I felt like it."

"It's a good place, eh? Light, air, vineyards. Whatever they do, they will not let the breasts of their island run dry. But it will not be nice for a year or so now, there will be some kind of revolution, there will be curfew, no one will go out at night, ladies will not ride donkeys into the hinterlands. Forget that nasty place. You are in Paris now. Tomorrow London. The world is very big. On that island it is always business, business, and bang-bang.'' He rubs his thumb and forefinger together, then turns them into a gun. Laughs, scratches under his arms, stretches, appropriates in a familiar and already nostalgic fashion two chairs for his arms, two for his feet, sticks his chest out and begins to recite some long Greek incantation, passionate, and somehow appropriate to the beginning bustle of Paris. I do not understand all the words, hardly any of them but sea and stars. Across the river, cars are gunning down the Boulevard St Germain. Next door, an old woman is hanging caged birds outside her shop. The Louvre and the Mint stand fixed, his words go on. The river shimmers, fishermen appear. He beats his breast, grimaces and recites. The sky has a damp white light. I have forgotten how subtle it can be. His worn raddled masturbator's face is alight. He spouts and spouts and stops. Jumps up.

``What was it, then?''

``Homer. Omeri. The first book of the Odyssey. It is very nice, is it not? I have to go. There is a woman I have forgotten to see. Good-bye. Do not mourn for that island, it is not a person, only a place. If you wish to mourn, mourn the lost innocence of Simon Precious Blood.'' He winks, throws down coins, and is gone.

I send a note to Aphroulla's new address and go back to the Gare du Nord via the Palais Royale and the painted glass windows of the Grand Véfour.

&

England is leaden skies and dirty underwear and chimney pots, and a pale harrassed Maurice Henshaw at the station.

For a long time I haunt olive merchants, speaking to them in borrowed words.